PRAISE FOR THE SILVER SIX CRAFTING MYSTERIES

"Nancy Haddock has struck gold with the Silver Six!"

—Ali Brandon, *New York Times* bestselling author of the Black Cat Bookshop Mysteries

"The perfect mix of intelligence and charm. The characters are varied and appealing, the setting is engaging and so vivid you can smell the flowers and taste the fried okra, and the plot is intricate and clever."

—Jennie Bentley, *New York Times* and *USA Today* bestselling author of the Do-It-Yourself Mysteries

"A slew of townsfolk I'd love to meet—as well as a few I wouldn't—all combined into a delightful and tasty mystery full of intrigue and twists . . . *Basket Case* is full of Southern charm, food . . . and mystery."

—Linda O. Johnston, author of the Barkery & Biscuits Mysteries

"Ms. Haddock, a masterful writer, obviously has humor running through her DNA and mystery deep within her bones . . . I'm looking forward to many more Silver Six books."

—L.A. Sartor, author of *Viking Gold*

"A great small town, filled with eclectic citizens, an intelligent main character, family fun, [and] wonderful writing."

—Open Book Society

Berkley Prime Crime titles by Nancy Haddock

BASKET CASE

PAINT THE TOWN DEAD

A CRIME OF POISON

A Crime of Poison

NANCY HADDOCK

BERKLEY PRIME CRIME
New York

BERKLEY PRIME CRIME
Published by Berkley
An imprint of Penguin Random House LLC
375 Hudson Street, New York, New York 10014

ISBN: 9780425275740

First Edition: December 2017

Printed in the United States of America
1 3 5 7 9 10 8 6 4 2

Cover art by Anne Wertheim
Cover design by Diana Kolsky
Book design by Kristin del Rosario

To Lynn Michaels and Julie Benson,
L.A. Sartor and Neringa Bryant.

I'm fortunate to have such fabulous friends.

Acknowledgments

I'm blessed to have an amazing immediate family by blood and marriage, and an equally fantastic extended family of "honorary" sisters, brothers, aunts, and uncles. Having their support, encouragement, and love means the world to me. Oh, and to Janie and Kay, I don't recall a time when I didn't know you and love you. Thanks for our lifelong friendship!

Hugs to my agent, Roberta Brown. I adore you, lady!

Allison Janice, you are a superb editor, and I was lucky to have you in my corner! All my best always! To my new editor, Katherine Pelz, thank you for adopting me! You are wonderful!

The entire crew at Penguin Random House is phenomenal. I particularly thank publicists Roxanne Jones and Danielle Dill, and artists and designers Anne Wertheim, Diana Kolsky, Sarah E. Oberrender, and Kristin del Rosario. You all have talents in spades, and I'm grateful you shared them with me.

Many thanks to the people of Magnolia, Arkansas, for welcoming me, answering my questions, and clarifying so very many points. Oh, yes, and letting me take photos of your homes and businesses, and supporting my charity book signing. Among my research angels and friends are Deena Hardin, managing editor of the

(Magnolia) *Banner-News*; Rhonda Rolen and all the incredible staff members at the Columbia County Library; Megan, CID secretary, and Heather, Sheriff's secretary, both of the Columbia County Sheriff's Office; Brenda, Columbia County Prosecutor's Office; and Randy Reed, Columbia County coroner. I can't forget Jerri Lethiew of Columbia County Co-op Extension Services; the Rev. Bruce T. Heyvaert, former vicar of St. James Episcopal Church; and Donna Pittman King of Pittman's Nursery. Jodie Westfall of Loft on the Square and her entire family are a delight, and the Loft is the perfect downtown inn. Thank you again for letting me extend my stay when Hurricane Matthew prevented me from getting home! I also want to mention "The Story Lady," Lois Gene Greer Russell. I loved spending time with you, Lois Gene!

Dana Thornton, Angela Flurry Lester, and Deb Baker of Magnolia Cove also provided inspiration and information in and on Magnolia. Deb also created the most amazing soap for me to give as swag. Aster's Garden Soap rocks, Deb, and so do you!

If I've forgotten to list anyone else by name, know that I haven't forgotten *you*!

Always deep and abiding appreciation for the caffeine and support to my friends at Starbucks #8484, Barnes & Noble #2796, Second Read Books, and the Anastasia Island Branch of the St. Johns County Library system!

Thanks to my hubby and my children for their love and unwavering encouragement.

So many to acknowledge, so little time. If you aren't specifically named here, please know that you are appreciated and thanked!

Chapter One

THE HANDCRAFT EMPORIUM BUSTLED WITH ACTIVITY late Friday morning, but not with shoppers looking for unique gifts or home décor. Today we prepped for the small army of artists who'd soon invade Lilyvale for the Fall Folk Art Festival. Many would soon come to the emporium to collect the items they consigned with us and move them to their festival tents to sell.

Sounds of packing tape being ripped from multiple rolls punctuated the cheerful chatter as we assembled cardboard boxes. Well, the Silver Six assembled. I'd helped with the taping until the third time I lacerated my fingers on the dispenser's teeth. Those little suckers were sharper than my cat's claws, and Maise thought blood on the boxes would be bad for business.

"Leslee Stanton Nix!"

"What did I do now, Aunt Sherry?"

She flashed me a grin as she finished taping the bottom of another carton. Since she was even shorter than my five foot three, she'd cleared a round display table to work.

"Nothing but be brilliant, child. I tell you, it was a stroke of genius when you suggested holding the festival in town, *and* making it a two-day event!"

"I'm happy you're excited," I answered, scurrying to shift her completed cube out of the way.

I placed the boxes near the goods the artists would be packing, but we were fast running out of floor space even though I nested as many boxes as I could. Of course, my critters weren't helping. Amber, a black-and-tan German pinscher–hound mix, came to my knees and weighed maybe twenty-five pounds. Her nose twitched like mad as she shoved the cartons around with her head. T.C., a short-haired brown-and-gold tiger stripe with only three toes on her front paws, jumped in and then out of the same boxes to startle Amber. Right. Like the dog didn't know her constant companion was in there. Still, it made me laugh, and Aster chuckled, too.

"We're all excited, Nixy," Aster assured me. Dressed today in black yoga pants and a flower-power tunic, our Earth Mother and herbalist worked at a folding table with her sister, Maise. Aster's famous lavender water in a spray bottle stood at the corner of the table ready to spritz. "Heavens, can you imagine having to move all this to the farmhouse for just one day? Even packing up our own art pieces would have been so much trouble!"

"It's a consarn pain in the patoot as it is," Fix-It Fred grumbled. "I thought the artists were bringin' their own crates."

Eleanor Wainwright, a model-lovely black woman dressed in tailored gray slacks with a royal-blue blouse, *tsk*ed at Fred. "I do believe they will have their own cartons, but it can only help to have extras handy."

She stood between Fred and Dapper Dab at the antique oak counter with its glass front and top. The three of them were the tallest of the Six, so Maise had assigned that duty station to them.

"The business owners on the square sure have been good about supporting us," Dab said as he handed me a box, then hitched up his dark gray pleated trousers. They fell right back to his bony hips, but with his full head of thick white hair, he still looked neat as a pin.

"That's because they know the value of having festival shoppers roaming the square *and* in the mood to spend money."

Sherry nodded as she folded the flaps of a small box. "Right, Aster, not to mention all our vendors and shoppers needing places to stay and good places to eat. I heard both the Inn on the Square and the Pines Motor Court were sold out for the whole weekend."

"That ain't sayin' much, seein' as how neither of them places has many rooms to begin with."

"Yes, Fred, but full is full, and that's a good thing," Sherry argued. "Why, I understand some of our artists are staying in Magnolia, Camden, and even El Dorado. That can't help but spread the word about the festival."

I grinned as I shuttled more cartons off the work spaces. The semiannual one-day event the Silver Six had held for the previous three years on Sherry's ancestral farmhouse grounds had drawn folk art aficionados from as far away as New Mexico, so the festival wasn't exactly a best-kept secret. Nothing in Lilyvale was.

"I still say getting everyone from the Chamber of Commerce and the city and county officials on board was the key," Aster said.

"Less talking, more taping, troops," ex–Navy nurse Maise ordered, rapping a knuckle on the folding table. She promptly countermanded herself by adding, "Nixy, are you certain you have signed waivers from all the vendors?"

I picked up another of her cartons. "Most mailed the release forms back to me, and I'll get the rest when they come to set up. I promise, I have duplicates of every form, permit, and license, and extra copies of the schedule, plus the diagram of where each tent will be."

"The traffic cones will be set up by one this afternoon to block off the parking lots?" she fired at me.

"One thirty, and I'll have the spaces for each vendor marked off by three."

"See if you can shave half an hour off that time. When will the large trash bins be out?"

"By day's end, if not sooner. I don't want the vendors to have to weave around obstacles when they're unloading their tents and whatnot."

"All right, then, go get us more tape. I'm almost out."

"So am I," Dab said.

"And I," Eleanor added.

I circled to the counter to snag their completed boxes and paused as Fred handed me his. "Don't you have more tape stashed in your tool belt?"

"No, and I ain't got any squirreled away in my overalls either, missy, so don't be teasin' me about what I tote around with me."

"I only teased you once."

"Yes, and she got you good," Sherry said on a chortle.

Nearly bald, no-nonsense Fred was famous for his many colors of overalls, which he usually wore with plain white T-shirts. All his overalls sported extra pockets sewn on by Aster and Maise. Every pocket held one gadget or another, never mind the loaded tool belt he kept fastened to his walker most of the time. The *clank-clunk*ing of the belt announced when he was coming, and the man had biceps like Popeye because he lifted the walker more than scooted it.

"Get on with you now," he said, shooing me with one hand. "I got a stash of tape in one of my workroom drawers."

"And get a few more boxes while you're there," Maise directed.

"Aye-aye," I said, resisting the urge to snap a salute.

When I opened the connecting door between the store and Fred's workroom in back, Amber and T.C. scampered around me and headed to their water bowls. I closed the door, scooched one of the bar stools we'd scrounged over to one of the four large, scarred wooden tables, and sank onto the seat. I needed just to breathe in the quiet for a moment. I loved the Silver Six, but most days they ran rings around me.

Not that I regretted relocating to Lilyvale. I'd come to town in April with every intention of heading right back to Houston, but in less than a week, I knew I belonged here with Sherry and her housemates. I'd moved in May and never looked back.

The Six had pitched in with gusto to make the emporium happen in record time. We'd primed, painted, and polished the structure inside and out. The only things we'd left alone in this room were the vinyl flooring, the cabinets, and the worktables. I traced a heart and then a spiral someone had carved into the wood, and smiled. No matter what logic I'd used, Fred wouldn't hear of sanding and refinishing the tables or cabinets. He said the tables he'd use as workbenches would only get battered again, and so would the pine cabinets lining two walls where he'd store his tools and supplies. The units had been built of local lumber at least seventy-five years ago, but he liked that the cabinets had yellowed with age. Gave them character, he'd insisted. Since this was his domain, if he was happy, the rest of us were, too.

I was proud of what we'd accomplished in just four months, and now we were mere hours from welcoming artists for the two-day festival. Not all of those who sold through us would have booths, and that was fine. I wasn't not sure how many more tents we could've accommodated.

Would heads roll if there were glitches? No, but when I'd suggested relocating the event for the convenience of being near the store, the Silver Six had supported me from the get-go, and I wanted to prove worthy of their trust. Besides,

I could be even more exacting than the Six were. Since I was in charge of this shindig, I'd do all I could to ensure it went off without a hitch.

Of course, I did notice that not one of my emporium co-owners wore our "uniform." I wore my green polo shirt with one of my many pairs of cropped pants with cargo pockets, but we also had green aprons in addition to the shirts. Both were embroidered with HANDCRAFT EMPORIUM over the left breast and were supposed to set us apart from shoppers. Or in the case of this weekend, vendors. Ah well, I knew by now to pick my battles with the Silver Six, plus the store shirts and aprons weren't a total bomb. Jasmine Young, our work-study employee from the technical college, wore them.

Which reminded me that Jasmine was supposed to come in at four thirty to help us straighten and reorganize, and she was bringing a friend from the tech school, Kathy Baker. Jasmine would be going to Southern Arkansas University in Magnolia in January to pursue a business degree, and though Magnolia was only about a thirty-minute drive away, she'd decided not to commute to work for us. I understood, and I was happy she'd wanted to introduce us to Kathy as her possible replacement.

Time for me to get moving before Maise had me keelhauled. Fred kept his space in apple-pie order, as Sherry said, so I quickly found three rolls of tape in a deep drawer. I turned to call to the animals only to see them curled up together on a spacious, fluffy dog bed. They'd been inseparable since I'd first found them in the alley, but seeing the girls spooned together, sometimes snoring, was too cute.

I hotfooted it back to the storefront with the tape and a few flattened boxes, renewed and ready to tackle the rest of the day.

BY THREE O'CLOCK, WELL OVER HALF OF THE VENdors had arrived, and setup was in full swing.

I stood on the sidewalk a few steps higher than street level just outside the Handcraft Emporium surveying the scene and inhaling the sweet hint-of-autumn air. Where cars customarily parked in two rows of diagonal spaces, a sea of ten-by-ten tents now stood, filling both the east and west parking lots of Lilyvale's town square. Gaily striped canopies fluttered in the pleasant early October breeze, happy voices rang out, and I returned cheerful waves from artisans.

So far, so good. The weather was forecasted to cooperate this weekend, being sunny but not too hot or humid. For southwest Arkansas in early October, having temperatures in the upper seventy-degree range was as perfect as I could've wished. Still, I knocked on the wood clipboard I clasped against my chest for luck.

My phone vibrated in the pocket of my pants. The screen showed it was Aunt Sherry calling.

"Are you standing outside for a reason, or just basking in the glow?"

"Basking," I said on a chuckle.

"Well, get it in gear. I need you to pack Diane Grindall's jewelry and deliver it to her. She has help putting up her tent, but she broke her leg last week, and the less she has to hobble on those crutches, the better."

"Be right there."

Inside, the store felt more like Party Central than a shopping destination. Smiling faces, excited greetings, and laughter echoed through the space. I'd barely placed the clipboard on the antique counter when Sherry snagged my elbow and towed me through the crowd to reintroduce me to everyone. I'd met some of the artists at Sherry's Spring Folk Art Festival in April, and others when they'd dropped off their goods at the store over these past months. The rest I knew only from phone calls and e-mails. Bless them, most had been at least agreeable if not enthusiastic about giving the new venue and the Saturday-Sunday time frame a shot.

We'd insisted that our vendors pick up any of their wares

consigned in the store for the duration of the festival. We didn't want to be in competition with booth sales, which was partly why the store was packed and the party was on. Our established artists had come to gather their items and stayed to visit, while our new vendors came to make connections.

Social obligation met, Sherry pulled me back toward the antique glass counter. We displayed extra delicate or expensive items on the three tiers of glass shelves.

"Diane's jewelry is on the bottom tier," she said. "There's a small box on the shelf behind the counter. Pack her things and run them over to her, will you, child?"

"I keep the earring and necklace sets together, right?"

"I'm sure that would be helpful."

Someone called Sherry from across the room, so she patted my arm and took off. I moved behind the counter and began packing the exquisite jewelry made with pearls and semiprecious gems while I watched the Silver Six work the room.

A few steps from me, Maise, the chief cook of the Six, talked recipes with BBQ Bo, a handsome black man who sold amazing meat rubs for grilling. A few steps away, Eleanor laughed with a stained-glass vendor, and, after assembling boxes all morning, she looked as elegant as ever.

Across the room, Aster seemed to be consulting with a vendor I didn't know. The younger woman pointed to a jar of Aster's balm, and Aster gestured at others. A master gardener, Aster used essential oils to create her line of lotions and potions. Shortly before our website went live, she changed her product name to Aster's Garden. The last of her redesigned labels hadn't arrived until after five yesterday afternoon, and then it was all hands on deck to carefully align the self-adhering stickers on every salve, balm, body butter, hand lotion, and room spritzer in her inventory.

As I watched, sure enough Aster sprayed a bit of what was likely lavender water over her companion's head, and the younger woman beamed. Since Aster kept small bowls of the lavender flowers around the shop, the scent subtly permeated the place. She declared that it was why shoppers lingered instead of dashing in and out, and since none of our patrons had been allergic to lavender so far, who was I to argue? Especially when she patiently taught me about herbs and plants so I could more knowledgeably answer customer questions when I was working the store alone.

Not far from Aster, Fred stood at a shelf that held metal art, carefully picking up this piece then that one to show the dollhouse maker. After I'd made an offhand suggestion to them a few months ago, Fred and Dab had teamed up to begin crafting metal art from Fred's surplus of nuts, bolts, washers, nails, and anything else they scrounged. Most pieces were small enough to display on shelves, but some were large enough to put on the sidewalk outside the store.

A burst of laughter near the bay window caught my attention, and I spotted Dab chatting with mosaics artist Mags Deets. To my surprise, he looked a little smitten, and so did she. I didn't hear every word he said but gathered our widowed, retired chemical engineer was telling Mags a story about distilling Aster's homegrown herbs in two honest-to-moonshine stills. They had originally been in the basement but were now snug in two small garages behind the farmhouse—electric-hot-plate-operated, of course.

As I finished packing Diane's jewelry, Sherry continued her rounds, speaking with everyone, just like the natural hostess she was. Her graying brown hair was cut in a wedge style, and this afternoon a sweep of long bangs covered her left eye. With the macular degeneration in that eye, covering it with her hair allowed her to focus better with her right eye when needed. How she managed to continue weaving baskets in a plethora of sizes and designs—and even crochet hemp and cotton twine baskets—amazed me. She'd begun working with gourds more and more, too. She preferred painting them rather than etching or wood burning, and wove the coils from pine needles, raffia, and vines to finish the top of her gourds.

I gazed at each of the Silver Six again, and smiled. Being with the seniors gave me a warm glow. Yes, even when they occasionally drove me a little crazy.

The wind chimes over the door tinkled, admitting another vendor coming to pick up her needlepointed pieces. Dang, it was after three. I needed to move out.

I tucked the last earring card into the box, waved at Sherry, and went to deliver Diane's jewelry.

Chapter Two

DELIVERING THE JEWELRY WAS NO HARDSHIP. I loved the ambiance of our historic town square anchored by the limestone courthouse set on a slight rise. Traffic split to flow around the courts building on Magnolia Road, our north-south two-lane highway. The street was aptly named because magnificent magnolia trees graced the courthouse grounds, lilies crowded the flower beds in every season, and a cozy white wooden gazebo nestled beside the building. Today traffic still eased by on Magnolia, but tomorrow the road would be blocked off.

Surrounding the courthouse on all four sides were brick and limestone buildings, including our store. Built with shared walls that formed the bulk of our town square, every structure dated from the late 1800s to the 1960s and housed family-owned businesses, some that had been passed down through generations. Each business boasted high-tech features, yet each treated their customers the old-fashioned way. Lee Street bordered the square on the north side, and

Stanton Drive, named for my ancestor and Lilyvale's founder, bordered the south end.

I crossed Magnolia to do a quick reconnaissance mission, as Maise would say, and see if vendors needed anything. Although we'd have city police and county deputies patrolling the square all night, and in the daytime, too, most artisans planned to put their wares out in the morning. Today was geared for tent setups and preparing the spaces for displaying their art pieces on tables and shelves.

Everything was in order until I arrived at Diane's assigned spot to put the box of jewelry directly into her hands. Her space was catty-corner from the emporium and in front of Wallis Computer Sales & Repair, right where it should be. Her daughter, Darlene, and her teenaged grandson, Beau, had done a fine job of setting up the tent and her display tables.

Trouble was, Diane's tent was being crowded by Dexter Hamlin's Gone to the Dogs food cart. Two months ago when I'd first met him, I'd instantly detested Dex, a fleshy man in his forties with greasy hair and a permanent sneer. Although we had okayed a multichurch bake sale to run on Saturday, Hamlin was the sole licensed food vendor admitted to the festival. He'd pulled political strings to get approved even though no one seemed to have the least liking for him. It made me wonder what hold he had over his connections.

I made my face as blank as I could manage as I approached him.

"Mr. Hamlin, you've set up your stand way off your mark," I said reasonably. "You'll need to move to the left."

"Hell I will. That puts me too far from the action and too close to the cross street."

"You have more visibility closer to Lee Street, especially if you angle the front of your stand in that direction," I pointed out patiently.

"Ain't happenin' and here's another thing. I'm selling energy drinks whether you like it or not."

"I don't like it," I said through gritted teeth, "and neither will the pharmacy or other stores that have stocked extra energy drinks. You agreed to sell only water. You need to honor your word."

Dex's answer was to spit in the parking lot and yell at a slightly older man with hunched shoulders to move a case of corn dogs. The guy wore dingy white from his floppy gardener's hat to his untucked shirt and baggy pants, all the way to his tennis shoes.

If I'd been the violent type and Dex had been less of a bully, I might've smacked him and been done with it. Instead I held my temper with both hands and an act of God and held my ground.

"You will move, Mr. Hamlin, and you'll do it now. In fact, you'll set up a full fifteen feet away from the nearest tent."

He let loose with a string of obscenities insulting my ancestors, among other things. "You think you can force me to move? Try it."

Since I knew the rules about spacing between artists' tents and exactly what Dex had been permitted to sell, I pulled out my smart phone to punch some numbers.

"Who the hell you calling?" he barked as he loomed over me. Not a tall order since I'm only five-three.

"I'm calling reinforcements, Mr. Hamlin. I don't have the time to argue or the patience to put up with your attitude."

Thankfully, the call was answered before Hamlin could mount a retort. On a Friday afternoon, this near closing time, it was a miracle to reach anyone at the county offices.

"Hi, Ali. Is County Health Inspector Clancy Edwards still there? I need him in the square pronto. It's about the food vendor we let into the folk art festival."

I paused, listened, and watched as Dex's complexion turned a mottled purple. It would solve my problem if he stroked out on the spot, but no such luck. Mean of me, but it was how I felt.

"Okay, you can tell Mr. Edwards that I'd just as soon shut down Mr. Hamlin's operation altogether, but I'll settle for him doing what I say to do. And he needs to watch his mouth, too."

Now I smiled, nodded. "I'll be right here waiting, Ali, and thanks."

CLANCY EDWARDS WAS IN HIS FORTIES, AVERAGE IN height, weight, and looks in general, but his black curly hair and intense gray eyes made him memorable. I explained my issues to him, then stepped away as he talked with Dex Hamlin. After Edwards pointed at the ground and Lee Street repeatedly, and Hamlin replied with wild gestures including an abbreviated sign language obscenity, creepy Dex called to his helper and they moved the cart. Edwards stayed until I gave him the thumbs-up that the cart was in a position I could live with, and I overheard the inspector warn Dex not to move the cart again or to sell energy drinks.

In spite of the positive outcome, I held enough residual anger to spit a whole box of Fred's nails. I was also a little spooked by the black glare Hamlin gave me before I walked away. Talk about killing looks.

I absolutely could *not* go back to the emporium in this state. Sherry would know in a heartbeat that I was upset. Nope, I needed to vent, and I knew just the person to see.

I pushed through the Great Buns Bakery door and sent the customer bell to jangling. The air-conditioning cooled me physically, and a deep breath instantly gave me a sugar high. An old-fashioned lunch counter lined with tall bistro chairs and a small grill behind it took up one wall of the bakery. To the right stretched a glorious glass display case of tray upon tray of delightful deliciousness.

I spotted Great Buns co-owner and my friend Judy Armistead immediately. "I need a chocolate croissant and Fred's Colt .45."

She calmly nodded. "Don't we all."

Judy, a five-foot fireball, turned from the grill behind the stainless-steel countertop. Her green eyes always seemed merry, and her short medium-platinum blonde hair made her look fey. "Exactly who are you gunning for?"

"Dexter Hamlin."

"Gone to the Dogs Dex?"

"That's him."

"Some people just need shootin', don't they?" She used the spatula in her hand to point at "our" bistro table. The one closest to the phone so she could reach it quickly. "Sit before your fidgeting wears me thin."

I wasn't aware I fidgeted, but I did catch myself checking the time on my phone and realized it was a minute later than the last time I'd looked. Geez. On the upside, I had fifteen minutes to spare before I needed to head back to the store to meet Jasmine and our potential new employee.

I skirted the tall and normal-height bistro tables and chairs arranged in the dining space, and sat as instructed. Meantime, Judy snagged the largest chocolate croissant in the tray and warmed it in the microwave. In no time flat, she set two latte cups that looked more like bowls on the table. Then she placed the warm croissant on a white plate, plucked utensils and a napkin from their round holders, and headed around the counter. How she kept her white Great Buns apron over white twill pants and a white T-shirt from being spotted with everything from grill grease to chocolate icing, I'd never know. Her husband, Grant, never seemed to have a speck or spot marring his clothes either, and he was the chief baker.

I used a fork on the croissant instead of ripping into it with my bare hands because, hey, I was raised right. But when I found myself savagely chomping instead of sanely chewing, I forced myself to relax. I savored, and swallowed, and repeated until only flakes remained on my plate. I thought about eating those with my finger, but I did have standards. I only did that in the privacy of my apartment.

"Better?" Judy asked when I pushed the plate away.

"Great Buns always makes it better."

Judy quirked an eyebrow.

"That came out weird, but you know what I mean."

"Yes, and Grant and I thank you for praising our humble bakery. So what did Dex do to get you so riled?"

"Besides being a total pig, Horrible Hamlin gave me grief about his assigned spot, and told me he was selling energy drinks whether I liked it or not. He's a slimy jerk, and talk about obscenities! I'm no prude, but the man must curse every third word. He takes low language to new heights."

Judy patted my clenched hand. "Breathe, girl. Dex is supposed to be selling corn dogs and hot dogs, right?"

"And bottled water, but not a single thing more or heads will roll."

"How many artists are set up near him?" Judy asked.

"Only one, and I made him move another five feet away from the original spot I'd mapped for him. The man snaps at everyone, and yells at that middle-aged guy he hired to help him. I called Clancy Edwards and—"

"The county health inspector?"

"The very same. He came right over and laid down the law with Dex. Promised to close him down if he didn't comply with the health laws and my wishes and stick to selling only what he was approved to sell."

"What happens if he keeps making trouble?"

I grinned. "That's where Fred's Colt .45 comes in."

Judy chuckled. "Well, Dex aside, I still think it was very civic-minded to hold the festival here in town. I mean, no one on the square really suffered when it was out at your Aunt Sherry's, but if today's sales are any indication of the weekend draw, we'll make rent for a year."

"That's fantastic! I hope everyone does as well."

"You know it. Oh, are you taking a maple donut back for Fred?"

I laughed. "I have to sneak it in the back so Maise doesn't see it."

"I'll bag it for you," she said, and rose, sweeping up my plate and her cup.

I finished my coffee, took the empty cup to the counter, and pulled a ten-dollar bill from my back pocket.

A minute later, I waved good-bye, told Judy to give Grant my best, and eased out the door, hoping no one would waylay me. Luck was with me, and I quickly hoofed it around the corner, then turned into the alley that ran behind all the stores.

A city office building sat on the corner behind Judy's bakery, but a parking lot took the rest of the space across the alley. The Handcraft Emporium, the last building at the end of the block, had started life as the Stanton General Store, established by my ancestors who founded Lilyvale. The name changed to Sissy's Five & Dime when my great-something Aunt Sissy had taken over the store. She and her husband had lived upstairs in the apartment I now called home. My Aunt Sherry had eventually inherited the building and had rented it to a variety of businesses over the years.

When I'd come to town last April to find out why booms repeatedly shook my aunt's ancestral farmhouse and smoke billowed out the kitchen windows, I'd learned that my Aunt Sherry had macular degeneration. Her condition had nothing to do with the incidents, and the disease hadn't worsened or slowed her down one iota. But Sherry Mae had been my mother's sister, and we were the last of the Stantons. Leaving my job at the prestigious Gates Fine Art Gallery in Houston and moving to Lilyvale was the right decision.

The question of what to do with myself in the small town was solved when I proposed opening the Handcraft Emporium not only to sell the Silver Six's folk art but also take other arts and crafts on consignment. With my background in fine art and marketing, and an eye for design and arrangement,

I became store manager. Since the Six were already connected to the folk art world, the idea quickly caught on. Now the store provided Sherry, Aster, Eleanor, Fred, Dab, and all their folk art friends a venue to sell art and crafts all year-round. At last count, we handled the work of forty-two artists, and the arrangement had succeeded beyond my dreams to benefit both the craftspeople and the store.

The Silver Six, in their late sixties to early seventies, were far from idle before the emporium project. They had volunteered at the technical school and in organizations in town, and they had resumed their volunteering, more or less staggering their hours at the store. After all, they supplied a good bit of the items we sold, so they had to reserve time to create.

I snapped back from my meandering thoughts and hustled the last few steps to the emporium's back door. Fred wasn't in his workroom, but my two wiggling fur babies greeted me as soon as I stepped inside. Amber wagged her tail so hard her whole body got into the act. She made excited *unh-unh* noises while T.C. wound herself through my legs, meowing like she hadn't seen me in weeks.

I bent to pet the critters that had found and adopted me in June, and both shoved their twitching noses at the donut sack. I held it out of their reach.

"It's not for you, girls, and you know it. Now chill a minute. I need to put this in Fred's cupboard before Maise catches me."

Amber sneezed and shook her head as if to say, *Not happening.*

I found his goodies stash in one of the cabinets. The plastic container had once contained coffee and still retained the coffee scent but had been acquiring an eau d'donuts aroma. Fred had printed NUTS & BOLTS on the container with permanent marker and had gone to the trouble to put some of those same items in sealable bags to give it weight in case someone—like Maise—hefted it. Why he bothered,

I didn't know. Maise might be head chef at the farmhouse, and she delighted in feeding people, but she never came off as the food police.

Okay, maybe with me she did. She knew cooking was not my thing, so she loaded me up with leftovers several times a week. Hey, I knew when I had a good thing going.

As I recapped the container, my cell phone vibrated against my hip, and I grinned at the photo on the screen. Eric Shoar, Lilyvale Police Department detective. Six-feet-one of brown-haired, brown-eyed handsome with a deep, dreamy drawl.

He was the other good thing I had going. The very, very good thing.

I leaned against the closest worktable and answered the call.

"Hi, Eric." I grinned at Amber and T.C., who sat two feet from me, ears perked. I'd swear they knew Eric's name.

"Is the setup coming along well? Have the artists collected all their goods?"

"Far as I know, yes. And if the usual number of folk art buyers attend this shindig, the artists may sell out."

"Shindig? Is that a Fred-ism?"

"Nope, that's a Dab term. So how is it going at your end? Are the traffic issues under control?"

"If people follow directions, we'll be fine. A few business owners are complaining that we're closing Magnolia Road at eight."

"You're leaving Lee Street and Stanton Drive open, though, right?"

"Have to, for safety if nothing else. Emergency units need ready access."

I sucked in a breath and let it out in a whoosh of words. "Bite your tongue, Eric. Right this minute. We're not having an emergency this weekend. We're not having so much as a hangnail at this festival."

"It could be a happy emergency. Like a woman going into labor."

"Nice save, but if you just jinxed us, you will *never* hear the end of it."

He chuckled. "You're a hard woman, Nixy."

"Not me. Sherry and Maise and Eleanor will come after you."

"Not Aster?"

"No, but maybe I should have her break out the lavender water and spritz everything in sight."

"Ah, yes. Invoke the calm."

"Always. So, how is the new detective working out so far?" I asked, referring to Charlene Vogelman. Hired to replace the detective who'd had complications from surgery and then retired, Charlene was mid-thirties, tall, and blonde. Her athletic body had curves to spare, but I liked her every time we'd met and chatted. A recent widow taking care of her disabled father, she'd taken the job here to enjoy a slower pace and a slightly lower cost of living.

"Considering she came from a big city, she's getting the hang of things here."

Having lived in Houston, I didn't consider Tulsa, Oklahoma, that big, but then, I'd never been there. I'm sure Lilyvale was an adjustment.

"Good deal. Maybe you'll have more free time now."

"I'm counting on it. Speaking of which, I know I haven't seen you much in the past two weeks since I've been showing Vogelman the departmental ropes, but if you're not exhausted on Sunday night after the festival closes, let's go to dinner."

"Adam Daniel's?" I named the restaurant on the highway north of town that had been damaged in a storm in June and since been repaired. We'd had our first date there but had never made it back. Maybe this time would be the charm.

Still, I had to tease him. "Wait. You're really giving up *Sunday Night Football* for me?"

His dreamy voice deepened as he said, "You're more important."

"You sure know how to turn a girl's head, Detective," I purred.

He laughed, and then I heard a shout in the background. "Everything okay at the station?"

"Officer Benton just dropped that ancient ten-pound stapler on his hand. See you later."

I disconnected with a smile on my face but came down out of the clouds when I realized it was very quiet in the store. Too quiet.

Chapter Three

I'D NEVER KNOWN EXACTLY WHAT A FROZEN TABLEAU looked like until I threw open the door from the workroom and entered the emporium.

His walker nearby, Fred stood with Dab at the shelves, each with a small metal-art piece in hand.

At one round display table, Aster and Maise looked like they'd been arranging potions and lotions.

At the display in the bump-out window, Sherry held an egg basket suspended over the table as if she'd stopped in midplacement.

Behind the counter, Eleanor protectively stepped in front of Jasmine and a second young black woman I presumed was Kathy.

They all stared at a man who hovered inside the front door. Stooped shoulders, white shirt and pants, white tennis shoes.

"What are you doing here?" Eleanor asked, her voice low and harsh, completely different from her usual sweet tones.

I wouldn't have recognized it as hers if I hadn't seen her speak.

The man I'd seen fetching and carrying for Dex Hamlin took off his floppy gardener's hat and twisted it in his hands. His graying hair was thin and lank and somehow made him appear more pathetic.

I slid by Aster and Maise to stand on the outside of the counter, but I kept my mouth shut. Whatever was going on, the air vibrated with animosity and more than a little fear. Instinct told me it needed to play out.

"I'm not here to make trouble, Ms. Wainwright." His gaze roved the room to stop on Aster and Maise. He spoke again, slowly, as if measuring his words. "Ms. Parsons, Ms. Holcomb. I came to apologize to you."

"Apologize?" Eleanor gave a genteel snort. "A sadistic bully who not only made lives miserable but caused people physical injury? I do believe I take leave to doubt your sincerity."

I blinked at her angry rush of words.

"I understand, but it's true." He glanced at the rest of us, still as sculptures, then looked at Eleanor again and held her gaze. "Once I was fired with no money and no reference, I hit bottom. Some church folks up in Camden took me under their wings, and I changed. I'm determined to make amends where I can."

"What happened? Did you suddenly find religion?"

"Actually, I did," he said a little shyly. "Hard as it is to believe."

We were all silent for a moment. Talk about hearing a pin drop. Then Eleanor shook her head.

"If you're expecting forgiveness, lower your expectations. I don't know about Maise or Aster, or anyone else you wronged, but I had hoped never to see you again. I must insist that you leave our shop and not come back."

He nodded, turned toward the door, and then looked back

at Eleanor. "Thank you for your time. Even if you can't believe me, I am sorry for what I did and who I was."

The wind chimes rang as he opened and closed the door, but the happy sound sure didn't lighten the mood. Or break the tension. I did.

"What on earth was that about?" I asked the room in general.

Tension snapped in a torrent, everyone speaking nearly at once.

Eleanor: "That's the horrid man who drove me away from Ozark Arms."

Aster: "He managed the complex where Eleanor used to live, and Maise and I lived there for a few months, too."

Dab: "He bullied residents, neglected repairs, and worse, was drunk half the time."

Maise: "He was a mean drunk. Should've been hung from the yardarm instead of just fired."

Fred: "Tigers ain't changin' their stripes and neither has he."

The Six paused for a collective breath when another voice said, "I can't believe he came back."

I crossed to the counter where Jasmine and her friend still stood. "Are you Kathy Baker?" I asked.

She blinked at me. "Yes, ma'am."

"I'm Nixy, and I'm sorry we've had a scene on your first visit here."

"It's not your fault, Ms. Nixy," Kathy said, "but that man terrorized my mother and me."

Eleanor took the girl's hands in hers. "I know he did."

"He made fun of me, and he made my mother fall down the stairs. She broke her arm and couldn't work. He said if she pressed charges, he'd do worse." Kathy's eyes glistened with remembered pain, and her voice hardened. "Just now, though, he didn't even recognize me. He didn't apologize to me."

Eleanor drew her into a hug, and a moment later the front

door flew open, wind chimes sounding more discordant than they should've. Eleanor released Kathy and whirled as if on her guard, then relaxed as Detective Shoar strode in. Eric wore his usual attire of jeans, a button-down shirt, and western-style boots, and right now, his cop face, too. He didn't so much as share a smile with me, but with one sweeping glance that touched each of us, he knew something was wrong.

"Eleanor, I'm glad you're here."

He paused and did a double take at Kathy. "Excuse me if this sounds rude, but I know you, don't I?"

Kathy squared her shoulders. "Yes, sir, we met a few years ago. I'm Kathy Baker."

Eric snapped his fingers. "Yes, Connie's your mother. She moved over to El Dorado, didn't she? How is she doing?"

Kathy looked pleased he remembered both of them. "Yes, sir. We moved when my mom lost her job here, but she's fine now, thank you."

Eric jabbed a hand through his short hair. "I'm sorry to be the bearer of bad news, but you and Eleanor both need to hear this. Cornell Lewis is in town."

"We already know about Cornell Lewis," Eleanor said, tucking Kathy into a sideways hug. Jasmine stood at her friend's back.

"You do?" He looked from her to me. "Don't tell me he came in here. What happened? Nixy?"

I moved to stand beside him, and that seemed to finish unfreezing the tableau, because then Sherry, Dab, Fred, Maise, and Aster gathered with the rest of us at the antique counter.

"Mr. Lewis was just in here," I confirmed. "He said he came to apologize."

"Which he did, not that we believe a word of it," Maise said tartly.

"Claims he got religion," Fred grumbled. "Day that happens is the day I stop fixin' things."

Eleanor cleared her throat. “Eric, can you force Cornell to leave town?”

“Not if he’s a law-abiding citizen.”

Aster snorted. “Citizen? We don’t want him living here again. I don’t expect anyone who knew him would.”

Eric laid his palms flat again the glass countertop. “Did he threaten any of you? Was he abusive in any way?”

I had my opinion but let Eleanor answer.

“I wish I could say yes to that, but I must own that he was respectful enough.”

“With all of us present,” Dab said, “he wouldn’t have acted any other way.”

“True,” I agreed, “but Eleanor asked him to leave, and he didn’t put up a fuss. I don’t think he’ll be back.”

“What makes you think that?” Maise asked sharply.

I shrugged. “Just a vibe I got from him.”

Eleanor tilted her head at me and gave me a small smile. “I do believe your vibes have proven accurate in the past.”

“Most of them,” Sherry said, and turned to Kathy, who had stepped away from Eleanor. “I hope this incident won’t keep you from working for us over the weekend. Jasmine speaks so highly of you, and we very much want this to be a good fit.”

“These people are really great to work for, Kath,” Jasmine said. “I wouldn’t have suggested it to you otherwise.”

Kathy gazed toward the door, then rubbed her hands up and down her arms as if she was chilled. “I like all of you, but I don’t know. It’s been three years since I saw him, but that man scares me.”

“You won’t be alone in the store,” Maise assured her. “We’ll be here all weekend.”

“I wish you’d reconsider, Kathy,” Eleanor said. “I feel like I’m repaying your mother for all her kindnesses to me in some small way if you’d join our little family.”

“You’re positive I won’t have to be alone with him?”

"As Maise said, you won't be alone at all." Aster grinned. "In fact, we'll probably drive you nuts with our chattering."

Fred harrumphed. "And if they do, you come visit me back in my workshop. You can play with Nixy's critters."

"Amber and T.C.," Jasmine put in. "The sweetest dog and cat. You'll love them."

"And they'll love you," I said dryly, "as long as you give them treats."

Fred snorted. "They ain't beggars, and you know it. Speakin' of which, one of us should look in on them. Kathy, you want to come meet 'em now?"

"Go ahead," Maise encouraged. "We'll take ten and then get back to cleanup duty."

"Nice to see you, Kathy," Eric said as she headed off with Fred and his walker. Then he turned to me. "Nixy, walk out with me?"

Dab returned to shelving metal-art pieces, Aster began spritzing her lavender water all over the store, and the other women simply shooed me off.

Outside, Eric took my hand, and we headed south away from the square.

"I feel awful not knowing in advance that Lewis was back."

I squeezed his hand. "You told Eleanor as soon as you could, and it's not like you could've stopped him from showing up."

"Except knowing would've put her on her guard so she didn't feel ambushed."

"Yes, well, speaking of which, there's something else you need to know."

Eric stopped in front of the shoe repair shop. "Regarding Lewis?"

"Yes. He's working for Dex Hamlin."

"The obnoxious hot dog guy? How do you know?"

"Because I had a set-to with Hamlin about an hour ago.

He didn't set up in the space I'd marked off for his stand, and then he demanded to sell energy drinks when he's only approved to sell the food and bottled water."

"And you saw Lewis at the stand?"

"Uh-huh, and if Cornell Lewis was a bully, he's getting a taste of his own medicine in spades."

Eric smiled without humor. "Hamlin is the kind of guy who gives rednecks a bad name. Did you set him straight or do I need to have a word with him?"

"No, thanks. I took care of it, and I don't want him any more riled than he already is."

"Understood. I'll alert the patrols to keep an eye on both of them."

"I appreciate that, Eric, but the point is, I didn't tell anyone that Cornell is working in the square for the next two days."

"Anyone meaning the Silver Six?"

"And Kathy and Jasmine. I really don't think the man will darken the emporium door again, but—"

"Any one of them could spot him while they're strolling the square," he finished.

"Yep, and I have to tell them so they'll be prepared."

"You do."

"Of course, it's unlikely the Six will be buying hot dogs or corn dogs."

"But Jasmine and Kathy might. They should know the score."

I sighed. "I'll round 'em up and break the news when I go back."

"Good. And I'll have the guys patrolling pay extra attention to what's happening at the food stand."

We came to a corner, and Eric tugged me to the side street, where he grasped my waist and pulled me closer.

"Why, Detective Shoar, are you frisking me?"

"Nah, just stealing a kiss."

* * *

I BROKE THE NEWS THAT CORNELL LEWIS WAS working for Dex Hamlin at Gone to the Dogs as soon as I returned to the emporium. No point in putting it off any longer. Besides, the seniors knew me well enough to know when I was holding back. Darn it.

The Silver Six took it more in stride than I'd hoped, and not even Kathy seemed too fazed.

"He's working for Dex Hamlin?" Eleanor shook her head. "That man might be a worse bully than Rotten to the Core."

"Who?" I asked.

She smiled. "That's what we residents called Cornell Lewis. A little levity went a long way."

"We wouldn't patronize Hamlin's stand anyway," Aster sniffed, "but we'll be bringing our noon meals and snacks to the shop. Maise has everything ready to go."

"We'll have plenty for you girls, too," Maise added, "so come to work hungry."

With that, the subject of Cornell Lewis seemed to be closed. That suited me. I'd had enough drama for the day.

I pitched in to rearrange the art and craft items so that the store didn't look quite so bare. The emporium was crowded with goods more often than not, and I tended to feel a little claustrophobic in the store. In my former job at the Gates Art Gallery, I'd arranged shows with ample negative space. White space between the pieces let the eye settle on each one. I can deal with the crammed store now, partly because I do all I can to space out the displays, and partly because my uncluttered apartment is a respite.

We sent Kathy and Jasmine home at six. I was having dinner with Sherry and the gang, but I wanted to do a walk-through of the square first, just to make sure all was as ready as possible for tomorrow. With Amber and T.C. on their leashes, I locked the door and stepped out front.

The temperature had dropped, but the humidity seemed higher. Maybe because the breeze had all but died. Hopefully we wouldn't have gusty winds to play havoc with the tents.

Only a few vendors remained at their booths, and they had everything under control. The festival would run from nine to five tomorrow, and nine to four on Sunday. We'd thought about opening later on Sunday in deference to church services, but shoppers would gather early whether we were technically open or not, and every hour of sales time counted.

I reached Dex's Gone to the Dogs food stand and paused. It was closed tight, so I'd check on him in the morning. Unobtrusively check on him. I didn't want to rub his nose in my victory, but I needed to be absolutely certain that he followed the rules. I'd never suffered fools gladly, and I wasn't about to let one jerk ruin our event.

A sharp bark took me out of my head, and I focused on Amber and T.C., who sat at my feet.

"Bet you're bored just sitting there, huh?"

Amber got to her feet first, then T.C.

"Ready to go eat at the farmhouse?"

I didn't know if they understood "farmhouse" as well as "eat," but Amber barked and T.C. loudly *rrreowed*, and both pulled at their leashes. Time to mobilize, as Maise would say.

Chapter Four

WE DINED SIMPLY THAT NIGHT ON LEAN HAMBURGERS grilled courtesy of Dab and Aster, and all the fixin's courtesy of Sherry and Eleanor. Maise had prepared southern-style potato salad, too, and conversation at the table revolved around our readiness for the festival. Make that my readiness.

"I saw the stack of paperwork on the clipboard," Sherry said, "but are you certain everyone has signed release forms?"

"I'm sure, Aunt Sherry. I got the last of them this afternoon, and checked off artists as they arrived."

"And the police are patrolling the square tonight?" Aster asked.

"And deputies, too. The artists have their stuff locked up tight."

Maise gave a curt nod. "Sounds like everything's ship-shape."

"It will stay that way so long as Dex Hamlin doesn't give me more trouble." I paused, then decided to ask the question that had been burning in the back of my brain. "Maise, when did you and Aster live in Eleanor's apartment complex?"

"After our house burned to the ground. Kids shooting off fireworks on New Year's Eve."

Aster picked up the story. "We were away for the holiday visiting friends, so we had some clothes, toiletries, and whatnot."

"And that clunker of a car," Fred put in.

"We knew Eleanor from church functions," Maise continued. "She mentioned an empty apartment in her complex."

"We thought we'd have to sign a yearlong lease, but we only needed a place for a few months."

"I do believe Cornell pocketed their rent without formally leasing the apartment," Eleanor said. "Once they moved in, I feared I'd lose their friendship for suggesting the complex."

"He was truly rotten to the core, but it was the perfect, inexpensive, temporary place to stay until the insurance company finished investigating our claim and paid us," Maise said.

"When did you come to live with Sherry?" I asked.

"In early March," Aster said. "We'd met her volunteering at community events. When she learned Cornell had a long-term tenant lined up, and we had to move, she offered her home."

"It was supposed to be temporary," Maise added.

"But we got along so well, and I was tired of rattling around this big house without Bill. I asked them to stay—"

"And we took her up on it," Aster said, beaming. "The three of us organized the very first folk art festival."

I had heard them talk about the first few festivals, and knew the inaugural one had been held three and a half years ago.

"When did the rest of you come? I've heard bits and pieces, but never heard the real stories. I'm interested."

"Curious and nosy is what you are," Fred said on a chuckle, "but I don't mind tellin' you. Sherry took me in next. Broke my fool hip, and wouldn't you know I lived in an upstairs apartment."

"Bill and I had known Fred forever," Sherry said.

"Knew my missus, too."

"Ester, yes," Sherry said with a warm smile. "When I heard about Fred's predicament, I offered him the room I'd had converted for Bill after his stroke. That was three years ago this past summer."

Dab nodded. "I lived across the road in that newer development." He meant the one dating from the 1970s, but that was new around Lilyvale.

"We all knew Dab's wife, Melba," Sherry put in.

"She'd been gone a year, and I needed a change."

"He also came to our fall festival that year, and we got to talking about distilling flowers and herbs," Aster said.

"We invited him to join the gang," Sherry said, "and he moved here in October, wasn't it?"

"First of November," Dab corrected, "and Eleanor joined us after Christmas, didn't you?"

"As soon as my lease was up," Eleanor said. "Cornell didn't push Kathy's mother down the stairs, but he was yelling and crowding her. She stepped back and fell. I lived in one of the other upstairs apartments and saw Connie fall."

"She took Kathy in," Aster said, "while Connie was in the hospital."

"That was the last straw for me with Cornell."

"I'm glad he was fired before his bullying killed anyone," I said.

"I heard tell it nearly did," Maise said, "but I don't recall the details."

An odd look crossed Eleanor's face, but Maise distracted me.

"Nixy, you run those extra burgers and potato salad over to Old Lady Gilroy before you go. We'll take care of KP."

Though I enjoyed doing dishes a lot more than I did cooking, I hadn't seen Bernice Gilroy for a week. I always looked forward to visiting with the elfin woman, for however long she let me stay. Which usually wasn't more than ten minutes.

As usual, she opened the front door of her tiny two-bedroom house, grabbed my arm, and jerked me inside. I'd taken to packing her meals in a large basket with handles instead of carrying containers in a box, or worse, food on paper plates. Less chance of dumping food all over her wood floors.

"Get on in here, Sissy," she said, leading the way to the kitchen that had been out of date since the 1970s.

At least she still called me "Sissy." She'd known my many-times great-aunt and likened me to the woman. At first I worried for her memory. Mrs. Gilroy had celebrated her ninety-fourth birthday on August seventeenth—same month as mine but mine's on the second. I soon realized Bernice used the name Sissy to tease me, or get my attention if it wandered. Now I worried if she called me Nixy.

Wearing one of her signature housedresses that buttoned up the front, and anklets with moccasins—today's anklets the same shade of yellow as her dress—she didn't look as frail as the last time I'd seen her. Her grip on my arm was far from frail, too. She towed me through the small living room with its two faded plaid wingback chairs, a scarred wood coffee table, and a massive flat-screen TV. Sherry actually owned the property, but Bernice wouldn't hear of allowing us to freshen the house and décor for her. At least she now routinely opened the brown kitchen curtains. The windows faced south and east, so she got a good amount of sunlight. The south window looked out to the farmhouse, and this was where Bernice sat, her binoculars resting on the 1950s table. The solitary chair at the table always made tears prick the back of my eyes.

"I suppose the art festival is all ready to go in its new location," she said as I put the basket on the table and began unloading the food. "You know I'm still peeved with you about that. How am I going to keep up with news if I can't see what's happening yonder through my own windows?"

I grinned at her. "I thought you had your spies reporting."

"I prefer to call them sources," she sniffed, "but I'd rather see it live in color than hear about it secondhand."

"You could always come to town."

She looked at me like I'd suggested she strip and dance on the roof.

"Ruin my image as an eccentric recluse? I'd have people knocking at my door day and night if I went jaunting off to town. You know I don't like company. Except for you. And then only if you don't disturb my shows."

"Yes, ma'am." She still wouldn't let a single one of the Six in the house, even though they'd been setting food on her porch for years.

"Of course," she added, a sly gleam in her gray eyes, "I'm still willing to meet that hunky boyfriend of yours."

"He's been busy with the new detective the department hired."

"A woman, I hear. She pretty?"

"She is, and very nice, too."

Bernice snorted. "Pretty is as pretty does. I don't condone chasing a man, but when are you going to kick things up a notch?"

"Excuse me?" I said. Bernice must've been watching Emeril Lagasse on TV as well as *NCIS*. She loved Mark Harmon.

"I mean get engaged," the little gnome said tartly, "though there's nothing wrong these days with testing out your physical compatibility. If you know what I mean."

"Uh, yes, I know," I stammered, sure I was blushing. "I'll see about bringing Eric around to meet you. I know he's wanted to."

"Humph. He may feel different when I set him straight about putting a ring on that."

"'Put a ring on that?'" I echoed on a laugh. "Bernice, do you listen to Beyoncé?"

"I'm not just any old lady, you know. Now let's see what you brought over for me."

She peered at the sealed containers—cooked burger patties, the potato salad and a bit of leftover slaw, sliced tomato, red onions, and bread-and-butter pickles, and buns in a zippered plastic bag.

Then she shook her head.

"I hope Maise is making heartier meals next week. I haven't had a slice of pie in a while either, and I wouldn't turn down a piece of cake."

"How can you not weigh more feeding that sweet tooth the way you do?"

"Clean living, Sissy. Now scoot. I have a late show coming on."

I left with my delivery basket and a smile. Even though Bernice could seemingly conjure some things she wanted, sweets were apparently not on that list. I made a mental note to get her some goodies from Great Buns. Now if only I could get her to tell me how she bought her flat-screen TV and her smart phone, and how she got them set up without leaving her house. My money was still on faeries.

I BOUNDED OUT OF BED EARLY THE NEXT MORNING to feed and walk the critters. Amber pranced around my feet as I poured her kibble, and T.C. rubbed her cheek against my leg.

For someone who'd never had one pet, much less two, I'd adjusted quite quickly and quite well to my critters since they'd come to me in June. I didn't even mind the shedding. Much. I simply cleaned my white overstuffed sofa, chairs, and comforter every few days with a special pet hair removal tool that actually worked. Okay, it got most of the stray fur.

Amber and T.C. had lived with an elderly woman in Minden, Louisiana, who'd passed on a few months before they appeared at my alley door. I'd gleaned that small bit of their history from their owner's neighbor when she'd learned they were with me and came to visit. She didn't know where they'd gone to or who might've taken them after their mistress died, but imagined they'd had a Disney-worthy adventure on their way to me. I could easily see that, because from the state their paws had been in, the vet thought they had walked long and far.

The fur babies had tended to be very quiet, and creepily well behaved at first. As if they were waiting for me to accept them before they showed their more playful sides. They were still inseparable, but their individual personalities had emerged in full force.

Now, as I sat at the kitchen peninsula eating cereal, T.C. swiped at Amber's near-empty food dish, then sprinted off in a blur. Amber gave chase, her paws slipping on the original pine hardwood floor that I'd refinished.

I washed my bowl and went to get dressed. The day was supposed to be beautiful, so I donned cropped jeans, another Handcraft Emporium tee, and sports socks with my navy-and-white tennis shoes. The critters parked themselves behind me in the bathroom, where I added eye shadow and mascara and put my brown hair in its usual ponytail.

The animals knew the second I'd finished. Amber's golden eyes looked more eager than T.C.'s green ones, but when does a cat ever look eager?

"Ready to go, girls?"

Amber gave a short bark, trotted to the basket of pet paraphernalia by the apartment door, and carried both her leash and T.C.'s to me. Amber wore her collar all the time, but T.C. stepped into her harness only for walks. She'd seemed to know how to get into it from the start, so she was just as cooperative for Fred and Dab when they walked her as she was for me.

Of course the collar, harness, and leashes matched. Eric had seen to that when he'd gone shopping for them. He'd insisted when we found the critters that he couldn't keep them, but he played with them plenty. We'd even taken them to the dog park, and yes, I had the okay to include T.C. We usually went at dinnertime when the park was empty. Which reminded me I needed to take them back after the festival.

We took one of our usual routes along residential streets off the square that offered grassy areas between the sidewalks and curbs for them to do their business. T.C. had a cat box and used it, but if Amber was doing her thing, T.C. had to make her mark, too.

By the time we got to the emporium, the Silver Six were there and raring to go, judging by the chatter coming from the store space. As usual, I left Amber and T.C. in the workroom along with their leashes. T.C. had a litter box there, both animals had toys, and Fred liked for them to keep him company.

Although Fred wasn't in the back at the moment. Must be out front.

"Nixy, good, you're back," Sherry sang when I entered the front of the store to see the Six lined up by the counter.

Surprise, surprise. They all wore the Handcraft Emporium aprons. I must've looked as astonished as I felt, because Sherry grinned.

"Yes, child, we're all dressed in our official store uniform and ready to rock. Are you?"

"I am."

"Good. The vendors are arriving, so why don't you go check that they have everything they need?"

All the artists should need were their wares and lots of shoppers to show up, but I headed out the front door with blank sheets of paper fastened to my clipboard for note taking—just in case.

WE WERE ALL SYSTEMS GO BY NINE O'CLOCK. THE tents were open, the booths in each parking lot facing the other to form comfortably wide, easy-to-shop aisles. The city works department had placed large trash cans at either end of the corridors and one each in the middle, too. The better to keep the streets clean, we hoped.

I'd helped several artisans tweak their displays for maximum buyer appeal, and people streamed into the square from the side streets where they'd parked. Most businesses on the square that normally didn't open until ten o'clock had decided to open early, and I noticed that both the Lilies Café and Great Buns Bakery had people flowing in and out, some likely having come for breakfast.

Gone to the Dogs wasn't open yet, and I hadn't expected it to be. Not a lot of call for hot dogs or corn dogs this early, and vendors had brought their own water. However, the ecumenical bake sale tables were loaded with every kind of cookies, brownies, cakes, pies, and tarts imaginable, and I imagined there were yet more goodies in reserve. I spotted Ida Bollings's pear bread, and the lemon bars from Judy's bakery. The cake brownies with a single pecan half on top that Sherry and Eleanor had made were out and ready to sell, and so were the snickerdoodles Maise and Aster had baked. Each paper or plastic plate was wrapped with plastic wrap because the churches required it, but the Silver Six ladies used fitted bowl covers over the wrap. They looked like clear shower caps but were made for food storage. All the goodies carried a label naming the kind of item, whether it contained nuts, and the name of the donors. In addition to the plain white label, Aster had stuck one of her Aster's Garden labels on the elasticized cover.

I thought about scoring a pie or cake for Bernice Gilroy but decided she'd be better off with slices rather than the whole enchilada. So to speak. Ida's pear bread tempted me, too, but she and Fred had been keeping company, so the Six were well stocked and shared generous slices with me.

The event was running even more smoothly when I checked at ten thirty and again at noon. The bake sale was still going strong, though Ida's pear bread, Judy's lemon bars, Aster and Maise's snickerdoodles, and Sherry and Eleanor's brownies had been snapped up between my rounds. The hot dog stand had opened just before eleven and was doing almost as much business as everyone else.

At one thirty, the temperature was a perfectly pleasant seventy-five degrees and a light wind ruffled the tent canopies. I did the barefoot test on the concrete and decided it wasn't too hot to take Amber and T.C. with me on my next swing through the festival.

The two critters were a hit with both adults and children, so it took a while to wend my way through all the booths. One tyke of about three asked to play fetch with Amber, so his mother and I took him up to the grassy area around the courthouse at the opposite end from Dex's food truck. Amber put her head and shoulders down, her haunches in the air, and wagged her tail for all she was worth. Each time the little boy threw the stick we'd found, Amber bounded after it, sometimes leaping like a deer. The little boy laughed so hard, he fell on his behind. At that point T.C. pawed his head, then went to get her own smaller stick.

"Thank you for indulging us," the child's mother said. "Mark will be asking for a pet again, but he'll sleep well tonight."

I waved as she carried him off, then resumed my rounds. I purposely didn't have my wallet with me. I didn't even have a ten-dollar bill in my back pocket. If I had, I'd have been buying art and craft pieces right and left. I really was too lazy to dust a lot of bric-a-brac in my place, even though I had nearly a whole wall of built-in shelves in my dining room. I didn't know that many people to buy gifts for either. Although . . . hmmm. Christmas was coming.

With that thought, I allowed myself to do some semi-serious browsing instead of barreling through my rounds.

One thing I'd noted at the April festival was that the types of items were unique to each artist. There were virtually no duplications, and the few who did make similar goods priced their pieces the same as the others did. No price wars, no undercutting. The same was true now.

Deb the Soap Lady had large bars in absolutely divine scents, magnolia being one I thought Sherry might enjoy. I loved the gardenia and rosemary mint, and put those on the list to give myself. One of the textile artists had a handwoven scarf that was meant for Eleanor. Maise wore small pieces of jewelry, but Aster still loved her hoop earrings. Diane had both at her booth, and I debated whether to buy them from her at the festival or simply buy them from the store. Of course, they could be gone by the time I came back armed with cash. I shrugged. If they were sold before I got to them, then I was meant to buy something else.

Finished at Diane's booth, I looked over at Gone to the Dogs. The vendor stand featured a large, boxy stainless-steel-and-glass hot dog rotisserie. A sign reading DOGS was displayed across the top, facing customers. Two people were in line, but I saw only Cornell Lewis, not Horrible Hamlin. About that time, Amber and T.C. both pulled on their leashes, straining toward the food cart. Since they were good about letting me walk them instead of the other way around, I figured they were drawn by the aroma and let them lead me nearer.

After the last customer in line was served and walked away, a boy about six years old dashed up to the stand. His jeans looked a little too short and his superhero tee a little too small. His wide smile revealed a missing tooth. I reined in the critters and watched.

"Mister, mister," he called, his chin just topping the food stand counter.

Cornell aimed a broad smile at the child and bent slightly closer to his young customer. "Would you like a hot dog, sir?"

The boy reached up, opened his fist, and dropped fifty-two cents on the counter. Up came the other hand, and he plopped a small plastic bag of peanuts next to the coins. Cornell wrinkled his nose and straightened.

"Can I buy a hot dog for this money and my peanuts?"

The vendor scratched his chin. "Well, sir, I can't have your peanuts. I'm allergic to them."

The child canted his head. "What's *'lergic* mean?"

"If I eat even one peanut, I itch something fierce, and break out in big spots, and then I can't breathe."

The tyke's wide eyes sparkled with fascination. "Wow. I better get these away from you."

He plucked the bag off the counter, and then frowned as Cornell pushed the coins toward him. "Does that mean I can't have a hot dog?"

"It means you get one for free."

"But why?"

Cornell smiled down at the upturned face. "You were going to share your food with me, so I'm sharing mine with you. Do you want mustard or ketchup?"

"Both, please."

Cornell used tongs to place a bun in a white paper tray and the hot dog in the bun, then made a show of carefully squirting condiments over the meat and bread. That done, he palmed a short stack of napkins.

"There you go, sir," he said as handed the tray to the boy with flourish.

"Thank you."

When the boy started to turn away, Cornell stopped him. "Sir, you forgot your money."

The child waved a fistful of napkins. "You keep the change, mister. Mama says to always leave a tip."

He bounded off, and Cornell watched a moment before he reached for the roll of paper towels and sprayed it with what smelled like a cleaning solution. He first blotted the coins the child left on the counter and moved them aside. After that, he wiped the counter itself, trashed the paper towel, and used the hand sanitizer on the counter.

Amber and T.C. had patiently sat on their haunches, noses twitching. Now T.C. *reeeowed* like a banshee, and Amber gave a sharp bark. That was when Cornell Lewis spotted them. And me.

I saw the flash of recognition in his eyes, but he didn't seem perturbed. He put down the cookie he'd just bitten into, and with his tone casual and polite, he said, "Hello. May I get you something?"

Amber barked again and T.C. meowed as if saying, *Yes, please.*

I stepped closer to the counter and saw that the cookies he'd bought were Maise and Aster's snickerdoodles. The cover with their labels sat beside the plate containing only four cookies, plus the half he'd just put down.

"I see you've been to the bake sale."

"I've had a weakness for snickerdoodles since I was a boy, and the nice lady sold me a whole dozen for three dollars." He looked at the plate. "I need to ration the rest of these, but once I start eating them, it's hard to stop. Say, I don't suppose you let your dog and cat have sweets."

"They wish, but no. Thanks anyway."

"How about a little bit of hot dog?" He pulled one out of the cooker. "Is it all right if they have a bite of this?"

I scanned the area, then fixed my gaze on Cornell. "Uh, thank you, but not if Dex Hamlin is around."

"He isn't. He went off to have a smoke. And probably a beer. He won't know, if that's your worry." He paused. "Or maybe you don't want to accept anything from me. I guess that would be associating with the enemy."

"I don't know all that happened in the past, but I'm willing to give you the benefit of the doubt for now. As long as you stay away from Eleanor, Aster, Maise, and Kathy."

"Kathy?" he echoed, brow furrowed.

"Her mother fell down the stairs and broke her arm because of you."

He paled. "Oh, yes, Mrs. Baker's daughter. I'd forgotten the child's name. I'm ashamed I was a mess for so long, and

I want to make amends, but I won't push. I'll be gone by Monday."

"You aren't moving back here?"

"No, I took this job hoping to reach out to some people I wronged."

"Where are you staying?"

"In my car for now," he said ruefully. "It beats living on the streets, and it's easier to keep clean than an apartment."

I couldn't help but smile. "I hear that."

"So what do you say to a few bites of meat for your pets?"

Whether he'd found religion or not, I read regret and sadness in his eyes, and his steady, calm gaze convinced me of his sincerity. I must've conveyed some cue to T.C. and Amber, for they moved closer and did what they seldom do. Haunches down, they sat up and full-on begged.

"They'd obviously love it. Thank you."

Cornell chuckled and cut the hot dog in half, then into smaller pieces. With the treats in a paper tray, he came out the back of the booth, set the food on the ground, then backed up a few steps and hunkered to watch the fur babies eat. I decided to snap a few pictures with my phone camera.

Was I surprised the animals didn't growl or act skittish with the man who'd been a bully? Absolutely. The critters surprised me again, and so did Cornell, when my pets finished eating and went to him to lick his hands and be petted. Yes, he had essence of hot dog on his hands, but they seemed to be thanking him, not merely copping another taste. I took two quick photos before Cornell retrieved the paper plate. I thanked him again, and he wished me a good day before returning to the food cart. No trauma. No drama.

I was reviewing my pictures when the critters suddenly pulled me backward on their leashes. With a death grip on my cell, I spun around, off balance. In the blink of an eye, I crashed into a man, jostling his hand that held his cell phone.

Chapter Five

"OH, NO!" I CRIED AS THE MAN'S PHONE FLEW IN an arc.

We both lunged toward it, but Amber leaped and caught it in her mouth, just like she did when Eric and I tossed a soft disk for her to catch. Except the phone was heavier.

"Good girl," I said quickly, "but don't bite down and don't drop it."

She sat on her haunches looking proud.

"Okay, Amber, give me the phone," I said as I reached for it. She didn't run off with it as she sometimes did with the play disk but delicately laid it in my hand and happily panted.

I peered at the screen looking for damage. It wasn't cracked, but a photo of Cornell feeding the critters, with me off to the side, showed on the display. I turned it over but didn't see teeth marks on the black plastic cover.

"Here you go," I said after wiping the phone on my emporium shirt. "I don't think my dog's teeth scratched the screen or the case, but I am sorry I knocked into you. I hope I didn't make you drop a call."

"Better a dropped call than a shattered screen," he replied. His tone was reserved, but without heat. The average-looking guy was dressed in jeans, a red Arkansas Razorbacks polo shirt, and work boots. "Your dog saved the day."

"Glad she could help, and I hope you aren't allergic to dogs or cats."

He shook his head but didn't extend a hand to my critters as most people did, and while they were perfectly calm, they didn't seek his attention either.

I gestured at the cell. "What I mean is I'm sure there's a bit of hair and slobber on that."

"It's fine, really."

"I'm Nixy," I said to make conversation. "Are you enjoying the festival?"

"Lee Durley, and I am, but I've lost my sister."

"She's not a small child, is she?" I asked anxiously.

"Oh, no. I had her on the phone, but the reception isn't great here."

"I'm all too aware of that. You can try Great Buns Bakery or Gaskin's Business Center. They recently installed signal boosters that might help."

"Thanks for the tip," he said affably. "So you live here?"

"Since about six months ago. I'm in charge of the festival."

"Really? You've done a good job."

"Thank you. It's our first time holding it on the square, so I was a bit nervous."

He smiled. "I'm only nervous about how much money my sister is spending. Her husband will have my head."

"Then duck," I advised with a grin.

He laughed. "I'll remember. If you'll excuse me?"

"Of course, enjoy the rest of your day. Oh, and pig sooie."

He gave me a blank look, so I waved a hand at his chest. "Your shirt."

He glanced down. "Oh, yeah. Go, Razorbacks. Excuse me, I need to get a couple of hot dogs."

I watched as he strode toward the hot dog stand, wondering why he hadn't picked up on my Razorbacks reference until I prompted him.

Okay, so maybe football wasn't the religion here that it was in Texas, but why wear a team shirt if you weren't a fan?

AFTER RETURNING THE CRITTERS TO FRED'S WORKroom, where they fawned all over him, I found I wasn't needed in the store, so I went up the block to Great Buns. I hadn't forgotten my vow to get some pie and cake for Bernice Gilroy, so I grabbed some cash from my apartment and sped on my way. Now was as good a time as any to see what kinds of desserts Judy and Grant had available.

I glanced over the crowd of shoppers, looking to see if Durley had found his sister, but didn't see him. I must've worn an odd expression as I entered the empty bakery because Judy looked up from wiping a table and said, "What's wrong?"

Since the store was empty, I told her, "I met a guy at the festival."

"Does Eric have competition?"

"Nowhere near. This man struck me as weird."

"Dex Hamlin and Cornell Lewis weird or regular weird?"

Earlier, when I'd seen her between the breakfast and lunch rushes, I'd told her all about the ex–apartment manager's visit to the emporium. Appalled at his nerve, and especially concerned for Eleanor and Kathy, she'd promised to text or call me if she saw Cornell Lewis so much as headed toward the emporium.

"Regular weird. His name is Lee Durley. Does that ring a bell?"

She looked at the faux-tin ceiling in thought, then eyed me. "I can't place anyone by that name, so he's not a regular customer. What's twitching your antenna about him?"

"He's wearing a Razorbacks polo shirt, but when I said 'pig sooie,' he didn't immediately come back with 'Go, Razorbacks.' He looked completely bumfuzzled, like I'd spoken Martian."

Judy frowned. "That *is* odd, especially considering the team is doing well this year. But men don't pay as much attention to their clothes as we do. Not until they have to dress up."

"I never thought about it like that." I paused. "Is it odd that he had a photo of the critters and me with Cornell Lewis on his cell?"

"Explain."

I gave her the highlights of the cell sailing through the air, Amber snatching it, and me looking for damage.

"Nixy, you know how many people here are taking pictures to post on every social media site on the planet?"

"Hmm. I hadn't thought about that. He could be an amateur photographer. From the glance I had, it was rather a nice human-interest sort of photo."

"There you go." She gave me an evil grin. "Or he could be a spy for another festival. Maybe you should tail him."

I rolled my eyes. Judy had provided some key information last June when a woman was murdered, and she'd caught the let's-investigate bug.

"I'm too busy."

"Too busy to be Nixy Drew?"

Nixy Drew was Eric's not-so-fond nickname for me. "I knew I shouldn't have told you about that."

"Hey, what are friends for if not to throw these little things in your face? Now, do you want a chocolate croissant today?"

"Believe it or not, I'm passing on the pastry for myself, but I'm shopping for Mrs. Gilroy."

"Old Lady Gilroy? The woman who lives next door to Sherry Mae?"

I chuckled. "That's her."

Judy gaped. "She's still letting you in her house?"

"She won't for long if I don't feed her sweet tooth. What kinds of pies and cakes do you have today?"

"Lorna is the one you need to see about pies. Remember my deal with her? We aren't in that much competition to begin with, but we decided she'll serve hot breakfasts, salads, and full lunches instead of sandwiches, and limit the dessert menu to pies."

"So you're doing breakfast biscuits and lunch sandwiches. Hot and cold?"

"In this weather, most customers are ordering cold. I do have cake, though. The bake sale lured a lot of my regular cake customers," she said, walking to the display case. "What did you have in mind?"

"I know she likes white cake with chocolate icing," I said, keeping my drool in check with supreme effort.

"Will this do?" she asked, pointing to a plate of two-layer Nirvana.

I almost got two slices but settled for one large one. That ought to keep Bernice happy in case Lorna Tyler at the Lilies Café had already closed or was out of pie.

I dropped the cake off at the emporium. Maise wasn't thrilled I'd bought cake at Great Buns instead of asking her to make one, but I told her I didn't want to add to her to-do list right now. She could bake whatever she liked for Mrs. Gilroy later. I did warn her I was after pie at Lorna's place, but she merely waved me away. I didn't know what I could do to—pardon the pun—turn her up sweet later, but I'd think on it. Fortunately, none of the Silver Six held grudges.

Except maybe in Eleanor's and Kathy's cases against Cornell Lewis. And, really, who could blame them?

I liked Lorna Tyler. Her husband, Clark, not so much. I rushed into the café, steeling myself to see him, and was delighted when I found only Lorna there. I crossed the original pine floors to where she stood at the bar, a huge stretch of oak with a beautiful patina. The bar was one of the two original fixtures dating from the late 1800s, when the building had been a saloon downstairs and a boardinghouse upstairs. Or maybe "boardinghouse" was too polite a word. The back staircase was also original, though I'm sure it had been repaired from time to time. I could easily imagine cowboys taking their ladies of the evening to a room for a little female comfort. Now the downstairs housed the Lilies Café, and the upstairs was known as the Inn on the Square.

Lorna smiled as I approached.

"You'll be happy to know that all four of my rooms are rented to lovely families. Not a troublemaker in sight."

"Excellent, Lorna!" After some unfortunate incidents with—shall I say—some unruly guests, she had finally installed some much-needed security cameras. Clark didn't like it, but I'm not sure he liked anything but golf these days. The cameras might never be crucial again, but better safe than sorry, right?

"So what brings you here? If you're checking on how business is doing, it's booming in spite of the bake sale. I made omelets this morning until I was clucking. At one point, we had a line out the door."

"Lorna, that's fantastic."

"It is. Clark didn't once complain about us hiring extra help for the weekend, and Lamar, Jasmine's boyfriend, was a godsend." She paused and beamed a smile. "And get this. I caught Clark humming while he loaded the dishwasher."

"Humming?"

"He didn't even complain when I sent him to the store for more provisions. Between the omelets for breakfast and the quiches I made for lunch, we ran out of eggs."

When she paused for a breath, I blurted, "How about pie? Judy said you might still have some."

She tilted her head. "You have a hankering?"

"Not me. Mrs. Gilroy. She has an unbelievable sweet tooth."

Lorna looked momentarily startled, then smiled. "Now

that you mention it, I remember she used to come in here when I was a girl and my parents ran the café. That woman loved my mother's chocolate meringue pie with graham cracker crust."

"I don't suppose you have that, do you?"

"Sorry, but I do have one slice of apple pecan. I made it in honor of Halloween and the other holidays coming soon, but the plain apple and cherry pies were more popular today. Wait here, and I'll box it for you."

I plopped on a bar stool with a sigh. Lorna could talk about as fast as anyone I knew, and sometimes just listening was enough exercise for an entire day. Not that Lorna gossiped. She shared news her customers imparted. Granted, some news was on the titillating side, but she was never catty.

She bustled back from the kitchen with a paper take-out sack, the Lilies Café logo printed on the front.

"Here you go, all boxed up, and I added the half can of whipped cream I had left over. Clark will get more, and I'm making cream pies for tomorrow, so there won't be as much call for this. I doubt Mrs. Gilroy will remember me, but give her my best."

"Done," I said, and paid for the pie, though Lorna didn't want to charge me.

Not wanting the canned whipped cream to get warm, I hoofed it back to the emporium again, put the sack in the dorm-sized fridge we kept in the tiny kitchenette, and went to see how our sales were going for the day.

At the festivals held on the farmhouse grounds, Sherry, Aster, and Eleanor had routinely sold two-thirds to three-fourths of their stock. And those were one-day events. Granted, we wanted our vendors to do a brisk business all day long, but I wanted us to do our share, too. The Silver Six might be family and part owners of the emporium, but I insisted they be paid something for each of their items we sold. We paid the other artisans. Only fair to pay the Silver Six.

Fred and Dab weren't in the store, but one glance at the depleted shelves and display tables, and I didn't have to hope the Six had done well. I could see they had.

"Y'all will have to work double time to make new products," I said.

Eleanor gave me her gentle smile. "I do believe you're correct, Nixy."

"It was wonderful," Aster said. "Why, we had to rotate two at a time to wolf down our lunches."

Kathy was wide-eyed. "I had no idea the store would be so busy."

Sherry chuckled. "And here you thought we hired you to make Jasmine happy."

"You earned your stripes today," Maise declared.

"Are Dab and Fred in the back?" I asked.

Sherry shook her head. "Nope. They sold out of the Razorback metal-art pieces, so they went out to Big George's hardware store for supplies."

"Sold out of the cannons, too," Maise put in.

"So they're aiming to make more tonight," Aster said.

I stared. "They aren't watching football?"

Eleanor laughed. "I do believe your innocent suggestion to them back in May has created two metal-art monsters."

"But it's keeping them even younger," Sherry said. "It's good to see."

Maise clapped her hands. "Ladies, we still have to get this place shipshape for tomorrow morning. Speaking of which, Nixy, it's almost five. You need to make another run through the festival. See how things went today for everyone else."

Since I couldn't execute a salute that met Maise's standards, I simply said, "Aye-aye, ma'am. I'm gone."

THE ARTISANS WERE PLEASED WITH THEIR DAY'S sales and looked for many browsers to return and buy. They told me they were tired but psyched for Sunday.

Cornell Lewis was in the process of shutting down Gone to the Dogs. Dex was there somewhere. I heard him shouting orders but didn't see him. Good deal.

I also spotted Lee Durley with a brown-haired woman who appeared to be talking a mile a minute. Both held multiple bags, and I silently thanked Lee's sister for spending money at the festival. They crossed the street and continued down Magnolia, and I quickly lost sight of them.

Back at the emporium, I declined dining with the Silver Six, begging off because I was tired and I had the leftovers Maise had sent home with me for the past two evenings. Since I was having dinner with Eric on Sunday night, I wanted to eat all the food I had in the fridge before it went to waste.

I did, however, take Bernice her desserts an hour later.

When the door didn't fly open, I frowned. Was she okay? I heard noise inside. It sounded like a commercial on TV. Maybe she hadn't heard me arrive. I knocked.

"Go away, Sissy. I'm watching a show."

If she was busy watching TV, she was fine. "Okay," I hollered. "I'll just leave your cake and pie on the porch."

I counted to three before I heard her little feet hit the floorboards. In another count of three, she opened the door and jerked me inside. Since I hadn't stopped by the farmhouse for my handy-dandy food delivery basket, I had the forethought to hold the goodies in a death grip.

"Hurry up and put those in the kitchen," she snapped. "I've got the game paused, but I want to get back to it."

"Game? Are you watching college football?"

"Soccer," she said absently as she eyed the goodies and cackled with glee.

"You watch soccer?"

"Men in shorts and tight shirts? A'course I watch soccer. Besides, once the game starts, they don't show commercials except at halftime. I don't get bored. Halftime is almost over, so scoot."

I stood on the porch a moment after she kicked me out. I knew my mouth was hanging open, but I couldn't help it. Soccer? Bernice? Good grief, she must have more than regular cable TV. She must have a special sports package. Who'da thunk?

The woman really was a puzzlement.

AT MY APARTMENT, I STAYED AWAKE LONG ENOUGH to eat while I watched a rerun of *The Big Bang Theory*. Yes, I'd finally broken down and bought a TV when Huff's Fine Furniture ran a Fourth of July sale. Eric and I had been seeing just enough of each other that I didn't have all that much time to get attached to any particular programs, but I did watch *NCIS* so I could converse about it with Bernice, the Mark Harmon nut. I accidentally found that Amber and T.C. liked Animal Planet and had begun leaving it on when Eric and I went out.

The fur babies had dined on their regular kibble, of course, but I gave them a few bites of grilled chicken breast and one morsel of macaroni and cheese. That finished off my leftovers from two days ago. And, yes, I know I wasn't supposed to feed them people food, but at least I didn't conveniently drop French fries on the floor for them like Eric did.

After showering, I donned a sleep shirt with a big bluebonnet bouquet on the front and curled up in bed with the book I was reading. The romantic comedy with its snappy dialogue reminded me of the old screwball comedies I'd watched with a guy I'd dated. We'd quickly become just pals, but I'd enjoyed the movies he'd introduced me to.

Eric called before I finished the chapter.

"Hey, Nixy, how was day one of the festival? Any more problems?"

"No, and the vendors were happy."

"That's most of the battle, isn't it?"

"Yep. How did your day go?"

"I took Charlene through some old cases, and the one open robbery case we have."

"She'll be bored in a month."

"Nah. I'll talk you into taking a little trip with me and leave the law enforcement to her for a few days. Maybe something exciting will happen while we're gone."

My mouth suddenly went dry. Was he suggesting that—as Bernice would say—we kick our relationship up a notch? Except for the one real romance I'd had in grad school, my dating forays that might have promised sizzle had fizzled.

"Nixy, are you there?"

"I'm here," I choked out, and went for humor. "Are you asking me to run away with you, Mr. Shoar?"

"More like meander up to Eureka Springs."

"Any special reason why that spot?"

I could picture him shrugging. "It's historic and quaint, and the fall color in the hills is beautiful."

"That's what Sherry and the gang told me," I said softly.

"A buddy from college has opened some cabins up on Beaver Lake, and I'd like to support his business."

I wondered if that meant he could get a good rate on the cabins, but I wasn't offended. Nothing wrong with saving money. I knew that firsthand.

"Are you thinking about it?"

"You know I am, but it's a big step."

"The sex or the trip?"

"Both, but mainly the trip. What if I snore?"

He snorted a laugh. "Nixy, you're overthinking this. Get some sleep, and I'll see you tomorrow at some point, I'm sure."

We disconnected, but I forgot about reading my book. Instead I gazed into the alert faces of my critters. "Am I ready for this?"

Amber waggled her tan eyebrows. T.C. kneaded her paws on my leg.

I wondered if their antics translated to mean *Whatever you want, human*, or simply *Whatever.*

SUNDAY MORNING, I BOUNCED OUT OF BED WEARING a big grin and, eventually, a pair of royal-blue cropped pants and a trusty Handcraft Emporium tee. The grin was, of course, because I was still thinking about Eric's phone call.

I carried my socks and tennis shoes to the living room. I'd put them on when I was ready to walk Amber and T.C. and then get on with my day. The critters waited patiently while I poured their kibble and refreshed their water bowls. I sat at the kitchen counter eating a piece of toast and drinking hot tea. I'd be downing icy water the rest of the day because, though the weather would be nice, it was likely to be warmer than yesterday.

While I ate, I mentally went through my closet for date clothes. Lilyvale was a great small town but wasn't overflowing with fine restaurants or swanky nightlife spots. My gussy-up-for-gallery-opening clothes had pretty much hung in the closet until I'd asked Eleanor for a fashion consultation. Between us, we'd reimagined and re-paired my suit pieces. Now I had combinations that worked for every kind of event I might attend in Lilyvale . . . and beyond.

The only question was, how sexy did I want to look for my dinner date with Eric? I did have a flirty black skirt to wear with a black lacy camisole and a red jacket, the red for that touch of zing. I'd even kept three pairs of Houston work heels in basic dark colors for special occasions. Considering that Eric had asked me to take a trip with him, dinner tonight should count as very special. I just hoped I could still walk in the darned shoes. I'd gone barefoot or worn sandals, ballet flats, or my trusty tennies for months now.

My dinner date duds decided, I took T.C. and Amber downstairs and clipped on their leashes, and off we went. Today Amber was less intent on sniffing every blade of grass for signs of other dogs, or of squirrels, rabbits, or other animals she loved to track. Today she pranced along the sidewalk, and as she always did, T.C. stayed right with her.

We were headed home on Lee Street when Amber suddenly stopped in her tracks, nose high and twitching as she smelled the air. T.C.'s ears perked and she stared intensely in the direction Amber sniffed. Then I heard shouts and curses coming from the square. What the heck?

I sprinted toward the ruckus, my critters leading the way to a crowd of vendors in a loose circle near Gone to the Dogs. With their attention riveted on whatever was happening, and their cell phones up and capturing the moment, I squeezed my way through. I arrived just in time to see Cornell Lewis attempting to rise from the pavement, Dex Hamlin standing over him. When Cornell was nearly on his feet, Horrible Hamlin drove a beefy fist into the man's jaw. This time Cornell didn't get up.

Amber rumbled a fierce growl, T.C. hissed like a deranged steam valve, and, without thinking, I charged into the fray.

Chapter Six

"HAMLIN!" I YELLED. "WHAT THE DEVIL DO YOU THINK you're doing brawling in public, and with our invited artists having to see this?"

"And on a Sunday," a woman called out.

He spun toward me, fists ready to go another round. "I was invited to be a vendor here, too, Miss Nose-in-the-Air."

"No, you were not," I said. "You weaseled your way into the event, and guess what? You can slither right on out."

Hamlin took a threatening step, and Amber lunged to the end of her leash in a storm of barking. T.C. puffed up to twice her size, danced sideways toward him, and *yeowled.*

"You keep them animals away from me," the brute warned. I'd never seen an angrier, uglier expression on any-one, and I'd faced a couple of murderers.

"My pets aren't a threat to you, but the police are." I waved at the artists around us. "I'm sure someone has called them."

"We did!" a male voice shouted from the crowd.

I didn't turn around. I didn't take my eyes off Hamlin's reddening face.

"We also took photos," another called.

"And video!" a female sang out. "That ought to cook your goose in court."

Hamlin scanned the crowd as if he'd spot the speaker. Fat chance. Especially when I spied the cavalry riding our way from behind Hamlin.

Officer Doug Bryant's long stride ate up the distance fast. At six feet and two hundred pounds of solid muscle, Officer Bryant was an imposing guy. Especially in full uniform. Most especially with one hand resting on the butt of his gun.

"What's going on, Nixy?" he asked. Yes, he knew me well enough to call me by my nickname. We'd been on the same volleyball team during a summer police picnic.

"I'll tell you—" Hamlin began, but fell silent when Bryant held up a hand and gave him the laser cop stare.

"Are you Ms. Nix?" Bryant growled. "You are not. I'll get to you in a minute. Nixy?"

I'd moved aside with my fur babies and shortened their leashes so that they sat at my feet.

"I didn't see the whole incident," I told him in all honesty. "You'll need to ask these folks to get the bigger picture."

"Noted," Bryant said. "What *did* you personally witness?"

"I heard shouting, saw the crowd, and ran over in time to see Hamlin punch Cornell Lewis over there."

I waved a hand to the man a few yards away, still on the ground but regaining consciousness. A fiftyish woman in a denim shorts outfit knelt beside Cornell. I realized it was Mikki Michaels, one of our textile artists who specialized in batik pieces, but who'd worked as an ER triage nurse.

"This man didn't just hit the other one," one of the men in the back of the crowd said. I turned, but couldn't see who it was. "He was beating him."

Mags Deets stepped forward. "I videoed the whole thing."

"Thank you, ma'am," Bryant replied. "We may want to see that."

"There ain't nothing to see," Hamlin said. "I had a disagreement with my employee."

"Over what?" Bryant asked.

"I heard," he said, staring at me, "that he gave away hot dogs yesterday. To a little kid and this chick's pets. I can't make no money that way, can I?"

"A simple warning not to do it again should've sufficed," I snapped.

"Ain't your business how I discipline my help, now, is it?" He punctuated that remark by spitting in the street, the mess landing not far from my shoes.

Officer Bryant was not amused. "That's enough, Hamlin. Turn around. I'm taking you to the station."

"What for?" Hamlin cried, backpedaling a few steps.

"Assault, and you're disturbing the peace. And my patience. Now turn around before I add resisting arrest to the charge."

Hamlin complied but spouted a litany of obscenities as he was cuffed and Mirandized.

Before Bryant led Hamlin away, he paused and jerked his chin at the crowd. "Nixy, take care of that."

I got the message. He wanted me to disperse the onlookers.

"Everyone, I'm so sorry this happened, but we have a wonderful last day of the festival waiting, and I'm sure you want to get your booths ready to open."

"What about our evidence?" Mags asked, waggling her phone.

"If you have photos or videos, let me know when I make my first rounds. I'll give your names to the police."

"Right-o," a voice said from the back, and with that the artists moved off, chattering among themselves.

It would take a while for the artisans to wind down. Heck, it would take me a while, too, because adrenaline continued to pound through my body.

Amber whined, tired of being tethered so tightly. I loosened my grip and gave Amber and T.C. each a behind-the-ears scratch.

"Okay, girls, we'll go in a minute. I need to check on Cornell."

Mikki was still with him, steadying him as he stood. His swollen nose looked especially painful, but I couldn't tell if it was broken. He also had scrapes on his hands and arms, and bruises bloomed all over his face. His white pants and shirt bore dirt smudges, blood droplets, and one ripped seam.

"Is anything broken?"

"Just the last of my pride." He shook his head as if to clear it. "I can't believe you went after him like you did."

I gave him a rueful smile. "Sometimes I act before I think."

"It's your strong sense of justice," Mikki said. "You're fair to a fault with your consigners. I don't know how the emporium makes any money."

"Volume," I said with a grin. "Sheer volume."

She chuckled. "I'd best get going. You really should see a doctor, sir."

"I will, and thank you for your kindness, ma'am."

"Do you need a ride to the hospital?" I felt a bit uncomfortable asking, but the man had been kind to my pets, and that was one of the reasons Hamlin was enraged. "I know you have a car, but—"

"No, thanks," he said, wincing and touching his split lip. "The medical center is only two blocks from here. It'll be faster to walk. If they can't see me, I'll see the doctor I know when I go back to Camden tomorrow."

"Okay. Uh, Mr. Lewis—"

"Please call me Cornell."

"Right, well, you know that you'll need to press charges against Dex Hamlin. The officer who arrested him is Doug Bryant."

He nodded. "Yes, I remember him from when I lived here before." He paused, gazed at the blue sky, then back at me. "Ironic, isn't it? Me being the one bullied. The shoe is on the other foot."

"I know the stories of what you were like, but it appears to me that Dex Hamlin is worse."

"Perhaps, perhaps not." He shrugged, then winced again.

"Cornell, go on over to the emergency department. They might not be too busy at this hour, and you can come back to open Gone to the Dogs later. That is, if you want to."

"Again, my thanks, Ms. Nix, is it?"

"Nixy," I said. "I'll check in on you later."

He limped some as he walked south between the rows of tents, headed toward the hospital. That was when I noticed spectators on the east square sidewalk. Among them were Deb the Soap Lady, Stained Glass Sarah, and Lee Durley—the shopper I'd collided with yesterday. A brunette wearing a big hat that shaded her face stood next to him, and, yikes! So did Pear Bread Lady Ida Bollings, leaning on her walker. Dang. There were likely more gawkers on the west side of the square, too. If the Silver Six hadn't already heard the scoop, they soon would. Time for round one of damage control.

IF I'D THOUGHT FOR A MINUTE THAT ELEANOR, Kathy, Aster, and Maise would do happy dances over Cornell's beat-down, I'd have been completely off base. The seniors were more concerned about how the unfortunate incident would affect the final day of sales, never mind the artists' willingness to return for the spring festival. They dissected, discussed, and dissed Hamlin, and ultimately decided that the less said the better.

Even Kathy seemed unaffected by the news. And Jasmine, who was more outspoken than not, didn't comment either. If anyone thought Cornell got what he deserved, it wasn't spoken.

After the unexpected excitement on their walk, I left T.C. and Amber with Fred in the workroom, then went off to make my first visits of the day to the vendors. I took my trusty clipboard, paper, and pen, and recorded the names of the artists who'd taken pictures or video of the fracas as well as getting phone numbers and e-mail addresses. Yes, I had all the artists' contact information, but I'd scribbled all over those pages. Better to give the police a clean list, even if it was handwritten instead of typed.

Over the course of the morning, the number of shoppers went from good to wow to holy cow. Every booth had at least five customers eyeing the wares, and people bought, not just browsed. The artisans would be pleased, which meant the Silver Six would be ecstatic.

Gone to the Dogs remained closed at noon. I considered calling the hospital to inquire about Cornell but knew they wouldn't give out patient information. Not to me, but perhaps they'd give Eric an update.

Call him or go to the station? Was he even working today?

I whipped out my cell phone and called.

"Hey." I heard the smile in his voice.

"Hi, are you at work? Can you talk?"

I heard a chair creak. "I'm at the station, but what do you need?"

"I want to ask about Dex Hamlin's arrest this morning."

"According to Officer Bryant, you were a witness. You know what went down."

"Yes, but I have a few questions. First, Hamlin is still there, right?"

"He's in holding at the county jail."

"So Cornell Lewis came in to press charges?"

"I don't know. I talked to Doug, but he went off duty after he processed Hamlin, and Detective Vogelman and I have been using the chief's office to finish reviewing case files. You want me to go ask if Lewis came in?"

"No, it's not critical. I just wondered if he had. He hasn't returned to the festival to open the hot dog stand."

"Returned from where?"

"I talked with him a minute after Officer Bryant left with Hamlin, and I thought he meant to go to the ER. At least he was walking in that general direction when I last saw him."

"You want me to put in a call to see if he went in?"

"If you don't mind. I don't know how to get in touch with him, and Gone to the Dogs has to come down this afternoon at four o'clock. With Hamlin in jail and Lewis MIA, I'm not sure what protocol is."

"The city maintenance crew can take it down."

"Will they store the tent and the equipment? I don't want Hamlin on my case if anything is lost or damaged."

"It'll be considered abandoned property, like a car. I'll alert the department of the situation."

"Thanks, Eric. Oh, and I have the list of the vendors who took pictures and videos of the fight. Want me to drop it off, or should I give it to one of the folks patrolling the festival for us?"

"If you have a chance, bring it by." He paused. "Are we still on for dinner tonight?"

"You bet your nuts and bolts."

"Ah, there's a Fred-ism," he said on a chuckle. "Later, Nixy."

A VERY SMALL ISSUE PREVENTED ME FROM GOING directly to the station with my handy-dandy witness list. An artist ran out of small bills, so I jogged to the emporium to see if we had enough in the till to make change. We did but had to dip into cash from the day before. Not a huge deal, but Maise wanted to be sure we kept the totals for Saturday's sales separate from Sunday. Nursing had been her primary career, but she'd taken accounting classes to help her husband in his insurance business. Now we shared bookkeeping duties, and it made sense that she'd want to know if the store sold more on one day than the other.

By the time I returned to the vendor with her money, then speed-walked the two blocks to the police station, Eric and Charlene had gone to lunch. The reception desk wasn't usually staffed on the weekends, but Officer Taylor Benton greeted me, and I turned the list over to him. Taylor Benton was in his mid-twenties, I guessed, with unblemished black skin. He was intelligent, eager, and earnest, and I'd felt horrible when I spiked a volleyball at the picnic game and gave him a bloody nose. Not broken, though. That was a plus, and we'd laughed about assaulting a police officer while he held a bag of ice on his face.

Speaking of assault, had Eric phoned the hospital? I didn't want to ask Officer Benton. But, hmm, I could pop over there myself. Say I was there to pick up an ER patient. Worst case, I wouldn't learn a thing. Best case? Okay, so given all the circumstances, all the trouble Cornell Lewis had caused my dear Eleanor, Kathy and her mom, and others in the past, I didn't know what the best case would be. But, hey, nothing ventured.

I set off at a leisurely pace, past the fire station and the small parking lot adjacent to it. Our trees weren't showing fall color yet, and Aster explained that the chemical changes hadn't begun. Leaves were still producing chlorophyll. Since Aster was a master gardener, I believed her. At least the leaves hadn't all dropped yet. In this older part of town closer to the square, stately trees spread their branches over homes dating from the late 1930s to the 1960s. I loved waving to people sitting on their porches or tidying their gardens, and today at the man repainting a picket fence.

There were fewer bungalows and more ranch-style homes as I neared Lilyvale Hospital, even though it was only two blocks south of the square. The health center, with its twenty beds, four emergency department treatment rooms, and a surprising variety of surgical services, was affiliated with the University of Arkansas. I'd read that in a pamphlet when Sherry was rushed here in April after eating poisoned chocolate candies. The ambulance entrance was around back, but I hurried through the side entrance.

The whooshing of the automated door alerted the man who sat at the check-in desk. He was in his sixties, thin with a smart goatee, and wore the hospital's volunteer uniform. I'd seen him around town but didn't know his name. And wouldn't you know, the identification badge that hung from a lanyard was turned backward. Darn it. I'd learned long ago that it helps any quest to greet people by name.

"Hi, I wonder if you can help me," I said.

"I'll try." Clear green eyes twinkled. "What do you need?"

"I'm here to pick up a patient who came to the emergency department this morning. He called a while ago, but I was delayed. Can you find out if he's ready?"

"Who is it?"

"Cornell Lewis."

The man's face turned stormy faster than a blue norther swept through the plains. "That son of a rattlesnake was here?"

"Um, well, yes, I thought he was."

He looked at his desk surface, shuffled some papers, then typed on his keyboard and pinned his narrow-eyed gaze at the screen.

"He isn't here," the man snapped.

"Was he treated earlier?"

The man's mouth thinned even more. "I don't have a record of him being here at all. I haven't personally seen him, and I don't want to."

"Okay," I said as I backed up. "Uh, sorry to have bothered you."

"That's an understatement," he growled. "If he's a friend of yours, lady, you're running in bad company."

"Got it, thanks."

With that I scooted out with another whoosh and hot-footed it back toward the square and my duties at the festival.

Obviously, I'd just run into another person Cornell had done wrong. I wondered who he was and what had happened. Eleanor would likely know, but did I want to raise the subject with her? Not unless it came up. Probably wouldn't.

I made another sweep of the booths when I returned, checking in with the artists to be sure all was well. I lapped the hot dog cart but didn't see a sign of Cornell. Maybe he'd gone on back to Camden. Come to think of it, he might not have health insurance, and I didn't know if our hospital would treat uninsured patients. He might have called Lilyvale a bust and gone to see his doctor friend.

I spotted Durley at the corner of Lee and Magnolia as I headed back to the emporium. He again wore jeans and work boots, today with a faded brown shirt, and he appeared to be window-shopping at the men's clothing store. I didn't see his sister but sure hoped she was spending more money at the festival.

IT HAD AMAZED ME IN THE SPRING WHEN I'D WITnessed the artists packing up at Sherry's farmhouse, and it amazed me now. Tables and shelves and tents and signs were stored in trucks and SUVs in record time. The vendors who consigned with us took items to the store, and every last one wore a happy, if tired, smile. Each one also thanked me for organizing the event and confirmed they'd come back in the spring. The morning's brouhaha had been put aside.

When they'd all driven off, there wasn't a gum or candy wrapper or a stray piece of paper in sight. Not even a cigarette butt, though we had designated a smoking area, and most had complied. The city maintenance crew had little to do but dismantle Gone to the Dogs.

Maise had scheduled a meeting for five o'clock. She called

it an operational debriefing. Back at the gallery in Houston, we'd called it a postmortem. The term caught on with us because an employee was fired following our first after-the-art-show discussion. *Debriefing* sure sounded better.

Jasmine and Kathy had gone home, so the seniors and I gathered around the antique counter, where the Six had rung up a record number of sales. It hit me again how they worked together like one of Fred's well-oiled machines. Each did jobs here, and at the farmhouse, according to their strengths. That was one of the first things I'd noticed when I came in April. Their attitude was all for one, one for all, and they lived it each day.

None of my little family looked worn to the bone after two long days, but I imagined they were riding more on adrenaline than on energy. Fred, Sherry, and Maise looked pleased as they took off their aprons. Aster looked a little frayed, wisps of graying hair escaping from her customary braid. Eleanor didn't have a speck of dirt on her apron or a single wrinkle in her emerald blouse. Dab didn't look as dapper as usual, and that stopped me.

There were circles under his eyes I hadn't seen before today, and were his pants riding lower on his hips? Had he lost weight? I hadn't noticed anything off about him when he and Mags flirted on Friday, but I made a mental note to ask Sherry if he was feeling all right.

Maise announced that not only had the emporium done well, the artisans reported excellent sales on both days, and three more artists had asked to consign their wares with us. That brought us to forty-five, though I wondered where we'd put everything. There were boxes of art pieces stacked over half the floor space.

"Never fear, child. We'll make room," Aunt Sherry sang.

"I do believe it's a good thing we decided to close tomorrow and Tuesday," Eleanor said. "It will take at least a day to rearrange the store."

"And another one to tweak it," Fred chuckled.

"I thought you were doing your volunteer work tomorrow."

"No, Nixy," Aster corrected. "We'll be here to help you."

"We'll have things shipshape again in no time," Maise said.

Dab smiled and nodded but didn't comment. Which was not that odd. He didn't gab, but when he spoke, we listened.

"Now then, were there any glitches we need to address for the spring festival?" Maise asked as she surveyed our little group.

I leaned an elbow on the glass top. I'd be cleaning the smudge later, but I didn't care. I stretched my back while I answered.

"Aside from Hamlin creating a scene, no. Luckily, most of the vendors seemed more excited than appalled."

"You be sure that varmint don't get into the next event," Fred growled.

"When our sponsors find out he was arrested, they'll ban him."

We were silent a moment, maybe contemplating what other events Hamlin might find himself booted from.

"I hesitate to ask this," Eleanor said slowly, "but what happened to Cornell Lewis?"

"Mikki Michaels told him he should go to the ER, but he didn't. I didn't see him the rest of the day."

"How do you know Cornell wasn't at the hospital?" Aster asked.

"I went over there and said I was supposed to pick him up. The man volunteering at the reception desk isn't a fan."

Eleanor leaned over the counter. "Did you get the volunteer's name?"

"The badge was backward. He's thin and has a goatee."

"Marshall Gibson," Eleanor said with a decisive nod. "Has to be him. He had trouble with Cornell, too."

"Everyone who so much as visited a resident in the complex had trouble with that man," Aster said.

I missed my chance to ask what Cornell had done to Marshall when Dab spoke up.

"Cornell will need to file charges against Hamlin, won't he?" We all turned to him. "What? On TV the police can hold someone for twenty-four hours, but can Lilyvale's finest?"

"Good question," I said. "The sleazeball pulled strings to get permission to vend at the festival. He may pull more to get out of jail."

"Nixy, child, you carry your pepper spray at all times, you hear me? I don't want Hamlin coming after you."

"Done and done, Aunt Sherry." I paused and looked at Maise. "I don't mean to bug out on the meeting, but I have a date with Eric in an hour, and I need to walk the critters."

"No, you don't," Fred said. "Dab and me walked 'em less than an hour ago. You feed 'em and fuss over 'em a bit, and go have fun." He narrowed his eyes. "The boy ain't takin' you to the Dairy Queen, is he?"

"Never fear, we're going to Adam Daniel's."

"Well, still, you be sure to order expensive vittles. You're worth it."

Chapter Seven

THE FUR BABIES WATCHED ME GET READY, AMBER on the bathroom floor with her chin on her paws, and T.C. sprawled on the rim of the claw-foot bathtub. How she didn't slide off was one of those cat mysteries.

I never used much foundation makeup, but I brushed on a bit more eye shadow than usual, applied an extra coat of mascara, and finished with lipstick in a light shade of pink that wouldn't clash with the red jacket. My hair ought to have a permanent crease in it from being up in a ponytail all the time. It didn't, or the mark didn't show because my blah-brown hair was just wavy enough to hide it. I wore it down tonight, brushing my shoulder blades. Would Eric mess it up after dinner? I counted on it.

The black-on-black outfit topped with the red jacket was perfect. Since I was tired from several long days and the stairs were steep, I'd carry my black heels for now. Tumbling into Eric's arms at the end of the date was one thing. Breaking a bone before I ever left the building was another.

"All right, you two, behave and maybe Eric will come up for a while later."

At Eric's name, T.C.'s ears twitched and Amber lifted her head and panted. I took that to mean *Oh, boy!*

Right there with you, Amber. I'd panted around him myself a few times, though I hoped I didn't sound quite as slavish. I *was* a lady.

A gentleman should always come to the door to call for his date, or so my mother taught me. That didn't work in my situation. My apartment could only be accessed from an interior staircase that emptied into Fred's shop space. I kept the emporium and workroom doors locked when we closed and the Six left for the day. I wasn't concerned about a break-in for my sake; the business was another story. Aside from the arts and crafts inventory, Fred kept the tools of his fix-it trade in the workroom. They were padlocked in the wall of cabinets, but a bolt cutter would break the locks quick and easy.

So, instead of Eric coming up for me, I met him out back, and I didn't mind a bit.

I'd just stepped out and locked up when his shiny dark-gray extended-cab truck turned into the alley. He parked, got out to escort me to the passenger seat as he always did, but stopped short and stared.

"You look amazing."

I grinned. "Thank you, kind sir."

He stepped closer. "Not that you don't look great all the time, but, uh, is this a new outfit?"

"Just a few old pieces I'm wearing in a new combination."

"It works." He cupped my cheek, and his dreamy voice deepened when he drawled, "Would it be tacky to kiss you in the alley?"

I held his gaze and swayed toward him. "What alley?"

YES, MY HAIR WAS A LITTLE MUSSED, BUT I FINGER-combed it into order as Eric drove to Adam Daniel's. Located on the highway running north to McNeil, the restaurant served a nice variety of meat, fish, and vegetarian meals. Not a swank place by any means, but the food was great. Since we'd had our first official date there, it was a sentimental favorite.

"How is Charlene acclimating to life in Lilyvale?" I asked.

He smiled but kept his eyes on the road. "She's getting the hang of small-town law enforcement."

I turned slightly in my seat to see him better in the twilight. "Is it that much different from the Tulsa force?"

"In terms of procedures, no. She's resigning herself that she'll be investigating more misdemeanors than felonies."

"I'd think that would be a good thing."

"It is, but for someone who worked major crimes, it's tame."

"Tame gives her more time with her dad."

"True."

"He uses a wheelchair, right? How is he doing?"

"Better. She doesn't talk about her personal life with me much, but she did say she hired a retired licensed practical nurse and the nurse's son. They're from outside Magnolia. The son has had some EMT training, but he's also been a short-order cook, so they come in on alternate days to make sure he's had his medications and eats."

"Did she get her dad to wear the senior alert button?"

He snorted. "Not hardly. The guy is more contrary than the Silver Six put together."

"You know her dad?"

"Oh, yeah. Mr. Kiddner used to complain about kids cutting through his yard. Looking back on it, I believe he wanted someone to jaw with more than he wanted the kids caught."

I digested that, thinking about Sherry and the gang. They weren't all *that* old, and they weren't the least bit infirm. Yes, Fred used a walker, but sometimes I wondered how much he really needed it for balance, and how much he just wanted a way to tote more tools around. Of course, Sherry had macular degeneration, but she didn't let it slow her down. An image of Dab's tired face floated into focus. Was the sweet man ill?

One thing was sure: I hoped to have my hands full with the sassy Silver Six for years to come. And when they began to fail? I'd deal with whatever came, and perhaps I'd have Eric by my side. The thought flooded me with warmth.

Charlene was a widow and a newcomer still meeting people, never mind making friends, and had no one to lean on. I promised myself to invite her to lunch or dinner. Maybe we could go do dinner and a movie, though we'd have to go to Texarkana or El Dorado to catch a film. Lilyvale didn't have a theater, and neither did Magnolia.

My stomach growled when we turned into the parking lot and the glow of lights spilling from the huge windows greeted us. The restaurant was cozily set in a clearing surrounded by pine trees, and the outside and inside décor was modern rustic. Not a style I'd want to live with daily, but I had to admit I felt hugged by the warm ambiance when Eric escorted me through the door.

The teenaged hostess wore black pants, a white shirt, and a thousand-watt smile. The place wasn't more than half full, and she showed us to a table in the far corner, one partly screened by climbing philodendrons and water reeds on steroids. Eric pulled out my chair, then instead of sitting across from me, took the adjacent chair.

Our waiter, who introduced himself as Phil, was also dressed in black pants and a white shirt and apron. He rattled off the specials, and I ordered a petite filet mignon medium well with a house salad and asparagus. Eric went for the fried catfish with a baked potato. We both decided on a glass of wine. Eric also ordered the banana icebox cake, which was part cake, part chocolate and white chocolate mousse, and all rich, creamy goodness.

"I'm sorry, sir," the waiter said, "but we're not serving that selection at this time."

"Why not?" I asked. "It's wonderful!"

"It's labor intensive to make," Phil said. "But you might check with Judy Armistead at Great Buns Bakery. I believe Daniel might have shared the recipe with her. We do have a delicious chocolate cheesecake."

"We'll take it," Eric decided.

Phil hurried away but was back in no time with our glasses of wine. As we sipped, Eric said, "Tell me about the festival. I only saw the booths in passing. Stick with the good stuff, though. I know about the fight."

"Okay, but I need to know one thing. Is Hamlin still sitting in a cell?"

"Far as I know, yes."

"He pulled political strings to get into the festival. Can he do the same to get out of jail?"

He heaved a sigh. "I didn't want to talk about this, but both he and his wife are connected around here, and that's all I'm saying."

I did a double take. "Wait. Some woman married him? By choice? Please tell me they didn't reproduce."

"No children," he said on a laugh, "and I don't think the marriage is good, but I understand Hamlin used to be a better man."

"Really? How many reincarnations ago was that?"

He shook his head. "Nixy, to answer your question, I don't know if Hamlin can call on enough clout to get out of jail. Now, let's drop this and talk about the festival."

"Want to see the pictures I took?"

While I ate my salad—and he snagged a few bites, too—we huddled together to look at the photos on my cell. I pointed out the artists who'd agreed to have their faces on our website. Most weren't camera shy, and some hammed it up for their shots. Then I came to the pictures of Cornell and my critters.

Eric smirked. "I thought you didn't feed T.C. and Amber people food."

I shrugged. "Cornell offered, and I felt bad about saying no. He didn't feed them much."

"Uh-huh."

When I swiped to the next photo, Lee Durley's face popped up on the screen. "Huh, I wonder how I got this?"

"What do you mean?"

I explained about the flying cell phone and Amber's save. "I must've accidentally taken the shot."

Eric peered at the photo, which was a bit too much of a close-up but pretty clear for an accidental shot. "He looks familiar. Is he an artist?"

"No, he said his sister was shopping at the festival. Actually, he did something that struck me as odd."

"What was that?"

He met my gaze, his expression telling me his cop radar had kicked in, but when I told him about the "pig sooie, go, Razorbacks" fumble, he only chuckled.

"Nixy, sometimes you think more about football than I do."

"But he was wearing a polo shirt with the team emblem."

"Maybe his sister bought it for him."

I conceded that with a shrug. "You said he looked familiar. Does the name Lee Durley help place him?"

He took the phone, enlarged the shot, and angled the screen toward better light. "I'm sure I've seen him, but I'm drawing a blank where or when."

"If you'd met him because he was connected to a crime, you'd probably remember, right? Even if he'd been a witness?"

"Imagine so."

"Ergo, he's probably harmless."

"Right, and here's our dinner."

We continued to chat over the meal about the festival's success. I mentioned we were on for the spring festival, as long as the city, the Chamber of Commerce, and the local businesses supported it. They should. It had been a success.

I threw out some ideas to tweak the event, too, the primary one being no food vendors.

"I'm all for having the bake sale again, if the churches want to hold it again. Oh, and the Handcraft Emporium now has three more consignors, but I don't know where we're going to put everything. The store is stuffed to the rafters as it is."

Eric grinned. "I'm sure the Six have a plan. They always do."

"I'm sure you're right, and I'll let them run with it." I sighed. "Sometimes managing the Six is like herding cats."

"Speaking of which, shall we go walk T.C. and Amber, and then have some alone time without them?" He gave me a smoldering smile and waggled his brows.

I fluttered my lashes and deepened my Texas-southern accent. "Why, Eric Shoar, whatever are you suggesting?"

"Come on, and I'll show you."

Be still my heart.

THE CRITTERS LOVED ERIC. HE WAS THE ONE WHO first spotted them sitting at the emporium's alley door, and the one who'd bought their food and water bowls, their first bags of kibble, and their matching dog collar, cat harness, and leashes. If they weren't so well behaved, they would've leaped into his arms every time they saw him. As it was, T.C. stretched high on her hind legs to paw at his hip, and Amber ran circles around him, first one way, then the other. As soon as he mentioned "Walk," Amber raced for the basket where I kept their toys and leashes, trotting back with hers. When I snagged T.C.'s halter, she nearly dove into it.

Had he foisted the animals on me instead of taking them himself? I'd felt that way at first. He'd insisted his schedule was too unpredictable, and splitting them up wasn't an option. They were inseparable from the time we found them. Besides, he pointed out, the critters had shown up at my door, not his, or anyone else's. They'd done the same with their former owner, and when she died, they'd quietly slipped away in the chaos of the authorities coming to the woman's house. As far as we knew, they'd walked from Minden, Louisiana, to Lilyvale. They must've had some adventures in their travels, but they weren't talking.

Well, except for T.C.'s meows and Amber's eager *unh-unh* sounds urging us to get a move on.

Tonight in the cool October air, Amber alternately wanted to sniff and prance. T.C. always let the dog set the pace of their walks, but she batted bugs in the daytime. At night, she peered into the dark, occasionally crouching while she waited on Amber.

We were returning to my apartment when a white pickup tore through a stop sign as we prepared to cross the street. I admit, I may have screeched, but Eric stared after the truck, then pulled a pen from his jacket pocket and jotted something on his palm.

"You aren't going after that yahoo, are you?"

"No, but I'm running his tag," he said in his cop voice.

"Did you recognize the truck?"

He ran a hand over his short hair. In the light from the streetlamp, the brown took on a reddish hue. "I have to confirm it, but the Hamlins own a similar vehicle." I must've looked stricken, because he added, "But so do at least seven other people in town. One of them is a teen I've tangled with over his reckless driving."

"Either way, somebody's in trouble," I said in a singsong voice, aiming to lighten the mood.

Eric shot me a one-brow-arched smirk. "At least it isn't you. Come on, let's have coffee. Or something."

I would *not* be happy if Hamlin had pulled strings to get out of jail, but Eric effectively distracted me when we arrived back at the apartment. I didn't even ask him to check on Hamlin's whereabouts—in jail or not—because, come on. When we kiss, we sizzle.

Making out with pets vying for attention was impossible, so I tucked Amber and T.C. in the bathroom with a handful of treats. Eric and I did a good deal of kissing before Amber began whining and gently scratching at the bathroom door. Maybe it was because I was still relatively new at being a pet mom. Maybe it was because I'd heard horror stories of pets wreaking havoc when they weren't used to being confined in a room. Bottom line, we released them and let them curl up with us on the sofa. We resettled, me cuddled into Eric's side, him playing with my hair.

"Have you thought any more about the trip?"

I tilted my head back to look at him. "Quite a lot, but I haven't mentioned it to the Six yet. I know Mrs. Gilroy would approve, though."

"Oh? This I have to hear."

I told him about kicking it up a notch.

"I wish I'd been a fly on the wall for that," he said, laughing.

"Anyway, I do want to go, but give me a few days before I broach the subject. We need to get the store in order tomorrow and Tuesday."

"Are you worried about taking time off, or that Miz Sherry Mae and the gang will be scandalized?"

"The scandal aspect. This is a small town and word gets around fast. Let me see how it plays out, okay?"

He brushed my hair back. "I'm not pushing, Nixy. I'd just like to have some extended time with you. Just us. No work. No one looking over our shoulders."

"Getting away together sounds wonderful."

"Good. I'll look into reservations. Say a month from now?"

Four weeks would put us near Thanksgiving, but not too near. Not unless the Six started holiday cooking a heck of a lot earlier than anyone else on the planet.

I nodded. "One way or another, I'm in."

We spent a little more sizzle time sealing the deal.

* * *

AFTER ERIC LEFT, I WAS, SHALL WE SAY, A LITTLE too stimulated to fall asleep. I hung my date clothes in the closet, washed my face, and donned the bluebonnet nightshirt but then headed for the kitchen. Not that I needed to eat, but I thought a few crackers would help calm the squiggly feeling in my stomach. Having some chamomile tea from the supply Aster had given me couldn't hurt either.

Thinking about taking the trip to Eureka Springs with Eric made my heartbeat trip. Okay, so I was on board emotionally. I curled up on the couch with my snack and tea and forced myself to consider the rationality of going.

It was a logical, and probably practical step to test our compatibility, and I didn't mean sharing a bed. Sure, we'd dated for six months and had often seen each other several times a week. He'd also seen me at about my worst at the picnic. I'd say I sweated a river during the volleyball game, but I'm a southern lady. We dew. Therefore, I'd dewed at least a small stream during that game, and my running mascara had given me raccoon eyes. Never mind the game of tug-of-war when I landed in the mud. Of course, we both had that mud bath, and it hadn't made him less desirable in my eyes.

We'd gone to Magnolia for dinner, and to El Dorado for a movie or four, but a longer car trip could be a challenge. And, eeks, sharing a bathroom! He might book separate rooms, but I doubted he had that in mind. I wasn't completely inexperienced in the romance department, but it had been years since I'd been more than a pal to a guy.

This was a huge decision, but when I shoved my fears out of the way, my heart told me to go for it. Eric was a good guy. He'd never rushed me. In fact, I often thought he was a little gun-shy. I never asked why, but I got that vibe.

I finished my crackers and tea, took the napkin and mug

to the kitchen, and then headed for bed. With Amber's warm body on one side, and T.C.'s rumbling purr, I soon conked out.

THE SILVER SIX HAD SAID THEY'D SLEEP IN AND BE at the store at ten. The day that crew slept past seven in the morning was the day I'd rush them all to a doctor. I, on the other hand, can be a world-class sleeper when I want to be, but I was up by six fifteen. Probably because I was still charged from my evening with Eric.

Since the Six and I hadn't had a chance to do a super-deep dusting of the shelves since June, we'd tackle that today before restocking and rearranging displays. My hair was fine in a ponytail, but I saw no point in getting one of my nicer outfits filthy dirty, so I'd elected to wear my work clothes. Frayed jean shorts, a faded, stretched-out tee with decorative paint stains, and ugly brown Crocs. I hoped I didn't run into any of Sherry's more refined friends. They'd have a fit and report right back to Sherry.

The critters and I were fed and out the door by six forty-five for our morning jaunt. We walked up Fairview, one of our customary routes, but instead of crossing at Troost to loop back, we went another three blocks to cross at Moccasin, and then turned left on McKinley headed for home. Amber sniffed everything in sight. The grass, the sidewalk, the gutter, the dirt, every tree, even the air. Nothing escaped her notice. T.C. batted at and pounced on bugs, a fallen leaf, a rock. Entertaining as they were to watch, the start-stop pace sure wasn't giving me aerobic exercise.

On McKinley I noticed an older-model sedan parked whopperjawed midblock under one of two oak trees. The front angled into the curb while the back stuck out into the street. Not enough to impede traffic, but nowhere near parallel to the curb. The paint might've been a cream color at one time, but now the car had more rust spots than not.

Amber and T.C. lifted their heads and sniffed as we approached. I wondered why someone going to work or taking their children to school hadn't called to report the badly parked car. It was the only one on the street.

The closer we got, the more my critters fidgeted, whining and meowing, all the while testing the air for scents. When we pulled even with the passenger door, they sat at the edge of the sidewalk. Amber bayed her odd *barkaroo*, and T.C. screeched a *reeoow*. All the windows were open a few inches, the back windows more so. They weren't tinted, and I noticed a man in the passenger seat. He looked to be asleep, his head tilted back, resting partly on the window, partly on the headrest.

I tugged gently on the leashes, planning to walk away, but my pets refused to budge. They gave me the big eyes and pitiful whimpers as if to say, *Aren't you going to do something?*

I sighed and carefully stepped nearer to the car window for a closer look inside. I didn't want to touch anything, but now I saw the man clearly.

A white floppy hat sat off-center over thin graying hair. Bruises colored his face. A split lip. White shirt smudged with dirt and blood droplets, and something else that looked like a dribble of vomit. Cornell Lewis.

In spite of the cool morning, I suddenly felt clammy, and my knees shook. I swallowed and bent lower to see his eyes, then clamped my free hand over my nose and mouth as a foul, sour smell seeped from the window. Cornell wasn't sleeping, not unless he slept with his eyes open and fixed on something he could no longer see.

His pale skin had a slight bluish tint. His face seemed a little swollen compared to yesterday, but that might have been from the beating Dex Hamlin had given him. But there were red spots on his face and neck that looked more recent. I dropped my gaze to his chest but didn't spot any rising and falling. Sure enough, Cornell Lewis was dead.

A wave of sadness washed over me as I scanned the inside of the car. Clothes were folded and stashed in plastic cubes in the backseat, and a small plastic bin held toiletries.

On the front bench seat, just beyond Cornell's hip, I spotted a plate of Aster and Maise's snickerdoodles with the elasticized clear cover. The Aster's Garden label on the plastic was plain as the rising sun. I didn't want to get closer to count them, but it appeared that the plate held six or seven cookies. Some were whole, some broken, or maybe partially eaten, but as of Saturday early afternoon, he'd only had four left.

I didn't see any other obvious injuries. No gaping wounds or blood. Cornell could've had a heart attack or a stroke. He could've died from any kind of natural cause, but instinct told me that wasn't the case.

Call me paranoid, but I wanted to open the car door and grab that plate of cookies and the plastic cover. I'd been up close and personal with a few crime scenes, though, and knew better than to disturb a single thing. And really, who would believe Aster and Maise guilty of killing Cornell? Certainly they wouldn't be stupid enough to leave that silly shower-cap-looking cover with their names front and center.

It probably hadn't been more than a few minutes since I'd first seen Cornell's body, but I had to stop speculating and call Eric. I straightened and pulled my phone from my cargo pocket, then fumbled it when a male voice boomed behind me.

"Good morning, little lady. Everything okay there?"

Chapter Eight

I WHIRLED, HEART RACING, TO FACE A MAN WITH A shock of salt-and-pepper hair. Crow's-feet accented his eyes, and smile lines bracketed his mouth. He wasn't smiling at the moment, though. His expression held concern, and perhaps a smidge of suspicion.

I let the "little lady" pass. I was considerably shorter than this man, never mind having bigger issues to deal with at the moment.

"What's going on?" he asked.

Amber pulled on her leash but didn't bark at the older gentleman. If she'd perceived any threat, I was certain she would have, so I allowed myself to take a deep breath as Aster had taught me, relaxing my shoulders on the exhale.

"It's the man in the car. I'm pretty sure he's dead."

Dark eyebrows shot upward. "Is he, now? Let me have a look."

"Uh, sir, I think we need to call the police right away," I objected, eyeing the back of his royal-blue sweats and black tennis shoes as he stepped past me.

"Hmm. You're right. Looks like anaphylaxis to me."

I blinked. "Are you a doctor?"

"Retired medical examiner for the State of Arkansas. I've seen this too many times. It's a reaction to an insect sting or a food allergy." He glanced up at me. "You know this poor fellow?"

"Not really, but his name is Cornell Lewis."

"And your name?"

"Nixy," I said, automatically extending my leash-free hand. "Actually it's Leslee Stanton Nix, but everyone calls me Nixy."

He cocked his head. "Herkimer M. Jones, MD. Are you related to Sherry Mae Cutler?"

"She's my aunt."

He nodded as if pleased. "Fine figure of a woman is Sherry Mae. You'd best make that call now."

I looked blankly at my cell screen for a moment. I wanted to ask Eric a specific question about Dex Hamlin, and I knew once I called the emergency line, I'd be on the phone with them until officials arrived.

"Nixy, hey, what's up?"

"Eric, is Dex Hamlin out of jail?"

"Yeah, as of last night. Why?"

"Here's the thing. I'll call 911 in a minute, but—"

"What?" he shouted. "Are you all right? Where are you?"

"I'm fine. I'm walking the critters, and I just found Cornell Lewis in a car. He's dead."

"Are you certain?"

"A man named Dr. Jones is here with me. He confirmed it."

Eric said something colorful. For a man who never, but *never* swore around me, he did it with flair.

"All right. Follow protocol, and I'll see you in a few."

Dr. Jones didn't say a word. He was busy looking at the body through the car window again. When I reached the 911 operator, I described my emergency, such as it was, told her who and where I was, and assured her I was safe. Then

I stayed on the line while she alerted the authorities, who'd soon be responding.

I didn't wait long. Two patrol cars pulled up first. Next, the EMTs came on scene, and within another minute, Eric's truck appeared. Eric exited first, wearing his usual uniform of jeans, a blue button-down shirt, and cowboy boots. Charlene Vogelman got out of the passenger side in a black pinstriped skirt suit, with the jacket, no less. All dressed up, and it seemed she'd have a felony to investigate in little Lilyvale after all.

I had managed to get Amber and T.C. under the shade of a tree while on the phone with the emergency operator. My knees didn't feel entirely solid yet, so I leaned against the oak's trunk, and my critters sat at my feet, surprisingly calm with all the emergency and law enforcement personnel milling about. In fact, from the way their ears perked and their heads swiveled, they were avidly watching the proceedings.

The EMTs snapped on gloves. The guy was movie-star-handsome Ben Berryhill, whom I'd met several times. The woman was Arlene Rollman. She was relatively new to the area but I remembered her from the police picnic. Ben did a double take at seeing Dr. Jones and stuffed another pair of gloves in his pocket.

"Doctor," Ben said as the older man moved back to stand with me.

"Berryhill, isn't it?"

"Yes, sir. How are you?"

"Better than that fella."

"Did you have a look at him?" Ben asked.

"Through the windows, yes. Not my place to do more unless I'm asked."

Ben gave Dr. Jones a lopsided smile and pulled the extra set of gloves from his pocket. "Just in case you're asked, sir."

Ben introduced Arlene before they both headed to the car. Ben opened the unlocked car door and braced a hand on Cornell's shoulder to keep him from falling out. I noticed that the body seemed more stiff than not. After Ben checked for a pulse, he looked at his female counterpart, shook his head, and closed the door just enough that it didn't pop open.

Eric nodded at me, but he and Charlene went directly to the first officers on scene, who stood at the hood of the car. I hadn't given a preliminary statement yet, except to confirm I'd made the discovery and the 911 call. When he looked up a few minutes later, I motioned him over. Charlene came with him, which made sense, but I was surprised when she took out a notebook.

Eric looked at my companion and broke into a wide grin. "Dr. Jones, how is retirement treating you?"

"Life's too quiet," he said, then motioned toward the car. "Except for this bit of excitement."

"Charlene, this is Herkimer Jones, forensic pathologist and former state medical examiner."

She shook his hand. "Doctor, nice to meet you. Did you discover the victim?"

"Technically, no. Nixy did."

Charlene's smile fell. "You two know each other?"

"We just met," Dr. Jones replied. "The young lady here looked a little green, and I stopped to assist her. Took a glance at the body, too, and I believe you're dealing with anaphylaxis."

"An allergic reaction?" Eric asked.

"I believe so, although I'd need a closer look to give you a more informed opinion. Obviously, that won't be official. The current state ME would need to present her own findings after autopsy."

Eric exchanged a glance with Charlene, and she nodded.

"If you wouldn't mind having a look, we'd appreciate it," she said. "Let me get you some gloves."

"Already have a pair courtesy of young Ben," the doctor said cheerfully.

Vogelman spared me a glance. "Nixy, please wait here."

She strode off toward the car with Dr. Jones. Eric gave

me an encouraging smile before he followed. I wished he'd touched my arm or patted my shoulder. I could've used the physical comfort. I gave Amber and T.C. a scratch instead and kept an eye on the police activity, which had drawn a handful of people from their homes up and down the block. I spied Lee Durley at the corner, a bit surprised he lived in the neighborhood. I waved, but he looked over his shoulder at a white house about then and didn't see me.

The city shared some law enforcement personnel, deputies picking up the slack for the police force and vice versa. The crime scene techs were attached to the Hendrix County Sheriff's Office but recorded and gathered evidence at all crime scenes in the county. Their van rolled up, and three techs hopped out, two female and one male. The one tech I'd met, Jan Blair, pointed to the back, and the other two began unloading.

While Ben assisted Dr. Jones as he examined Cornell, the techs hung back. I could hear the doctor's voice, though not everything he said. Having his upper body in the sedan muffled some words, but I caught "full rigor," "liver temp," and "heart condition." Then Dr. Jones straightened, and I clearly heard, "That was one hell of a reaction. Bad way to go."

"You don't think he was poisoned?" Charlene asked.

"Detective, in the broadest sense, any substance harmful to the human body in sufficient concentration is, in fact, poison. Doesn't matter if it's cyanide, tobacco smoke, medicine, or food."

The doctor's words slammed home the finality of Cornell's life, and tears for a man I'd barely known prickled my eyes. He'd been kind to a child, and kind to my pets. He'd deserved a chance at redemption.

Vogelman called to Jan. After a brief conversation, Jan took photos of the driver's-side door, then opened it and aimed the camera inside.

Vogelman faced Eric then, and she said something that sparked a short but serious exchange—if the frowny faces were any indication. Seconds later, the detective walked around Eric and came back to me. Again he followed, and now his expression was guarded. I wanted to ask him what was wrong, but now wasn't the time.

If cops had a mantle of attitude, she had donned hers and buttoned it tight. I got the cop stare, and that made me go queasy all over again.

"Miss Nix, tell me what happened."

She gave my clean-the-store outfit the stink-eye as if looking for bloodstains. I glanced at Eric, but he remained mute.

As I gave her the short version of finding Cornell, the coroner arrived. That distracted me momentarily, but I remembered to address her as Detective Vogelman. I emphasized that I didn't touch the car, and when she glanced down at the pets, I added, "They didn't lay a paw on it either."

That got a small smile from her. "Dr. Jones mentioned anaphylactic shock as a possible cause of death. Do you know if he was allergic to anything?"

"Peanuts," I said, and related the exchange he'd had on Saturday with the little boy.

"Did you see the plate of cookies in the car with Aster Parsons's and Maise Holcomb's names on that plastic cover?" Vogelman asked.

"They're called snickerdoodles," I corrected, "and, yes, I saw the plate."

"Why would the dead man—"

"Cornell Lewis," I supplied.

"—have them in his car?"

"He bought that kind of cookie at the bake sale on Saturday."

"You know this how?"

"Maise and Aster made a batch for the multichurch bake sale. When I talked to Cornell early Saturday afternoon, he had the plate of cookies on the hot dog stand counter. I saw him munching on one, and he had four whole ones left on the plate."

"How do you know Mr. Lewis?"

I shrugged. "I don't really *know* him. I know of him. He managed the apartment complex where Eleanor lived, and Aster and Maise lived there for a while, too. And Kathy Baker."

"Who is that?"

"A work-study student from the technical college. We're training her to take over Jasmine's position." At her perplexed look, I added, "Jasmine is moving to Magnolia after Christmas."

"Considering you don't know Mr. Lewis, you know a lot about him."

"Just bits and pieces." I explained about Cornell coming into the emporium on Friday, our hot dog stand visit on Saturday, and my short conversation with him Sunday morning when Dex Hamlin assaulted him. "Basically, Detective, I know what my family said about him, what I witnessed, and what he told me himself."

"When did you last see Lewis alive?" she asked.

"Sunday morning."

"And what were the circumstances?"

I sighed. "One of our artists, Mikki Michaels, used to be a nurse. She was tending to Cornell while Officer Bryant was on the scene. She suggested he go to the ER, and I asked if he wanted a ride. He said he'd walk, and he left on foot heading south toward the hospital."

"That's the last you saw of him?"

"That's it," I said, purposely not mentioning that I'd gone looking for him at the hospital. Explaining my concern and flat-out curiosity would raise more questions, and my spirits were flagging.

"It appears he was living in his car," the detective said. "Did he mention that to you?"

"Matter of fact, he did. He also said something about seeing a doctor in Camden if the ER wouldn't treat him. It didn't occur to me until later that he probably didn't have insurance."

Vogelman didn't comment. She gave me the silent treatment, but it didn't work. I didn't say a word. Well, except to Amber and T.C. They'd stood up and now strained at their leashes, smelling the other side of the tree.

"Almost done, girls," I told them. T.C. ignored me and stretched up to claw the bark, then jumped back when a chunk of it few off. Amber gave her a *What the heck?* grunt.

I glanced at the time on my cell phone. Yikes, it was past nine. The Six would be at the store soon if they weren't already there. I met the detective's steady gaze and arched a brow.

Eric cleared his throat. "Are you finished with the interview, Vogelman? The coroner is waiting for you."

She blinked as if coming back to the moment. "Yes, we're done for now, but I may have more questions later."

"Fine. I'll be at the emporium all day with the Silver Six. That's my Aunt Sherry and her housemates."

"I know who they are."

"Okay, but we're closed today and tomorrow so we can put the store back together. Knock on the front door if you come by."

"Got it."

With that, she hurried toward Terry Long, the coroner.

I slanted a glance at Eric. "Dr. Jones says Cornell died of an allergic reaction to peanuts?"

"He can't be that specific, and you know the routine."

"Yeah, yeah. The body and evidence all go to Little Rock, and it could be weeks before you have answers, but what about that grant the county got to improve the forensics lab?"

"It's more for training than equipment, Nixy."

"But you have that fingerprint analysis program, don't you?"

"We do, and Maise's and Aster's prints are sure to be on the shower cap thing."

"I know that. So what? The snickerdoodles could have nothing to do with Cornell's death. They aren't made with peanuts."

"I understand that, but if they were a factor in any way, Charlene Vogelman will follow every scrap of evidence she has, circumstantial or not."

"In other words, this could get ugly for Maise and Aster?"

"I'm afraid so."

This time I said something colorful.

DEX HAMLIN WAS MY PRIME SUSPECT, AND I TOLD Eric so before I left. Maybe Hamlin rubbed peanuts on Cornell's face. Hamlin was mean enough to do something like that. Eric assured me he'd discuss Hamlin with Charlene, and I felt marginally better.

Still, I jogged the critters back home, and I *never* jog. That's how pressed I felt to talk to Aster and Maise.

As expected, the Six hadn't waited until ten o'clock to come in. Fred's red truck, Dab's dark-gray Caddy, and Sherry's blue Corolla sat parked in the lot behind the emporium. I didn't want Amber and T.C. underfoot, but they might provide some comfort. Or be a nice distraction. I could always put them in the workroom if they caused a problem.

"Nixy, child, are you all right?" Sherry said as I ushered the animals into the store.

I tilted my head at her worried tone. "I'm fine, Aunt Sherry. Why?"

"You've never been so long when you walk these two, and then we heard sirens."

"We also heard that Dex Hamlin got out of jail last night," Dab said.

I blinked. "I'm the one dating a cop, and y'all know more than I do."

"So you didn't know that Hamlin character was free?" Aster asked.

"Not until about an hour ago."

"Debrief us, Nixy," Maise ordered. "I can tell by looking that you know why the police and ambulance tore past the square."

"I do, but you might want to have a seat."

"To the workroom," Maise said, and it sounded like, "To the Batcave."

"Aster and I will bring the coffee and biscuits in," Eleanor added.

We had gathered a variety of bar stools to use at Fred's solid wood worktables when we held crafting classes. Now we pulled them to the nearest, most scarred table and took seats. This was our customary planning place, or as Maise called it, the war room. Since I was the focus of the meeting, I sat at the end with Sherry on my left. Aster showered me with lavender water mist before she took the chair on my right.

With coffee and one of Maise's to-die-for buttermilk biscuits at each place, I launched into my report. Except for the occasional exclamations of dismay, they let me finish without interruption.

Aster sighed, and I put my hand over hers. "I'm sorry, but you and Maise needed to know about y'all's snickerdoodles being in the car, and about Cornell's peanut allergy."

She flipped her braid over her shoulder. "I don't see what there is to worry about. We don't use peanuts in our snickerdoodles recipe."

"I don't know of anyone who does," Maise added. "I know Herkimer Jones, though, and if he thinks Cornell had a severe allergic reaction to something, he did. Let's hope it was a wasp sting."

"Nixy, child," Sherry began, "didn't you tell us once that the autopsy is done in Little Rock?"

"I did. Dr. Jones just gave Charlene and Eric his opinion based on observations and experience. The local crime scene technicians will pull fingerprints, but all the evidence goes to the state crime lab and the body goes to the state medical examiner."

"So it could be weeks before any reports come back," Dab said.

"Depending on how backed up the workload is," Eleanor added.

Maise nodded. "Meantime, Vogelman is obligated to investigate the incident as an unattended and possible suspicious death. I went through this with two private patients I saw years ago. We'll probably be questioned because of the snickerdoodles. I'd question us if I were in charge."

"You're right, Maise," I said, "but not liking the man one little bit isn't much of a motive. Not for you or Aster, and not for Eleanor or Kathy."

"What if something about the cookies *did* kill him?" Sherry asked.

"Half the county and most of the festival shoppers bought bake sale goods, Sherry. As for opportunity, I'm betting once y'all got home last night, every one of you stayed there. And you got to the emporium within minutes of each other this morning, right?"

Six heads bobbed in agreement.

"But we need to be prepared if Detective Vogelman decides to zero in on me or Aster or Eleanor, or any of us for that matter," Maise declared.

Sherry clapped her hands. "Which means the Silver Six just may have another case to solve."

I glanced at each senior and stifled a groan. This was déjà vu all over again, but I would be right there with them. They were family.

WE WORKED STEADILY THROUGH THE MORNING. ABsolutely everything came off the shelves, and once we wiped them down with damp cloths, we dusted each item before putting it back. That alone took two hours, even with all hands on deck, as Maise said. Yes, I watched the clock we'd hung above the door and listened for a knock at the front door. When it didn't come I finally lost myself in the task at hand.

Since the Six were part owners, I'd insisted they have first choice in where and how to display their wares. After our thorough cleaning, they got busy consolidating, rearranging, and tweaking their goods, while I dealt with the boxes left by our consignment artists after the festival.

In spite of my fine art degree, I couldn't draw worth spit. However, I did have an eye for spatial design. At the Gates Gallery, where I'd worked in Houston, I'd aimed for an uncluttered serenity in the space no matter what kind of exhibition we were hosting.

Uncluttered didn't exist in the emporium. Sherry's baskets hung from the ceiling. Textiles were draped on dress forms and on a decorative ladder leaning against the back wall. Stained-glass art lined the bay window at the store front, and paintings and mosaics were either propped on newly acquired easels or hung on the walls. Every last shelf in the floor-to-ceiling wall unit opposite the antique counter was filled. Painted and primped-out gourds lay on shelves and on our display tables, and we even put them on the two lipped benches outside along with fancy throw pillows.

I worked to create as much space as possible between displays by putting out a good representation of each artist's work and a sign instructing shoppers to ask to see more. I'd also insisted that we separate similar crafts so they wouldn't be lost in the visual shuffle. So we had different types of items sprinkled throughout the store, and it seemed to work just fine. The Handcraft Emporium was still colorful chaos, but it didn't feel as claustrophobic to me as it once had.

The least-crowded shelves were those in the glass-top-and-front antique counter. We just didn't carry that many delicate or expensive items, but we dusted them, of course.

I stepped back from hanging fabric tote bags on an antique coat rack, stretched, and looked at the clock. Twelve thirty in the afternoon. Five hours since the police responded to my call, and no word from Eric, or from Vogelman. Was that a good thing, or not?

Maise clapped her hands behind me.

"Okay, troops, time for lunch. We have tuna salad, chicken salad, and cold meat loaf sandwiches with a veggie tray. Nixy, I put everything in your fridge, so we'll help you carry the food while the men put out paper plates, cups, and napkins."

Again, I wanted to salute, but instead I climbed the stairs to my apartment with the four senior women. Soon we had lunch fixin's spread out on the same worktable where we'd noshed during the morning meeting. I did step back upstairs to get T.C. and Amber a few treats, but my real mission was to phone Eric.

He didn't answer his cell, so I left the message that the Six and I would be in the back room for an hour. If he or Vogelman needed to reach us, they could come to the back.

We finished our meal in peace, chatting only about the success of the festival and community news. The subject of leaf-peeping in northeast Arkansas came up, and I almost mentioned Eric's proposed trip. Talk about a diverting topic! In the end, I let the moment pass. While the ladies and Dab might be fine with it, Fred would give me grief about knowing my worth and making sure Eric knew it. Yes, I knew he was teasing. Mostly. I just wasn't in the mood.

Truth be known, I felt a bit raw from having discovered another body, and saddened that I'd never know if Cornell Lewis had changed his ways for good. I liked to think he had. He'd been kind to my animals and a child. In my book, that earned him the benefit of the doubt.

Then I wondered if anyone would mourn him, and the thought made my heart ache a little.

BY FOUR THAT AFTERNOON, WE HAD EMPTIED almost half of the boxes but had yet to finish arranging all the merchandise. And, in spite of lunch and other breaks, I began to drag, and I could tell the Six were wearing out, too. Dab looked particularly tired, so I waylaid my aunt in the workroom as we returned from throwing flattened boxes in the Dumpster.

"Is Dab okay, Sherry?"

She tilted her head, and the lock of hair fell over her left eye. "Why do you ask, child?"

I shrugged. "He looks like he's lost weight, and his eyes seem dull."

She nodded. "He hasn't seemed as hale and hearty as usual, but, honey, his wife died in October not quite four years ago. He goes through a rough patch as the anniversary gets closer."

"Ah. I understand."

"You've been thinking about Sue Anne's death?" she asked.

"It'll be two years since we lost Mom."

"It's nearly five since my Bill died," she said, folding me in a hug.

Both my mother and Sherry's husband had died after having strokes, but Bill lived another few years. My mother had passed quickly, and Sherry had come to Tyler to help me sort things out. That was when I'd first come to know my aunt beyond a few childhood visits and greeting cards for birthdays and holidays. I'd done the right thing moving here to be with her.

When we pulled apart, she captured my hand and squeezed. "We'll keep an eye on Dab, Nixy. Not to worry. Now, in all the craziness this morning, I forgot to ask how your date went."

I blushed a little. "Dinner was fantastic."

A sly grin spread across her face. "And afterward? Did it get hot and heavy?"

"Sherry Mae Cutler, how you talk!" I exclaimed, mimicking a phrase of hers. I paused, then decided to take the leap. "Aunt Sherry, how would you feel about me taking a trip with Eric?"

She arched a brow. “I don’t think that’s any of my business.”

“In the normal course of things, it isn’t, I guess, but this is a small town with a giant gossip mill. I don’t want you to be the target of any maliciousness. Besides, I’d need to coordinate the work schedule to be off for a few days and arrange to board Amber and T.C.”

“There will be no boarding of those dears,” she declared. “We’ll look after them at the house, but we do need to arrange the schedule. When did he have in mind?”

“About a month from now. In early November. He talked about seeing the fall color up in Eureka Springs.”

“I’ve been there for leaf-peeping. It *is* spectacular. There are wonderful historic hotels there, and a number of bed-and-breakfast inns, of course.”

“So, you don’t have a problem with me going?”

“No, and no one else will either.” She paused and grinned. “Except Fred. He’ll tease you something fierce about getting married, but he does it because he cares.”

“I may have to tease him back about Ida Bollings, then.” I pictured the tiny woman in her big blue boat of a car driving through town like a bat out of hell. “I swear, I thought I’d see them sporting matching walkers by now.”

“Honey, you still might. Now come along. We need to help tidy up so we can go home.”

We had taken two steps toward the door leading to the shop when it banged open and Fred *clank-clunk*ed over the threshold.

“There you are. You two best get in here pronto. That new cop is here and she ain’t being respectful.”

Chapter Nine

SHERRY AND I RUSHED PAST FRED. I FEARED THAT Aster or Maise or both would be in handcuffs or zip ties or whatever, but that wasn't the case. They stood at the counter next to Charlene Vogelman, who held a manila file folder. Eleanor and Dab stood guard behind the counter. I didn't look around to check, but the door banged and Fred's walker clunked, letting me know the gang was all here.

The detective turned as I stomped closer, Sherry behind me. Eric was conspicuously absent, and that niggled at me, but I stayed focused.

Vogelman narrowed her eyes at me. "Detective Shoar said you knew how to keep your mouth shut, but you told these people about the crime scene, didn't you? They know some of the details."

I shrugged. "In the first place, 'these people' are my family. Second, half the neighborhood people were gawking, and gossip spreads fast here. Last, when I'm asked to keep quiet, I do. You didn't ask."

"I won't make that mistake again."

I snorted. "And I sincerely hope there won't be an again."

She turned back to Aster and Maise.

"I had these photos blown up. Is this the plate of snickerdoodles you made for the bake sale?"

Neither Aster nor Maise wore readers often, but Eleanor passed one green-framed pair and one brown-framed over the counter from the stash of cheaters in various strengths we kept in the store. Each woman leaned over to peer at the 8 × 10 photo, and then Maise picked it up and angled it toward the overhead light. I stood behind her, so I had a clear view, too. Vogelman waited. I wondered if she'd heard the disrespectful dig from Fred. I also wondered what she'd done to earn his anger. Besides questioning Maise and Aster at all, that is.

"I can't attest to those being the snickerdoodles we made," Maise said, "but that's the kind of plate and bowl cover we use."

From beside her sister, Aster pointed at the photo. "That's my Aster's Garden product sticker. I figured it couldn't hurt to advertise a little."

"Wouldn't you say it's a logical assumption those are your cookies?" Vogelman asked.

"I suppose it would be," Maise said calmly. "Would you like the recipe?"

The detective pursed her lips. "How many other people made snickerdoodles for the bake sale?"

Aster waved a hand. "You'd have to ask the ladies in charge. They keep a list of donors and the items donated. We dropped off our cookies and Sherry and Eleanor's brownies Friday morning, and came right to the store. We had artists' items to box up for the festival."

The detective frowned at the photos. "How many plates of cookies did you donate?"

"Just one each. A dozen cookies, a dozen brownies."

"Does your snickerdoodle recipe call for nuts?"

"No, why?" Maise asked, all innocence.

"Then there were no peanuts in the cookies?"

"Peanuts?" Aster exclaimed. "Heavens, no."

Sherry cleared her throat. "The cake brownies Eleanor and I made had pecan halves on top, and the churches insisted that donors label anything with nuts to avoid allergic reactions."

"Are you sure Cornell didn't react to an insect sting?" Maise asked.

"I can't discuss that," Vogelman answered, her tone neutral but her weighty gaze on Maise.

I nodded. "You'll have to look into his medical records, I suppose."

She ignored me, gazing in turn at Eleanor, Aster, and Maise. "At one time or another, you all lived in the apartment complex that Mr. Lewis managed until he was fired approximately fourteen months ago. Were any of you aware of his nut allergy?"

Maise snorted. "Like we ever broke bread with that man."

"And we certainly didn't offer him our baked goods," Aster added.

Eleanor held her hands palms up. "My stove and oven were broken half the time I lived there. In addition, I don't believe I ever saw him eat. Just drink beer."

"I should think that if the man had a severe allergy," Maise said, "he would've carried an epinephrine injector. Although those are expensive."

The detective smiled like a cat about to pounce until I spoke up and said, "Maise was a nurse, in case you didn't know."

The detective huffed a breath, gathered her photos, and crammed them in the folder. "That's all for now. Please stay available for more questions later."

With that, she left the store. The wind chimes we used in place of a customer bell sounded discordant as the door closed behind her.

The Six and I exchanged solemn glances.

"I do believe she has gone without a civil good-bye," Eleanor said.

"I believe she told us not to leave town," Aster added with a rueful smile.

"And it's a bad sign that Eric wasn't here, isn't it?" Sherry asked.

"T'ain't good. Nixy, call the man and find out what's goin' on."

"It's obvious, Fred," Maise snipped. "If Cornell Lewis in fact died from an allergic reaction to peanuts, those cookies make Aster and me persons of interest. Eleanor, too, I suppose, since she lived at Ozark Arms longer and had more dealings with Cornell. We may all be under the microscope because of our close association."

"Eric is too close to us because he's dating my niece," Sherry said. "He's either recused himself or been pulled from the case."

"Then we'd best call that criminal attorney, Dinah Souse," Dab said, "because that Vogelman woman is going to be trouble."

BEFORE THE SIX LEFT FOR THE DAY, MAISE TOLD ME to eat the leftover raw veggies and the last cold meat loaf sandwich already in my fridge upstairs. Her meat loaf was perfect hot and perfect cold, so I wasn't about to demur. I could tell she was gung ho to hold a war council, but she only said we all needed to rest.

I also learned what had set Fred off earlier. Eleanor told me Vogelman had given them attitude when she'd first come in. She'd demanded to see our tiny kitchenette and said she'd get a warrant if Aster didn't cooperate. Fred might've beaned her with a wrench then and there if he'd been standing closer. As it was, Dab and Maise had held him back while Vogelman opened and closed the few cabinet doors and looked in the wastebasket. That was when he'd taken off to find Sherry and me.

I was surprised Charlene Vogelman would come on so strong with the Six. Then again, except for one hint of a smile, she'd been coldly formal with me at the crime scene. Professional distance I could understand. Wanting the truth, I could get on board with, and I knew from Eric that she'd had an excellent track record for closing cases in Tulsa.

That gave me some comfort. She didn't settle for the convenient suspect. She searched. She'd better do so in this case, because I wouldn't stand for her railroading a member of my family.

I TOOK THE CRITTERS UPSTAIRS, KICKED OFF MY Crocs, and tossed a ball to Amber while I enticed T.C. with a long, feathery cat teaser. After a while, Amber decided to chase the teaser as I snaked it across the floor, and T.C. went after the ball. She didn't fetch, but she liked batting it around.

I couldn't help but wonder if I'd hear from Eric. If I did, what would I say? I had to admit Maise was right about him having a conflict of interest. He knew us all too well, and because of that, wc wouldn't be high on his suspect list. And I definitely should not ask questions about the case.

Then again, I wasn't big on "should dos" and "ought tos."

At six I was pouring kibble into critter bowls when my cell played the whistling *Castle* theme song, the ringtone I'd assigned to Eric. In my dash to get to the living room, I tripped over T.C., then stubbed my toe on the coffee table.

"Ouch. Hello?"

"What was the ouch for?" he asked.

"I stubbed my toe. How are you?"

"Okay. Uh, Amber and T.C. haven't been to the dog park in a while. It'll be dark soon, so there shouldn't be anyone there."

Eric's friends who spearheaded the dog park had given me the okay to bring T.C. along with Amber, as long as it was empty. That was normally shortly before sunset.

"Nixy? You there?"

"Are you sure you want to be seen with me?"

"That's what I want to talk to you about. Will you let me pick you up in about five minutes?"

"I'm still in my work clothes."

"Not a problem for me if it isn't for you."

It should be. I should have jumped in the shower when I came upstairs, but I'd chosen to veg out.

"Please, Nixy. I need to see you."

The edge in his tone swayed me. "We'll meet you in the alley."

We disconnected, and I turned to find a set of amber and a set of green eyes staring at me.

"Want to go to the park, girls?"

They perked their ears and tilted their furry heads.

"Go with Eric?"

That truly magic phrase had Amber racing to the toy basket. This time she dug T.C.'s harness and leash out first, then her own leash. I got them ready to go, stretching my back as I straightened, and then slipped on my Crocs. By the time I got downstairs, Eric stood by his truck with the back door open. Both animals nimbly leaped inside, and then he lightly laid his hand on my back and escorted me to the passenger side. The good ol' butterflies took flight in my belly. Hard to be angry with a guy who makes you feel treasured.

Or with a guy just doing his job.

The park wasn't far, and I filled the time telling him the progress we'd made in the store. I wasn't ready to grill him about Cornell yet.

"As often as I've seen y'all dust, I'm surprised it needed cleaning," he said as we pulled up to the park.

"It wasn't too bad, but Sherry called it fall cleaning. I'm sure we'll do it again after the spring festival. Yes, Amber, we're here." My dog gently pawed my arm from where she'd perched herself halfway on the console to see out the windshield. She knew exactly where she was, and so did T.C. She'd balanced herself atop the passenger seat and my shoulder.

Though neither critter had ever shown the least interest in running off to chase something, and no one was in the adjacent children's playground to tempt them, we snapped on their leashes as a matter of course until they were inside the first of the dog park gates. Actually, there were four gates altogether if one counted the two leading into the area exclusively for small dogs. The combined space was an acre and half and partly shaded by mature trees. I'd figured the native grasses covering the park would be torn up by doggie nails by now, but other than beginning to turn autumn brown, the mown carpet of grass remained intact. Thick mulch lined the chain-link fences, circled the trees, and marched along the row of bushes planted along the fence line that separated the large and small dog areas.

The main attraction in both areas was the doggie playground, aka the array of agility equipment, their bright colors not the least bit faded from the summer sun. Amber immediately leaped through hoops and over hurdles. T.C. was at her heels until she spotted a squirrel on a low tree branch. The cat was perfectly capable of climbing the tree, but she merely circled and meowed.

Meantime Amber ran back to us and danced around Eric's feet. She'd seen him holding the soft disk she loved to chase. He threw it and she bolted after it, nearly catching it in the air. She pranced back with it in her teeth, and the two of them played toss and retrieve for a while before Amber romped off to check on T.C., and then get a drink from the kiddie splash pool.

"Come sit with me," Eric said, and grasped my hand to

lead me to one of the half-dozen benches with dog-bone-shaped backs.

"Are we going to talk about the elephant in the dog park?" I asked.

He gave me a level look. "Charlene is investigating this as a suspicious death, but there's a possibility Cornell Lewis was murdered."

I strove for calm. "Okay, considering how many people he apparently hurt, insulted, or otherwise annoyed, I figured that. How can you be sure he was deliberately killed?"

"Right now, we can't be. Or rather Charlene can't be. It's her case."

"Go on."

"Dr. Jones's opinion is that Cornell died of a food allergy rather than an insect sting. I don't know what he saw that led him to that conclusion, and the state medical examiner will determine the official cause, but Charlene confirmed he had a peanut allergy this afternoon."

"I'm surprised she got his medical records so quickly."

"When you gave her the Camden lead, she tracked Cornell to a homeless shelter there and talked with the administrator, Scott Dowdell. A doctor who donates his services to community outreach made a note of his severe allergy, but also detected a heart problem."

"So the allergic reaction could've triggered a heart attack." He gave me questioning look and I explained, "After Vogelman asked Maise and Aster about nuts in their snickerdoodles recipe, Maise gave us a crash course in anaphylaxis. I don't suppose you found an empty bag of peanuts in the car."

He shook his head. "I wish we had."

"Does Vogelman remember my statement about the cookie plate Cornell had at the hot dog stand? He had only four cookies left, and there had to be six or seven in the car."

"I'm sure she's taking that into account."

I gave him a sharp glance. "What are you not saying? That Vogelman thinks I'm lying? That Aster and Maise made more cookies, and poked peanuts in them, or rolled them in peanut dust? All on the off chance they could first find Cornell, and then get him to eat them?"

He grimaced. "I can't say any more, Nixy."

I held his gaze, knowing one of my questions had hit an investigative nerve. But which one? I took a steadying breath.

"Listen, Eric, Cornell Lewis being killed is bad. He told Eleanor he'd changed, and in my little bit of dealing with him I think he really was reformed or well on his way. I feel bad that I'll never know if I was right about him, but what I can't stand is having the Silver Six suspected of his murder."

"I know, and I wouldn't have a one of them on my list as a serious contender for it, but I'm not working the case."

"Because we're dating, right?"

"And the Silver Six are your family."

"I'm not going to ask you about the case per se—"

"Or trick me into telling you anything?"

"No, but I want to ask why Charlene Vogelman seems to have them in her sights."

He looked toward Amber and T.C. playing one-sided tag on the tunnel. T.C. draped herself on top of the tunnel at one end, and when Amber ran through, the cat swiped a paw at her. The dog ran right around to do it all again, and the cat obliged.

"Look at it from her perspective. Aster and Maise made snickerdoodles for the sale, and Cornell bought them. Later he's found dead with the same kind of cookies on the front seat, and with a plate cover that was clearly theirs. You confirmed you saw Cornell with that plate, or at least saw the cover, and verified he had a peanut allergy." He stopped for a breath. "She can't ignore all that. It would be unprofessional."

"But Maise and Aster didn't have one reason to kill Cornell."

"Eleanor was angry that Cornell showed up. She wanted me to run him out of town."

"Eleanor isn't Aster or Maise, and you know she wasn't serious. Besides, you didn't tell Vogelman about that, did you?"

"I didn't have to. Kathy or Jasmine apparently mentioned it to someone, and Vogelman got wind of it."

"Does she think Aster and Maise bumped off Cornell for Eleanor's sake?" I shot off the bench and paced. "That's idiotic. Next you'll tell me Vogelman suspects we all conspired to kill Cornell."

He rubbed the back of his neck. "Not precisely, but you're all thick as thieves, forgive the expression. You've said it yourself. The Six are tighter and more loyal to each other than most families."

"None of the Six left the farmhouse after they went home on Sunday."

"Which only makes all the close friends each other's alibi. The same as having no alibi."

"Then you should talk to Bernice Gilroy. If she wasn't busy with her TV programs all night, she probably would've heard a car leave. She keeps binoculars on the kitchen table and spies on the neighbors. Mostly Sherry and the gang."

"Mrs. Gilroy lives in a house Miz Sherry Mae owns. Would she be honest?"

I snorted. "To a fault. That woman says exactly what she wants, and lets the chips fall."

"Then maybe *you* should ask her if any of the Six left Sunday night or very early Monday morning."

"Maybe I will. Wait, did you just let the time-of-death window slip?"

"Don't tell me you hadn't already figured that out."

"Well, it *is* a logical time span. Too many potential witnesses in daylight."

He put his hands on my shoulders. "Nixy, I don't want this to come between us."

I sighed. "I don't either, but I can't traipse off to Eureka Springs with you as long as the Six are in jeopardy."

A slow smile spread across his face. "You're agreeing to the trip?"

"If this case is resolved." I blew out a breath of pure frustration. "Eric, at least tell me Vogelman is looking at Dexter Hamlin. He put the beat-down on Cornell Sunday morning, for heaven's sake."

"We're looking for Dex right now. He's not in town, and his wife hasn't seen him since late last night."

"And that's not suspicious?"

He took my hand. "Nixy, Cornell Lewis hurt and angered a lot of people when he managed that complex."

"I met one of them at the hospital yesterday afternoon. Marshall Gibson. He about blew a gasket when I asked if Cornell had been in the ER."

"I'll mention him to Detective Vogelman, but she's interviewing the people who still live at Ozark Arms, and those who've moved but live in town." He squeezed my hand. "Please trust that she'll look at every potential suspect."

I nodded but didn't necessarily agree. Sincere as Eric was, and much as I thought he believed what he was saying, I also thought I might be getting a bit of the party line. If the police chief was as eager for swift justice as he'd been during the last two murders, Vogelman would be under pressure to solve the case fast. Never mind to prove herself. That was pure common sense.

Dusk had settled in, and we called the critters. Amber raced over, tongue lolling out. Bless her heart, she needed more vigorous exercise than I gave her on a regular basis. Or her breed usually did, according to Dr. Barklay, the vet. I did play with Amber in the parking lot, and at the farmhouse when we went out to visit. Dab and Fred ran her around, too.

T.C. always came along, and both animals seemed happy and healthy, so maybe I should just keep doing what I was doing, and let the worry go.

I had enough concerns about the Silver Six. I didn't need to borrow trouble.

Chapter Ten

ERIC ASKED IF I'D EATEN YET, AND WHEN I SAID NO, he admitted he hadn't either. Still in my work clothes, and having the critters with us, I didn't want to take the time to run them home, shower, and change. I know, I know. I'm months into dating a hot guy I'm kind of nuts about, and yet I'm too lazy to clean up for him. Maybe I needed my head examined, but my body was bone tired.

Instead I offered to share my veggies and meat loaf sandwich with him.

"I'm in," he accepted without hesitation, "but let's run by the Dairy Queen, too."

"Not if you're buying fries to accidentally drop on the floor for Amber and T.C."

"Who, me?" he asked with false innocence. "No, I thought you could use a latte or banana shake."

Two of my faves. I grinned. "Let's go."

I decided on the DQ version of a latte, and Eric went crazy with a black coffee and a banana split with two doses of chocolate and one dose of caramel topping. We were hardly five minutes from my place, but time enough for the soft-serve ice cream to melt.

Or so I thought. Eric put the little plastic boat in an ice chest. With plenty of ice to keep the banana split cold for our short drive.

"You always have ice in the chest?" I asked archly.

"I'm nothing if not prepared," he said with a grin.

T.C. didn't care for milk, and I'd learned since I had her that many if not most adult cats don't. But ice cream from Eric? That she wanted, so we dug out a dollop of it without chocolate or caramel for both her and Amber. Then with our treat in the freezer, we sat side by side on stools at the kitchen counter eating half sandwiches with celery, carrots, broccoli, and cherry tomatoes. He had ranch dressing dip with his veggies, but I declined. I was saving my calories for dessert.

"About the trip, Nixy," he began as we made short work of the banana split. "Did you mention it to Miz Sherry Mae?"

"I did, and she went into raptures about the historic hotels and scenery."

He chuckled. "No objections?"

"None, and she offered to keep the critters for me, too. I do have to coordinate the work schedule. Do you have an exact time in mind?"

"I thought we'd go the first weekend in November. Peak fall color is supposed to be that month, though it could be earlier or later."

"We'll have to take our chances."

"We'll make the most of it," he said, offering the last bit of banana to me from his spoon.

I held eye contact as I took it, chewed just enough to swallow, and then leaned in for a kiss.

We didn't get far into the action before his cell buzzed. He'd put the phone on the countertop, and now the vibration made it skid along the surface.

"Shoar."

I could've stayed right where I was and shamelessly eavesdropped. Instead, I grabbed the plastic ice cream boat and spoons, put them in the kitchen sink, and shamelessly eavesdropped. Not that I heard much.

"Already?" he asked. Then, "No, I can come back. Yeah, see you in a few."

His smile held so much regret, I went to him with open arms and we shared a long kiss.

"Go," I said when I stepped away. "I'll talk with you later."

He smiled, but I could've sworn he muttered, "I hope you will," as he closed my apartment door.

ERIC HADN'T TOLD ME ANYTHING ABOUT VOGELman's thinking that the Six and I hadn't already concluded, namely that one or more of us might be suspects. Particularly Aster and Maise, but I didn't like having our theory confirmed. With the shop closed again tomorrow, we definitely needed to make time for one of Maise's war councils.

Since it wasn't nine o'clock yet, I called the farmhouse landline. Even if the ladies were snuggled in bed, the men might be up watching *Monday Night Football*. After three rings, Maise answered.

"Something wrong, Nixy?"

"Nothing, I just wondered when y'all planned to be in tomorrow."

"You have somewhere else to be?"

"No, but I saw Eric for a while tonight."

"Ah, then we need a war council?"

"What's she saying?" I heard Sherry say in the background. "What's happened?"

"Here, you talk to her," Maise said to Sherry.

She must've put a hand over the receiver because I heard a *mumble-mumble* before my aunt came on the line.

"What's going on, child?"

"Nothing yet, but we need to have a meeting of the minds tomorrow."

"What time?"

"Not the crack of dawn," I said. "How about ten?"

"We'll be there by nine thirty. Want us to bring breakfast?"

"No, thanks. Not to hurt Maise's feelings, but I need to see Judy at Great Buns."

"Fine, fine. If you get there first, take one of the paintings in the store off its easel and get out the murder board."

She meant the flip chart, and we'd only used it once to list suspects for the murder we looked into in June.

"I'm on it. Are y'all taking it easy tonight?"

"Eleanor might be. She's up in her room. The rest of us girls are baking cookies, and the menfolk are watching the game." I heard male cheers erupt and Sherry chuckled. "I think Dallas is winning."

That I had to see. I signed off with Sherry, toed off my Crocs, and tuned into the football game. Dallas *was* winning, beating the Redskins by a touchdown. As I settled in to watch awhile, it hit me that Eric was right. I just might think about football more than he did. So sue me. I was a Texan.

TUESDAY MORNING, I REALIZED I MIGHT NEVER GET to sleep late again. Not with a pup licking the inside of my elbow, right where it tickled, and a cat parked on my chest.

"Okay, I'm awake, girls. Give me room to move."

They did, and I jumped in the shower, then threw on another clean but grubby outfit to work in. One that hadn't been completely destroyed when I'd worn it to help repaint, refinish, and generally refurbish the whole building in May and June. If I ended up going outside the store today to see anyone but Judy, specifically to ask questions about the case, I could run up and change. That was one of the many things to love about living above my workplace. That and buying so much less gas. I think I'd driven more in six days in Houston than I had in six months here.

The sky was streaked with high clouds, and the temperature hovered in the mid-seventies. I inhaled the crisp air as I strolled with the critters, thinking I could smell autumn. I idly wondered if the Ozark Mountains would have their own special scent when Eric and I were in Eureka Springs. Funny, now that I'd committed to go, I knew it was the right decision.

At Judy's urging, Grant Armistead had installed a teakwood and wrought-iron bench under the Great Buns awning for patrons to sit and enjoy their pastries. Judy had even put out a large bowl of water for those who came to town with their animals. Okay, primarily for Amber and T.C. I made good use of the convenient place to park the critters for a few minutes but didn't come by with them every single day. Hey, my waistline couldn't handle all the flaky richness of the goodies Judy and Grant made.

I'd picked up a small dog collar with a sturdy plastic closure, and it worked perfectly to loop through the leash handles and then snap around the bench arm. The animals had shade and water and could watch the morning activity on the square.

I'd only seen Grant a handful of times. He always seemed to be in the back baking or doing the books. He was a burly guy, five foot nine to Judy's five foot nothing, and he struck me as gruff. I wondered a time or two why the effervescent Judy had married such a quiet man, but when I saw them together, I knew. They were in Love with a capital *L*.

Today was no different in that Grant was out of sight, and Judy was loading a bag of croissants for Kay Gaskin. She and her husband, Carter, owned Gaskin's Business

Center next door to the emporium. Would she mention me finding Cornell Lewis's body? I couldn't make myself invisible, so I'd have to buck up and risk it.

"Hi, Kay." I greeted the middle-aged woman. How she endured wearing suits or dresses with sky-high heels day in and day out was a mystery. Made my feet ache just thinking about it.

"Why, Nixy, hello. I've been meaning to come tell you how much Carter and I enjoyed having the festival in town."

I smiled. "Did it bring you any business?"

"It did. A few artists came in for labels, and festival shoppers came for boxes and adhesive and packing tape. I'm sure glad we ordered extra stock of those items because we nearly sold out. We even sold some of the Arkansas kitsch items to out-of-staters."

"That's great! Do you think you'll want to support the spring festival?"

"Of course!"

She beamed at me, then at Judy as she took the bag of croissants and handed over her money.

"Don't be a stranger, and tell Sherry Mae and everyone hello."

When the door closed behind Kay, Judy planted her fists on her hips.

"Well, you went and found another body."

I rolled my eyes. "Guess I'm getting good at knowing where to look."

She snorted. "You joke, but I know it has to bother you."

"What bothers me more is that the Silver Six might be implicated."

"What? Why?" Judy's eyes could not have grown any wider.

Dang, I should've kept that to myself, but I needed her help.

"Judy, keep this to yourself, but there was a plate of Aster and Maise's snickerdoodles in Cornell's car. Or rather a plate of the same cookies and the shower cap cover thing they use." I braced my hands on the counter. "Have you heard anyone talking about the death?"

"You're pale and you need to eat," she declared.

"Judy, Amber and T.C. are waiting outside. What I need is information."

"Tell you what. Take these," she said as she passed me two dog and two cat treats, "and go check on the fur babies. You have one minute."

I sighed. I wasn't going to win this one, so I followed her instructions. T.C. and Amber were fine, getting attention from anyone who walked by. I told them I'd hurry and returned to the counter.

"Now, I'll tell you all I've heard while you eat whatever you're ordering this morning."

I arched a brow. "Need you ask?"

"One egg and cheese on a fresh biscuit coming up."

I sat at our customary table and watched, ever fascinated because Judy was a whirlwind behind the counter, a master multitasker. I hadn't even asked for coffee, but she broke an egg on the griddle, spun to pour a cup of plain coffee—nothing fancy for me this morning—then flipped the egg and snagged a Great Buns biscuit the size of Texas from the warmer. With the cheese and egg added, she plated my breakfast sandwich, put the plate and coffee mug on a tray, and came from behind the counter.

"Here, chow down," she said.

"And you talk."

She shrugged. "There isn't much to say. When Grant and I came here two years ago, we spent so much time getting the bakery ready to open, and then running the place, we didn't have much of a social life. Customers gossiped now and then, but we didn't pay too much attention."

"Do you recall anything involving Cornell Lewis?"

"Not by name. Several people complained about an obnoxious guy who managed an apartment building. That had to have been him, but the customers were talking to each other, not to us. We didn't know anyone well enough to ask questions."

"That's understandable. Is anyone gossiping now?"

"First, I heard all about the fight, and why didn't you come tell me about it yourself? You're gonna wear me thin if you don't keep me up to speed."

"It was a crazy day, Judy."

"Fine, you're forgiven this time. So, here's the scoop. Not a soul is broken up over Cornell's death. They think he got what was coming to him. I also overheard that someone Cornell had bullied ended up dead."

"What?" I choked out. "Who said that?"

"I think it was Debbie Nicole. Or it sounded like her voice. She came in for donuts for the library staff, but I had my back turned when she made that comment. But, Nixy, you know how stories get exaggerated."

I also knew there was usually a kernel of truth at the core of stories. I made a mental note to ask Eleanor about a death connected to Cornell.

"What about Dexter Hamlin?"

"Nothing but vague rumors about him. Seems he and his wife are connected to a bunch of movers and shakers all over southwest Arkansas, so no one speaks ill of him." She grinned. "Except you. Horrible Hamlin. That was a good one."

"Have you heard he's missing?"

She tilted her head. "Voluntarily or not?"

I chewed and thought about her question, then swallowed and measured my words. "If it turns out that Cornell was murdered, I want Dex to be the guilty party. I'd like to think that's why he's dropped out of sight."

"I hear that." She tapped a nail on the tabletop. "Nixy, what's the big deal about Maise and Aster's cookies being in the car? Half the county was at the bake sale."

I grimaced. Should I tell her about the peanut connection? Judy wasn't a blabbermouth, but to quote Maise and misquote World War II propaganda posters, "Loose lips sink ships." If Vogelman knew that details of her case were common knowledge all over town, she'd be even more put out with me. No, I needed to be on her good side as much as possible.

"Well? I see your wheels turning, so you might as well spill."

"The thing is," I began, "Cornell bought those cookies himself. He told me so, and I saw the plate with only four of the original dozen cookies left."

"When was this?

"Saturday, when he fed my critters a hot dog."

"Then why would the ladies be implicated?" She snapped her fingers. "You think someone slipped poison into the cookies?"

"I don't know what to think."

I called to mind the plate in Cornell's car. Were there seven cookies including the broken pieces? Eight? Did it matter? It did. Cornell hinted that he didn't have much money. The bake sale ladies had given him a discount on the plate he did buy. If he hadn't bought another plate of cookies from the bake sale, then it stood to reason someone had given them to him. Who? Would he accept food from just anyone?

"Nixy, hey," Judy said, shaking my arm. "You okay?"

"You just crystalized something for me."

"You're welcome. So will the Magnificent Seven be investigating again?"

I laughed. "I take it that's the Silver Six and me?"

"Yup. I like the rugged Old West image."

I shook my head and brushed the biscuit crumbs off my fingers. "You can call us anything you like if you'll keep your ears open for me."

She grinned. "An undercover assignment. I'm all over it."

* * *

AMBER AND T.C. WERE LAPPING UP THE *OOHS* AND *aahs* of a couple of preschoolers, their mother watching with an indulgent smile. When she saw me, she asked me to tell her children Amber's and T.C.'s names. They toddled off trying to one-up each other on which animals liked who best.

"Making friends wherever you go, huh, girls?"

Amber gave me a panting doggie grin, and T.C. simply looked smug.

Considering that I'd been with Judy for nearly half an hour, I was surprised the Six weren't at the store at nine thirty. I had time to snag an easel, set it up in the workroom, and get the flip chart and markers out. After waiting five minutes, I pulled seven chairs to the worktable, then began on the murder board. Besides tuning into *NCIS*, I'd caught just enough *Castle* episodes to have half a clue what I was doing. I wrote *TIME OF DEATH* and *CAUSE OF DEATH* on one sheet, then flipped to the next page and wrote *SUSPECTS.*

I could estimate the time of death as sometime between after dark on Sunday night and early Monday. Cornell had been in the passenger seat, so I envisioned two possible scenarios: One, he'd parked the car, moved to the passenger seat to sleep, ate tainted cookies, and died. Two, he'd eaten the cookies elsewhere, likely with the killer looking on, became ill, and the killer drove Cornell's car, parked it, and left him. The killer might have said he'd drive Cornell to the ER but let him die instead. If I went to the trouble to poison someone, I'd sure hang around to make sure the deed was done. Either way, I'd do the deed after dark.

I shook my head at the grisly images I'd conjured and got back to work. I listed Sunday night sometime after full dark to Monday morning before dawn for the TOD, and jotted *anaphylaxis* as the cause of death. Then I added a question mark beside the entry. Much as I had instinctively liked Herkimer Jones and tended to trust his opinion, the state ME had to make the final call. I wrote the name of one suspect: Dex Hamlin.

At nine fifty with the Six still MIA, I began to feel a smidgen of concern. I called Aunt Sherry's cell, but she didn't answer. When I texted, though, she replied they were on their way. The tightness in my shoulders loosened, until ten minutes later when the seniors spilled into the workroom all but growling remarks at one another. Not the happy chatter I was used to hearing.

Amber and T.C. blinked at me, then ran for the bed they shared.

"What's wrong, y'all?" I said as I hurried toward them. No one seemed ill. In fact, every last one of them looked livid.

"I'll tell you what's wrong, missy," Fred spat. "That highfalutin new detective showed up at the house at seven thirty this mornin'."

"With a search warrant," Sherry growled.

"She had officers trampling my garden," Aster said, dabbing her red-rimmed eyes with a snowy-white lady's hanky.

"They went through the property from stem to stern." Maise threw up her hands. "They didn't mind making a mess while they searched."

"What on earth was Vogelman looking for?" I asked, already getting a headache from the ping-ponging conversation.

"Peanut products," Dab spat.

"I do believe she hit the mother lode," Eleanor said.

"Did the police confiscate anything?"

"An empty jar of peanut butter," Sherry said. "Good thing we made our peanut butter cookies last night."

"They took Dab's sack of peanuts in the shells, too," Aster added.

"Plus that trail mix with peanuts Fred eats," Maise huffed. "The stuff is loaded with enough sodium to float a battleship, so he's better off without it."

"Give it a rest, woman," Fred growled. "My health is perfectly fine."

"I did a spot repair to my garden, but the plants need more attention."

"It'll take us half a day to put the house to rights," Sherry complained.

"And another half in the barn and work sheds," Dab said.

The barn had been used more for storage than for housing livestock. The sheds were two outbuildings a bit larger than one-car garages, and all three buildings were painted red.

The same color I was seeing right now. My mind reeling at the images of destruction, I held up a hand. "Wait, wait. Are you telling me she marched in with a warrant and had the searchers rip up Aster's plants and ransack the house?"

"Well, no, it wasn't quite that bad," Aster said.

"The detective did ask permission to search first," Sherry temporized. "You remember we gave Eric the okay to search in April when that woman was killed, but Dinah Souse told me never to do that again, so I refused. You could've knocked me over with a feather when Vogelman pulled out that warrant."

Maise stuck out her chin. "Still, the officers didn't put all our things back where they found them."

"No, they didn't," Dab said, "but I could tell Dougie Bryant and that young Taylor Benton were uncomfortable going through our home."

"And Deputy Paulson, was, too," Aster admitted.

Ah, so Megan Paulson, the mayor's niece and an inspector with the sheriff's office, had been with Officers Bryant and Benton. They all knew the Six and would've balked at damaging property. They'd been following orders, I knew, but they were stupid orders.

"Pardon the pun, but this is nuts," I said. "Have you called Dinah Souse yet?"

Sherry nodded. "We called her from home, and she's meeting us here."

"When?"

The door to the alley opened, and the criminal defense attorney stepped inside. Not a huge surprise since her office was on the square.

Eleanor glided across the floor to take Dinah's hand. "Thank you for coming so quickly, Ms. Souse."

The attorney's white chocolate mocha coloring was marginally lighter than Eleanor's skin tone, and she had the same kind of quiet beauty. In her mid-thirties, the lawyer oozed professionalism in a muted gold skirt suit with a white blouse. The outfit suited her willowy figure. Brown leather pumps and a matching soft-sided briefcase completed the ensemble. She didn't appear to wear much makeup, but I'd bet hers didn't melt off like mine did. She seemed too cool and collected to allow so much as a hair out of place in her elegant French twist.

"Hello, everyone," she said in her softly accented contralto voice, and shook hands all around.

I stood beside the flip chart, and when she got to me, her startling green eyes held the slightest twinkle. "So you're involved in another murder, Ms. Nix?"

"Please call me Nixy, Ms. Souse."

"Dinah," she said. "We all may as well be on a first-name basis."

"Thank you, but you need to know I am *not* involved in this murder, and neither are the Six."

She waved a hand at the chart. "Then why does it appear you are investigating?"

"Because Detective Vogelman has other ideas about us," I snipped.

Fred banged his walker. "Fool woman thinks we got

t'gether to kill Cornell Lewis. Damned dumbest thing I've heard in all my born days."

"All right, let's get started," she said as she sat on the bar stool Dab pulled out for her.

"Don't we need to give you a retainer first?" I asked. I'd given her one up front when she'd come to be with Aunt Sherry during questioning.

Aster dug her wallet from her purse. "I have it right here. Are you sure you don't want more than ten dollars?"

"This consultation is free. Having the retainer now only saves time making me your attorney of record should you be called in for questioning."

She opened her briefcase, wrote a receipt for Aster, and then removed a legal pad and pen and swept us with her gaze. "Now then, give me the highlights of what's going on so I'll have an overview. I'll ask for details later."

We looked at one another as if to decide who'd go first. In the end, I was the spokesperson since I'd found the body, and the others chimed in to clarify here and there. Dinah's notes covered three pages by the time we finished. She glanced over them, then turned to a fresh page.

"Good. Now then, tell me about this morning when Detective Vogelman brought officers to serve the search warrant. Did you bring your copy for me to see?"

Sherry withdrew the bulky document from her large faux-leather bag. As Dinah read the warrant, I held my breath. When finished, she frowned at the flip chart.

"Peanut products?"

"Ridiculous, right?" I asked, rhetorical as the question was. "Peanuts are a dime a dozen. Ninety percent of Lilyvale must have them in their homes."

Dinah responded calmly. "The warrant gave the police a wider leeway than I would like to see, but it's in order."

"We know the circumstances are somewhat suspicious, but how did the woman convince Leo James she had probable cause?" Maise asked.

"Not to bore you with legalese, but the detective likely presented her case to Judge James as more than reasonable suspicion simply because the cookies you and Aster made were in the car with the victim. Or rather the same kind of cookies with the cover you used. That alone has to make Vogelman's antenna twitch, especially since poison is traditionally a woman's weapon of choice."

"Peanuts aren't poison," I protested.

"They are to an individual with severe allergies," Dinah replied mildly. "Now, I did some brief digging and learned that Detective Vogelman has searched other premises with permission, except in one case. I can't say who refused her, but she applied for a warrant in that instance as well. You are getting equal treatment, more or less."

I frowned. "It's the less that I'm concerned about. Do you think Vogelman will search the emporium?"

"She insisted on havin' a look-see at the kitchenette yesterday," Fred groused.

"Did she? Without a warrant?"

"She came in loaded for bear," he answered.

"Technically, we gave her permission to look around," Aster added.

"Only because she caught us off guard," Sherry hastened to say. "I did remember your lesson from April, and that's why we denied her when she asked to search the house this morning."

"Well, I think you can count on her coming back with all her legal ducks in a row," Dinah said.

"I do believe Detective Vogelman isn't going to take us off her suspect list anytime soon," Eleanor said.

Dinah said as she smoothed the pages of her legal pad flat, "Maybe, maybe not, but if she shows up here to search, call me. Of course, you know to call me immediately if she takes anyone in for questioning, or into custody."

My ire rose again. I knew I might be overreacting, but for two cents, I'd march over to the station and ask Charlene what the devil she was doing wasting time on Aster, Maise, and the gang. Ranting at her wouldn't help matters, but I'd feel like I'd done something instead of stewing.

I hated stewing.

And if Eric knew about the warrant last night and didn't give me a hint, never mind a heads-up, let's just say he had some 'splainin' to do.

Chapter Eleven

DINAH LEFT SAYING SOMETHING ABOUT RESEARCH. I didn't know what she had in mind, but I was ready to do my own digging. With or without the Six.

Of course, they were gung ho.

Before we could confab, the ladies insisted on fixing tea for themselves and coffee for Fred and Dab. When we'd reassembled in the workroom, I uncapped a marker.

"Let's look at what we know," I said.

"From what you got up there, missy, don't seem like we know much."

"I realize that, Fred, but we have to start somewhere."

"What about Eric? Did he tell you anything?" Sherry asked.

I took one second to decide how much to share but decided they needed to know all.

"He didn't tell me much. As y'all predicted, he's off the case because of his relationship with me and with all of you. However, he did give me a general time of death, and he said Vogelman learned Cornell had a heart condition in addition to the allergy. She talked to a man who runs a homeless shelter in Camden."

"Did he mention what kind of heart ailment?" Maise asked.

"No, but I didn't ask. I didn't want him to clam up."

"Bet he did anyway," Fred said. "I ain't sure that boy is good enough for you."

I let that pass and pointed to the time of death on the chart. "I narrowed the time of death to after dark and before dawn, just because if I were the killer, that's when I'd act. I overheard Dr. Jones say something about full rigor, but I didn't hear if the body was in it or not."

"Full rigor takes eight to twelve hours, depending on how warm or cool it was in the car," Maise said, "so your timeline works. What's next?"

"If Dr. Jones's opinion ends up being verified by the state ME, then cause of death will be anaphylaxis. Is that right, Maise?"

"Actually, no. The allergic reaction would be a contributing factor, and those symptoms and their progression are different for everyone. But with a heart condition present, the official cause might be a coronary or asphyxiation. Either way, his death had to be most unpleasant."

"Then don't get into that," Fred commanded.

I'd learned in June that Fred had a weak stomach when it came to hearing about death scenes.

"You didn't see any other signs of violence, child?" Sherry asked.

"Violence, no. Other than the scrapes, cuts, and bruises from Sunday morning's beat-down, I only saw a few splotches on his face and neck. No gaping wounds or, uh"—I glanced at Fred, and he gave me a go-ahead nod—"pools of blood on Cornell or in the car."

"Then move on to suspects," Aster said.

I flipped the page to show them Dex's name.

"That's it?" Fred was unimpressed. So was I.

"He's the most viable one I have. First," I said, ticking the points on my fingers, "he beat on Cornell for giving away two lousy hot dogs. Second, he was out of jail or holding or wherever by Sunday evening. Eric was with me when his truck zoomed through a stop sign. Third, he's now missing."

"What do you mean, and who told you that?" Sherry asked.

"Eric. Dex's wife says she hasn't seen him since Sunday night."

"So, if Dex killed Cornell," Aster said, "he's done a runner."

"And if he did not," Eleanor said slowly, "Cornell met up with someone who took extreme exception to him being back in Lilyvale. Moreover, it was someone he trusted enough to accept food from him or her."

"Correct, Eleanor, and you just might hold the key to finding out where he might've been from Sunday morning until he was killed."

"She does?" Sherry asked.

"Yep. Eleanor, I need you to make a list of all the people who lived in your apartment complex when Cornell was the manager. The ones who are still there, too, if you know of any."

"I know of five counting a married couple, but, Nixy, there were thirty-seven residents all together. Or there were during the time when I lived there. Some I didn't know except to greet in passing, and most were students at the technical college. As far as I know, they've all moved on."

"That's okay. Just list everyone you remember and I'll reach out to them for a chat."

"All right, but the people who are still here might be more forthcoming if I went with you," Eleanor said.

"I'd love to have you. If Vogelman has already talked to the people on your list, and used her unique cop charm, they might be ready to unload to you."

"Nixy, child, you shouldn't mock Charlene Vogelman. She's doing a tough job."

"I just don't want her doing it at y'all's expense. By the way, Eleanor, do you recall Cornell bullying someone who died?"

"Died?" she repeated.

"Judy overheard something to that effect in the bakery."

"No one died while I lived at Ozark Arms, but I suppose it could've happened after I moved. I admit I was very lax in keeping up with the residents I knew, especially early on."

Maise tapped her chin. "I recall hearing a young man up and moved out of those apartments in a hurry. If I'm not mistaken, he worked at the library. You could ask Debbie Nicole about him."

"I will," I said, and hoped she'd talk to me.

I'd gotten off to a rocky start with the pixielike librarian, but we'd mended fences since. Of course, if I asked questions related to a murder, I might end up on her bad side again. Worth the risk, I decided as I hopped off my bar stool, flipped to a clean page on the chart, and started a *People to Talk To* list. Next to Debbie Nicole's name I wrote *Guy who moved*. While I was at it, I wrote Kathy's name.

"You don't suspect Kathy, do you?" Aster asked.

I capped the marker. "No, but she might remember some of the residents Eleanor doesn't. Plus, if a lot of students rent there, Kathy may know people who know people."

Sherry nodded. "Good thinking."

Maise clapped her hands. "Ladies and gentlemen, we need to mobilize before the day gets away from us. Nixy, go open the rest of the artists' boxes, and we'll put out the pieces."

I set the marker on the easel tray. "No, y'all are not working in the store today."

Six rebellious faces scowled at me.

"I can handle things here. You go get the house, garden, barn, and sheds in order."

Sherry waved a hand. "We can do that later."

"But it's better to do it now while you're fresh. You don't want to work all day and go home to a mess, do you?"

"My garden does need some TLC."

I hid a grin. Aster didn't merely talk to her plants and play classical music for them. She blasted artists like Jimi Hendrix and Aerosmith and sang along. She thought rock music gave her herbs more oomph.

"And I'd appreciate taking inventory in the stillroom," Dab said.

"Then go. Take care of things at home."

"What if that durned new detective shows up here?" Fred asked.

"I can handle her."

"Humph."

"You call Dinah to come over, just in case."

"Promise, Sherry. Now y'all get out of here," I said, shooing them toward the door. "I'll check in with you later."

Sherry stopped at the threshold and reached up to cup my cheek. "You're so good to us, child."

I swallowed a lump in my throat. "I'm glad I moved here, Aunt Sherry."

She beamed. "Come to dinner tonight if you want."

I muttered a vague agreement, but I intended to track down Eric and have a serious talk with him.

I MEANT TO GET RIGHT ON ALL THAT UNPACKING, but I needed to make notes on the flip chart first. Too many questions crowded in. Questions I hadn't brought up with the Six.

Where had Cornell gone after Sunday morning? Whom had he seen? Who had seen him? Having wheels, he could've gone anywhere, seen anyone, possibly to continue apologizing to those he'd wronged. I wouldn't want to face people I'd bullied with my face blooming full-color bruises, but perhaps he'd seen it as part of his penance.

Then there was Dex Hamlin. I presumed he'd been driving the truck that tore through the stop sign two nights ago, but where had he been going? Did he find and kill Cornell, or was he missing for another reason? For all I knew he'd gone hunting or fishing, or off to meet a woman. Nah. No woman with an ounce of sense or self-respect would have an affair with that man.

I finished scrawling points to pursue and went into the store with the critters to do my real job. I thought the hands-on task would quiet my brain. I thought watching Amber and T.C. bat wadded packing paper and jump in and out of boxes would distract me. No such luck. I knew the wheels of justice could move at a crawl, but the wheels in my head still spun like mad.

Although I'd worked largely on autopilot, by noon I had over half of the boxes unpacked and items arranged. It helped that the artists had sold most of their stock at the festival, but I was still pleased with my progress.

Until someone knocked hard on the front door, and Vogelman yelled she had a search warrant.

Dinah's office was just around the corner, but I didn't want to call her before I opened the door for the police. I was half afraid the detective would kick it in. Yes, I knew that was more cop show drama than reality, but no point in delaying.

I hollered I was coming, unlocked the door, and swung it wide open. The wind chimes seemed to clink off-key.

"Ms. Nix, I have a warrant to search the premises."

"Okeydokey, let me see my copy," I said as Officers Bryant and Benton and Deputy Paulson came in behind her.

For the briefest instant she looked surprised, but she handed over the warrant and then instructed the officials to start searching.

"Hold it," I said, and whipped the cell out of my pocket.

Vogelman's eyes narrowed. "If you attempt to impede my execution of the warrant, Ms. Nix, I will arrest you."

"I have no intention of impeding the search, but I have

the right to observe every step of the way. Since I'm the only one here, aside from my pets, I'm calling for backup. Unless you want to poke into one space at time. I didn't figure you'd want to be at this all afternoon."

I touched the screen a few times, then smiled at the officers while the phone rang. "Ms. Souse, hi, it's Nixy. Detective Vogelman is here with a warrant." I paused to listen. "No, I sent them back to the farmhouse to put everything back to rights." I listened. "Okay, see you in a few. Come on in the front door."

I disconnected, and Vogelman scowled. "You're really alone?"

"I am, but one of your officers can check the back. By the way, I've been out of peanut butter for over a week. I'm out of bread and jam, too." I shook my head in mock dismay. "I really need to get to the store."

She didn't roll her eyes, but I could swear she wanted to. Instead, she looked at Doug Bryant and jerked her head at the door to the workroom. When he headed toward the back, she eyed the boxes on the floor.

"What is in these?" she asked.

"Most of them contain the leftover art from the festival. The artists who consign with us brought items back here for us to unpack and put on display."

"You said most of them. What's in the others?"

"My cat was in one of them, and my dog pushed another one behind the counter." I paused and took a subtle half step toward her. "By the way, if y'all break anything in your search, you've bought it."

She held my gaze, and I thought I saw respect there. "We'll be careful."

"Thank you," I answered as Dinah swept in the front door and Officer Bryant strode in from the workroom.

"No one is here, Detective."

She acknowledged him with a nod. "All right, we'll get started."

* * *

DINAH WAS HAPPY TO TRAIL AFTER THE OFFICERS who searched the workroom and my apartment. I didn't know what her hourly rate was, but it was worth the cost to have another set of eyes. Not that I believed Vogelman would condone planting evidence, or that the deputy and officers would go along with such a scheme. Come on. Searching for all things peanut was bizarre enough, and in boxes of all places. Planting peanuts on the premises would surpass all reason.

Still, Dinah was legal muscle, and someone I trusted with the keys to my place and to Fred's locked cabinets. Since they'd propped the door open between the store and the workroom, I heard Bryant and Benton exclaim over some of Fred's cool tools. That made me smile.

I stayed with the art and craft items. Deputy Paulson did most of the hands-on searching and didn't seem to mind me observing.

The only hiccup occurred when Benton and Bryant first entered the workroom and saw the flip chart with all my scribbles. The last time we'd done a murder board, the Six had insisted we leave the first few pages blank. In other words, bury our notes so they could be easily hidden. I'd forgotten to heed that advice.

"Want to explain this?" Vogelman said when she saw it.

"It's my thinking board."

"It's a murder board. I've heard you stumbled around trying to solve two murders."

I resented the "stumbling" part but gave her a bright smile. "Apparently arranging art is a puzzle-solving skill, and I do like to use my skills to the fullest."

I thought she'd tell me to keep my nose out of the investigation. She didn't. She gave me a *yeah, right* smirk and then eyed the flip chart again. "Why did you pick this time-of-death window?"

"First, the body looked rather stiff when Ben Berryhill opened the car door to check for a pulse. Second, it's logical that the car was parked after dark, and after most people on the street had gone to bed."

"Whatever. It doesn't appear you have much to think about, Ms. Nix."

I shrugged. "There are a lot of blanks to fill in, aren't there? I hope you're turning up more answers." I paused, knowing I shouldn't say it, then did anyway. "Finding real evidence instead of dwelling on unlikely suspects."

She didn't answer. Just turned and stalked to the storefront.

I didn't so much as peek at the officers or Dinah. I simply followed and resumed watching Deputy Paulson.

In fact, the search proved rather helpful in one way. The deputy first searched the shelves and kitchenette, and then started on the boxes. As she set each box on the counter and unpacked it, I had the okay to put the items on shelves. Sure, I had to artfully arrange them later, but that was my specialty.

The last place the team searched was the wall of shelves behind the antique counter. The ones that flanked an old-fashioned lift with an ornate accordion-style door.

"Awesome," young Officer Benton breathed.

I grinned at him. "My way-back-great Aunt Sissy had it put in when she upgraded the building and turned the upstairs storage into an apartment. It's the only way to move furniture to and from the apartment."

"As long as you aren't moving bodies in it," Vogelman drawled, "I'm satisfied. Deputy, officers, we're done here."

When the door closed behind them, I turned to Dinah. "Thanks for coming over so quickly. Having you here helped me stay calm."

"Nixy, except for baiting the detective about unlikely suspects, you handled that well."

"I've learned a little tact from Aunt Sherry Mae and the gang."

She chuckled. "Detective Vogelman might disagree, but she's a reasonable and capable cop doing her job. You hang in there."

I CALLED AUNT SHERRY TO ADVISE HER OF THE search and told her Dinah had been with me from start to finish. She wasn't thrilled Vogelman had searched the building, but she didn't dwell on it. She asked instead if I was coming to dinner. I was, and that made her happy.

I worked steadily for two hours without hearing from Eric. I worked steadily for another hour, all the while arguing with myself about texting him. After another hour, I decided to do it.

R U in hiding? I typed.

Almost immediately he texted back: Caught a case. Talk later.

Uh-huh. Right. If I deigned to answer when he saw fit to call.

I didn't reply to that message.

At five o'clock I flattened the empty boxes, much to the annoyance of T.C. and Amber. They forgave me when I mentioned two words: "dinner" and "farmhouse."

Before I went up to my place, I stretched my back and critiqued the displays. They looked perfect if I did say so myself, and I'd already dusted and vacuumed, too. I'd even cleaned the window and the glass in the front door. In the morning, after the critters and I had taken our walk, I'd give the store a quick swipe to gather up any last pet hair.

While the fur babies had their kibble, I jumped in the shower and washed my hair. It took hours to dry, even with an industrial blow dryer, so I secured it with claw clips. In a ponytail, it would still be wet at bedtime, and I never went to bed with wet hair. I refused to sleep on a damp pillow.

So I'd hit it with the dryer later before I crawled under the covers.

After the search warrant trauma, and then straightening all day, the Six were more cheerful than I'd dreamed they'd be.

The men were setting the huge dining room table, and I joined the ladies in the kitchen. Maise beamed at me when I nearly swooned from the aromas of dinner and told her so.

"I cooked two roasts the size of battleships. We'll have leftovers enough for us, and you, and for Old Lady Gilroy, too. I made a chocolate cake for dessert."

"That's not Mrs. Gilroy's favorite, but she won't turn down a slice of that."

Late-afternoon sun streamed into the room from the south- and west-facing windows, lending a soft glow to the age-darkened wood of the table and sideboard. I helped put the dishes on the table—a platter of sliced beef, two bowls of potatoes, carrots, celery, and baby onions, and two gravy boats. When everyone had full glasses of sweet tea, I took my customary seat at one end while Maise sat at the other. The Six even allowed the critters to sit under the table so long as they didn't beg. They didn't, though Fred had been known to sneak them a morsel of meat now and then.

The Six filled me in on their day, saying the search turned out to be a good thing. They'd reorganized, located some things they'd forgotten about, and found some items to donate.

"I opened a box that had been shoved in the corner, and there were more beakers!" Dab beamed. "I guess when I set up the stillroom out back, I didn't have space on the shelves and just left them as they were."

"Now Dab doesn't have to order more," Aster said gaily, "and we've washed the dusty ones that were in the box. We're all set for another round of distilling."

We segued into the emporium search, including Vogelman's demeanor and Dinah's advice to hang in there.

"She has absolutely no reason to suspect us any longer," Sherry declared.

"No incrim'natin' evidence whatsoever," Fred added. "Dang foolishness wastin' time on us, lookin' for peanuts when they're as common as dirt. Eric Shoar woulda known better."

"He had to search here in April, though," Aster said.

"I do believe the new detective is doing her job the best she knows how," Eleanor put in, "but I'll be pleased to be off her suspect list."

"Amen." Maise clapped her hands. "Are we ready for dessert?"

Over the perfectly moist cake with rich frosting, I turned the conversation back to suspects.

"Eleanor has leads for you," Dab said.

"I started my list of apartment complex residents." She paused, drew a folded sheet of paper from her pants pocket, and handed it to me. "It's not complete, but it's a start."

I scanned the printout, which took all of two seconds since it was short, but smiled. "Twelve names and contact information, too? Eleanor, this is great! Thank you. I'll start contacting these people tomorrow."

"Actually, I took the liberty of calling a few myself," she admitted. "I thought it would break the ice, so to speak."

"Good idea," I said. "Were the people you called open to talking with us?"

"Once I assured them we were simply gathering information, yes, but I didn't reach everyone. Several had generic voice messages. The kind that confirm the number reached but don't give a name."

"We can only do what we can."

"I'm happy to hear you say that because I do believe we might want to take a few of them to lunch."

I blinked at her. "Are you saying some could use an itty-bitty bribe?"

"'Incentive' sounds more civilized," she replied tartly.

"But, Nixy, we need to be careful. Tactful. Detective Vogelman has already interviewed most of the people who still live at the complex, and a few who don't. They are skittish."

"I promise not to upset your friends and acquaintances, Eleanor. In fact, we can rehearse questions we need answered, and you can take the lead."

She nodded. "I can do that as long as you jump in if you need to."

"Excellent plan," Sherry said. "You do tend to speak your mind quite freely at times, child."

"I'll be on my best behavior. Cross my heart. Oh, Aster and Maise, will you have a look at Eleanor's list and note anyone with a special fondness for your snickerdoodles?"

The sisters exchanged a glance. "That will be a short list."

"I know it's a long shot, but any one bit of information might break the case. And, Eleanor, would you print copies for each of us? Maybe having it handy will jog a memory."

"Now you're cookin' with gas," Fred said, then pointed his fork at me and glowered. "Now, what's this about you goin' off to Eureka Springs with Eric Shoar?"

Chapter Twelve

FRED EARNESTLY LECTURED ME ABOUT MY "FEMALE mis-teek," and then expounded about cows and free milk, *and* about making Eric chase me until he caught me at the altar. He must've gone on for a full five minutes, and I could only guess at how many shades of red I'd turned before he ran out of steam.

Fred even knowing about feminine mystique baffled me. I didn't hear the term often, so where did he hear it? Embarrassed as I was, I would have been more so if I hadn't heard the rest of the Silver Six chortling in the kitchen.

Yes, they'd abandoned me to Fred's not-so-tender mercies.

If I were a lesser person, I'd plot a way to repay them, but I gathered the container of roast beef and sides and a large slice of chocolate cake. With everything securely in my delivery basket, I strode to Bernice Gilroy's house.

She opened the door before I knocked, snagged me by the forearm, and jerked me into the house. The little elf of a woman had strength, and it constantly amazed me how much.

"Heard you found another body," she said as I followed her into the kitchen. "What is it with you and dead people?"

"If I knew that, Bernice, I'd know how to avoid the problem."

She tilted her head. "You have a point. I heard it was Cornell Lewis who bit the dust. Was the crime scene grisly?"

"Uh, not particularly. Did you know him?"

"I knew his mother and father, and there was a man who'd make a terrorist look like a saint. Cornell learned meanness at his father's knee."

"He could've chosen a different path than his dad. I only talked to him a few times, but he seemed reformed."

"Maybe he was. I'll tell you one thing. That boy ate snickerdoodles by the handful. He ate so many at a church picnic once, he got sick." She chuckled. "You'd think that would've put him off the cookies, but it didn't."

"He bought some at the bake sale Saturday."

"Is that what killed him?"

"The police aren't sure yet."

"You fill me in when you know. Now then, put down the basket. I want to see what Maise sent over."

"The roast and veggies are divine and tender enough to cut with a fork," I told her as I unpacked the plastic container. She had ears like a bat and eyes like an eagle, but I'd bet money all her teeth weren't her own. "There's cake, too. A big slab."

"White with chocolate icing?"

"Nope, chocolate all the way."

She wrinkled her little nose. "It'll have to do, but you bring me more of the kind I like, you hear?"

I grinned. "Yes, ma'am."

"Don't sass your elders," she said as she put the food in the nearly empty fridge and slammed the door. "Rumor has it you're going away with your detective. Bet Fred gave you an earful about that, but I have some advice."

I braced myself. "What's that?"

"Pack lingerie. Something suggestive, not skimpy. You don't need to dress like a tart to offer him a little sweet. You take my meaning?"

The heat of a blush burned my face.

"Ah, I see that you do. Nothing to be embarrassed about, Sissy. The mating dance is old as time."

"You're a corker, Bernice."

"I know. Time for you to leave now. Mark Harmon will be on in five minutes."

I left the little house yet again pondering where Bernice got her intel, and if news of my tentative Eureka Springs trip was all over town.

Although, if I didn't straighten things out with Eric, there would be no trip.

THE CRITTERS HAD PLAYED WITH DAB AND FRED while I was at Bernice Gilroy's. Short a time as that was, they were tuckered out and had flopped on the bed as soon as we got to the apartment. Admittedly, I didn't love cleaning up pet hair multiple times a week—never mind a litter box—but my pets were a comfort, and they gave me someone to talk to besides myself.

They also gave me the excuse to walk them the two blocks to the police station. That wouldn't be happening tonight.

"So what do you think about Eric, girls?" Their heads shot up from their paws when I mentioned his name, but I shook my head. "He hasn't called. He hasn't texted. I have to wonder what kind of case has him so busy, right?"

Amber sighed and rested her head back on her paws. T.C. stood, circled, and then lay with her paws tucked under her, her tail curled around her.

Was that a show of support, or were they merely bored?

Okay, so Eric and I didn't talk every single day, but the longer we'd dated, the more often he'd touched base. That he hadn't connected with me since early last night meant either he was avoiding me, or he was very busy. With what?

I considered that as I blasted the blow dryer on my hair. Hendrix County wasn't that large. In fact, I'd been surprised it hadn't been absorbed into another county back when Arkansas was a younger state. Sherry had told me that the powers-that-be had left the county intact for historical reasons. The Widow Hendrix, her husband lost in the Civil War, had owned most of what was now the county. My ancestor and the town founder, Samuel Allan Stanton, and his wife, Yvonne, had bought the land when they'd cut out of Fort Smith, Arkansas, immediately after the war, bringing their five children.

My Aunt Sissy had been the youngest of the brood, and the one who'd lived the longest. Generations of Stanton family investments in land, including Sherry's own shrewd purchases, had allowed the clan to prosper in Lilyvale. Only in the 1920s and again in the late 1930s had the family sold land, and that was to invest in the oil boom, mostly in and around Magnolia. Thanks to a fund Sissy had set up long ago, one Sherry now managed, I lived rent free. I had finally convinced her to let me pay the apartment's utilities, and since my meters were separate from those of the emporium and Fred's workroom, it was easy for us to keep track of our business costs.

I turned off the dryer, put it away, and brushed my teeth. So, Hendrix County being minuscule by comparison to others, what kind of case *did* Eric have? Sure, we had residents in outlying areas. Most homes were situated on still-working farms, although there were some businesses outside the city, too. The Pines Motor Court, a cute, kitschy motel from the late 1940s or early 1950s, was a few miles out. There were branch offices and labs for a timber corporation and for a chemical firm, although Dab hadn't worked there. We also had a company that manufactured lamp shades, and a woman who made her soaps for boutique hotels. She wasn't Deb the Soap Lady from the festival, so I had yet to meet her.

Of course, Lilyvale wasn't Utopia. We had DUIs, thefts, vandalism, fights, and traffic accidents. We'd also had a lost child and two seniors who'd wandered off. Those incidents ended happily, but thinking of them made me think of Dex Hamlin's disappearance. Maybe Eric was pursuing leads to locate him and get him back to Lilyvale. If so, I sure hoped he got his man, and soon.

I WOKE ON WEDNESDAY WITH ONE DECISION MADE, one back on the burner. I'd wait for Eric to call me, and I'd reconsider traipsing off on that trip until I found out what was going on with him. I knew there were things he couldn't talk about during a case, but a hello-how-are-you would've been nice.

My decision not to call didn't stop me from strolling oh-so-casually past the police station with the fur babies. I spotted Charlene Vogelman exiting her car in the back parking lot, but she didn't see me, and I didn't wave. I also didn't see Eric's truck. Had he pulled an all-nighter on his investigation? Could be, but I didn't care, did I?

Not much. Denial had its uses.

Time to refocus on managing the store and investigating. Part of running the store meant updating the website. Or rather sending updates to Jasmine's boyfriend, Lamar Watts, who had designed and now maintained our site for a nominal fee. First step was to e-mail the festivals photos to myself. I did that, trotted up to my apartment to snag my tablet, and set it on the checkout counter to review the pictures. After selecting the best variety of shots, I e-mailed them to Watts the Web Wonder. When I reached the ones of Cornell with my animals and the accidental picture of

Lee Durley, my finger wavered over the delete button. I could e-mail these few to Gaskin's Business Center next door, have hard copies made. What to do with them? What's a murder board without photos of victims and suspects?

I sent those pictures in an e-mail with instructions to Kay Gaskin. Then I buckled down to finish getting ready to open. The Silver Six were due at nine thirty, so I had the till recounted for accuracy and was doing last-minute dusting for pet hair on the shelves when I came to the Aster's Garden display. Seeing her new labels made me flash back to seeing the one on the plate cover. Had the killer deliberately left the cover in the car to implicate Aster and Maise? Who would do that and why? The sisters never spoke a harsh word about anyone, and I couldn't imagine them having an enemy in the world.

Had the crime scene techs found fingerprints on the plate cover other than Maise's and Aster's? Yes, the evidence had to go to the state lab, but our local techs could lift and compare prints.

I went to our murder board and made a note to ask Eric. He might give me a yes or no without divulging anything else. Then I darted up to my place to get my copy of Eleanor's list and returned to the workroom just as the Six pushed through the alley door. Today I heard their happy chatter and knew they'd more or less left yesterday's drama behind.

WE DID A BRISK BUSINESS IN THE MORNING, BUT IT didn't take a village to run the shop. Dab was in the workroom with Fred, and although I didn't hang out with them often, I had wanted to discuss some new metal-art pieces with them.

"We're already addin' more team mascots, missy," Fred grumped, and pointed the screwdriver he held at a classic blender. "Can't ignore my fix-it work, you know."

Dab nodded. "We're creating a cowboy and covered wagon for the two big Oklahoma teams, a longhorn for the University of Texas, plus a bulldog, tiger, and bear."

"That's great, and if you don't like my new ideas, forget I said anything."

Fred set the screwdriver on the workbench. "What'd you have in mind?"

"Holiday-themed pieces for Halloween, Thanksgiving, and Christmas."

"I ain't doin' no zombies or pilgrims."

"That's fine, Fred. I had pumpkins, a cornucopia, maybe a sled for winter in mind, but you decide. The only reason I mention this is because I think they'll sell." I paused. "Your work is good, gentlemen. I know holiday stuff can be a dime a dozen, but not what you two will make."

"I swan, she's sure dumpin' the butter boat on us, Dab."

"She is, but why not give it a shot, Fred?"

Fred shrugged. "You design 'em, I'll help you build 'em."

With that, Fred resumed tinkering, Dab winked, and Eleanor sailed through the shop door calling my name.

"Nixy, I just received a call from one of the ladies on my list. Minnie Berry. She's living at the retirement home."

We had at least three retirement homes in and near Lilyvale, but I didn't ask which one. I cut to the chase. "I remember seeing her name. Is she okay?"

"Oh, yes, she's well, but she's having cataract surgery Friday, and she wants to talk with us before then. I told her we could come by today."

"What time?"

"Now. We'll catch her between lunch and her nap."

I'D NEVER HAD THE OCCASION TO VISIT A SENIOR living center, but I'd heard horror stories. Pines Breeze was a pleasant surprise.

Eleanor informed me that Pines Breeze was both an

independent- and assisted-living center. A sister facility housed those who needed round-the-clock nursing. There was a small Alzheimer's unit in that sister nursing home, but many families took those patients to El Dorado or all the way to Texarkana.

The aroma hit me first when we entered through the automatic doors. The place smelled like its name, as if someone had sprayed Pine Breeze air freshener to cover a slightly stale scent. Not completely unpleasant, but it made my nose itch. I followed Eleanor to the reception desk, noting that the entry décor was a bit tired but not shabby. After a woman with bright red hair and a name tag reading MADGE signed us in, she told us Minnie was waiting in the lounge across the hall.

Minnie sat in a brown checked wingback chair, one of four in a grouping. She wore a loose summer print dress, and champagne-blonde hair framed her face as she peered at us through her glasses.

"Eleanor!" she trilled. "How good of you to come visit. Come, sit."

Eleanor bent to touch a cheek to Minnie's. "It's always good to see you. How are you feeling?"

"Right as rain and ready to get these cataracts removed. I have the cutest doctor!" In spite of the film over her eyes, they twinkled. "Who have you brought with you? Is this the famous Nixy?"

Famous? I didn't know how Minnie came to that assessment, but I smiled and held out my hand.

"It's wonderful to meet you, Mrs. Berry."

"Call me Minnie, dear. Sit so we can gab. Would you like anything to drink? There's a fridge with soft drinks and water in the corner."

"No, thank you," Eleanor said as she sat on Minnie's right. I took the chair on the left. Slightly threadbare, but comfortable.

"So, you're investigating Rotten to the Core's murder?"

Good thing I'd turned down a drink or I'd have choked. "Oh, we aren't investigating, Minnie."

She wagged a finger at me. "Don't give me that song and dance. I know all about your sleuthing."

I glanced at Eleanor, who looked baffled.

"Eleanor, did you forget Dougie Bryant is my nephew once removed?"

Dougie. That was what the old-timers like Fred's special friend Ida Bollings called Officer Doug Bryant.

"I do believe I did forget, Minnie," Eleanor said faintly.

"Well, the dear boy comes to visit now and again, and he's regaled me with the story of how you got to the bottom of some things."

I winced. The bottom of one of those things had nearly meant the bottom of a casket for Sherry and me.

"Now then, what can I tell you about our former manager? You knew him longer than I did, Eleanor."

"We're hoping to learn who all he might've talked to when he came back to town." Eleanor hesitated, then added, "He came to our emporium on Friday afternoon."

"My dear, why?"

"He said he'd found religion and wanted to apologize."

"Humph. Making amends is a classic in those twelve-step programs, but how does one make amends for some of the things he pulled?"

I spoke up. "Eleanor didn't believe he'd changed, but I saw some signs that he might have."

"Oh?" Minnie asked, brows arched.

I explained that Cornell had been working at the hot dog stand and had given freebies to both my pets and a child. "And he didn't fight back when Dexter Hamlin hit him."

Minnie shuddered. "Hamlin. Now, there's a nasty piece of work."

I gave a small nod to Eleanor, our signal for her to go to the next question.

"Minnie, do you know of anyone else Cornell might've approached?"

"Can't say that I do, although he could've gone back to the apartment complex. If he was truly bent on apologizing, a few people from our days are still living there."

She rattled off names already on Eleanor's list, one of them the married couple, then narrowed her eyes. "You say you want know who Cornell talked to before he died?"

"Talked with or might've seen," I said, "if he did go to the apartments."

"You're not thinking one of them killed the man!"

Eleanor and I both reeled back, hands on our chests. We didn't choreograph that move, but it sure looked like we did.

Eleanor found her voice first. "Heavens, no, Minnie, and we wouldn't dream of accusing a soul. We're merely attempting to track his movements before he died."

"Was murdered, you mean."

Eleanor caught my eye and shrugged. That was the signal for me to lay it out.

"The main reason we're involved is because the new detective in town thinks Eleanor or Maise or Aster killed him. Possibly all of us."

Minnie snorted. "Ridiculous."

"To us, yes. To her, not so much."

"Hmm, well, if she comes around again, I'll give her an earful."

"So she did interview you?" I asked.

"Yesterday about my lunchtime. I eat early on Tuesdays so I can go to Walmart on the Pines Breeze bus. She near made me miss my ride, but I'll tell you what I told her. I can't think of a single, solitary soul who'd give that man two seconds of time. If I do, though, I'll let you know. Not the detective."

"Thank you," Eleanor said, covering Minnie's wrinkled hand with her own near-smooth one.

"Minnie," I said, "Did Detective Vogelman ask to search your apartment?"

"No, but then I told her I take all my meals in the dining room. I only keep pretzels and ice cream, protein drinks, and cola in my fridge." She paused. "Of course, I would've refused had she asked. I know my rights."

"I'm glad to hear it. May I ask two more questions?"

"Of course, Nixy. What are they?"

I wavered only a second before jumping in. "First, did anyone die at Ozark Arms while you lived there?"

"Oh, my, no! Why do you ask?"

"I'm following up on a rumor."

"Because sometimes there's a bit of truth in them?"

"Yes, ma'am."

"There was one young man who suddenly moved. Dennis Moreno. Remember him, Eleanor?"

"I do now that I hear his name again."

"He worked at the library, and he used to check books out for me—with my card, of course." She paused. "One day, Dennis was supposed to return some of my library books, but he never came by. Then a few days later, I saw someone carrying boxes out of his apartment." She shook her head. "When I returned my books and asked after him, Debbie Nicole said he'd moved home."

"Do you know where home was?"

"I want to say El Dorado, but it could've been Camden. Is that helpful?"

"Every scrap of information is more than we had before, Minnie. Now for the harder question."

"Spit it out."

"Do you know of anyone who'd want to kill Cornell?"

"Back when he managed the apartments, absolutely. As angry as he made the residents, I think one of them would've happily bumped him off long before he was fired." She winked. "Even me. To wait until now to do the deed? No. I have a saying, young lady. I can wish you well, and wish you well away."

I grinned. "I'm going to adopt that motto, Minnie. Thank you, and I hope I didn't offend you."

"Not at all. Now, Eleanor, tell me. Who do you see from the old place?"

I sat and smiled as Minnie and Eleanor chatted awhile, but Minnie soon announced she needed to get her old bones horizontal.

Back in my white Camry, I turned to Eleanor. "I'm thinking Minnie isn't the person Vogelman got a warrant to search."

"I do believe you're correct," Eleanor said with a smile.

"I hope just one of them told the detective something to get her permanently off our backs."

Chapter Thirteen

WE DISCUSSED GOING BY THE APARTMENT COMPLEX to see the four people Minnie had named, but in the early afternoon, Eleanor said three of them would be at work. Jim Diller, who had been given the manager's job when Cornell left, was technically working on-site, and she hesitated to bother him.

We swung by the complex anyway, and I cringed as we parked in a visitor's spot, then got out to have a look around. Built in the general style of the 1970s, Ozark Arms looked more like the Up-in-Arms. Okay, it wasn't slumlord bad, but I'd swear it had been outmoded when it was brand spanking new. Six two-story buildings roughly arranged in a wide U shape, the U to the back, made up the complex.

"How many apartments did you say there were?" I asked Eleanor.

"In all six buildings, there are thirty-six. Three downstairs and three up. Those to left of the main doors are the two bedrooms and all the others are one. I lived upstairs in the last building on the right." She sighed. "Did it look this sad when I was here, I wonder?"

She'd said the last almost to herself, but she was right. The whole place needed paint and landscaping, although I noted as we walked closer that the curbing, the few steps leading to the main sidewalk, and the main and branching sidewalks themselves were in good repair. The only saving grace to the grounds was the smattering of oak and pine trees providing shade. I just couldn't wrap my head around our own dear Elegant Eleanor having lived here.

"I'm so very grateful I live at the farmhouse now," she breathed at my side when we stood halfway up the main sidewalk, "but this place was affordable after my husband died."

I'd never heard Eleanor speak much of her past, other than how she and the others came to live with Sherry. I knew she had been a mechanical engineer, and in a male-dominated field, and that was something in and of itself. I opened my mouth to comment, but she seemed lost in her own thoughts. I let her stay there.

Three children spilled out of the left-hand building in front of us. One tyke carried a plastic dump truck almost as big as he was, and a boy and girl who might have been a year older carried soccer balls. Their chattering broke our quiet bubble. I turned to Eleanor.

"Are you sure you don't want to track down Mr. Diller while we're here?"

"We don't want anyone on our list to feel ambushed, now do we?"

"You're right. That's not the way to make friends and influence people to spill what they know."

But just then, a handsome black man stepped onto the stoop twirling a pipe wrench that looked two feet long. He caught sight of us, looked away, and then looked back.

"Eleanor Wainwright?" he called, breaking into a broad grin.

"Jim Diller, hello," Eleanor said, and moved toward him.

Diller was in his mid-fifties, dressed in jeans and a cotton shirt, both threadbare and paint splattered. The wrench in his large hands reminded me of the tools a guy I'd dated had shown me. Parker the Plumber and I had sprung a leak in the romance department, but I recalled how much heavy-duty wrenches weighed. If Cornell had been killed by a smack on the head, I'd suspect the wrench was the weapon.

"Eleanor! How are you?" he greeted.

"I'm well, Jim. How about you? Are you still liking this job?"

"I surely am. Between my regular maintenance duties and fixing problems for the residents, I stay busy." He paused and turned to me. "Now, let me guess. You must be Sherry Mae's niece."

"Yes, sir," I said, and shook his hand.

"I heard y'all had opened a shop all together, but I haven't been in yet."

"Quite all right, Jim," Eleanor said. "I know you're off to repair something, but could we have a moment?"

"This must be about Cornell Lewis, right? That lady detective talked to me on yesterday afternoon. I couldn't help her 'cept to say that Barbara Linden told me she saw him at that festival last weekend." He shook his head. "I was changing the filter on her HVAC unit when she got home, and she was pretty shaken."

"He came to the shop to apologize to Eleanor and told us he was making amends."

"So you thought he mighta come to look up folks here."

It was a statement, not a question, and I nodded. "We're hoping to track his movements, especially after Sunday morning."

His eyes narrowed. "Why?"

Eleanor grimaced. "Because that detective believes my friends and I might have contributed to Cornell's death."

"That's a crock, but I'll tell you what I told the police

lady. Cornell didn't come around here, or I'd have gotten calls to run him off." He shook the monster wrench. "And I would've, too. Fact is, I thought about driving downtown to confront him, but it wasn't worth the aggravation."

He glanced at his watch, and I knew our time with him was nearly up. Did I dare to ask if he let Vogelman search his place? Nah, I had more important information to get.

"Mr. Diller, may I ask you two more questions?"

"If you can make it quick."

"Do you know of a resident Cornell bullied who might've died?"

He frowned in thought, shook his head. "Nothing that drastic, although we had some injuries. Connie Baker's fall comes to mind. Oh, and we had a guy who up and moved out before his lease was up. He worked at the library, as I recall."

"I'll follow up on that with Debbie Nicole, then. Do you know of anyone who would kill Cornell? May be holding a grudge?"

"A grudge, no. Plenty of us thought about him dropping dead. If any of us had killed him, we'd have banded together to hide the body. He just wasn't worth the risk of going to prison."

"Jim," Eleanor said, jumping in, "we've kept you long enough, but thank you for talking with us. Will you call if you hear anything that can help?"

"You know I will, and don't be a stranger at church, you hear?"

We turned back toward the car, and I gave Eleanor a thumbs-up.

"That's two down and eight to go."

"No, only five at best. Remember, we are not at all positive we have the correct phone numbers for everyone."

"Would anyone else be at home right now? Seems a shame to stop when we're on a roll."

She shook her head. "We need to set up lunch with Randy Darby and his wife, and with Lorraine Chandler. Besides, I do believe Maise will have our hides if you don't get back to help her with the bookkeeping. You *are* the emporium manager."

I snorted. "Y'all can run the shop blindfolded and you know it."

"Perhaps, but you make it more fun. You're the one who finds the bodies."

I DIDN'T HAVE A MATH BRAIN, SO I'D TAKEN JUST enough college math courses to earn my degrees, and they had not included accounting. And bookkeeping? That was a whole 'nother skill set.

Working with Maise made that part of my job easier. She'd proven to be a good teacher, giving clear explanations and being patient. Sooner or later I'd have to take over this task on my own, but I voted for later. Figuring sales taxes gave me a headache.

At four o'clock, Eleanor interrupted us long enough to tell me she'd set up a lunch meeting with Lorraine Chandler and Randy and Billie Jo Darby for the next day at eleven forty-five. We'd take them to the Lilies Café. Barbara Linden, the woman who'd spotted Cornell during the festival, already had a lunch date, but we could see her at her office just across the street at one.

By five o'clock, Maise and I had finished the accounting for the four days before the folk art festival and the two days of the festival. We also had a list of items to reorder from the various artists. The craftspeople might send what we ordered, and they might send new art. We took what we got.

When Maise announced the festival days' totals to the Silver Six, all but Eleanor actually whooped with joy.

"I knew we'd been busy on Saturday, but I never dreamed we sold that much," Aunt Sherry gushed.

I grinned, tickled they were so happy. "I don't know why not. Your shelves were almost bare at the end of the day."

Aster nodded. "I remember we restocked what we could,

but we had slim pickings on Sunday. We're going to be working overtime to make more products."

I didn't dampen their enthusiasm by reminding them the expenses came out of those profits. It was enough to see them excited.

Dab hitched up his slacks, only to have them sink to his hips again. "You know what we should do? We should celebrate. How about going out to eat?"

Maise looked dismayed. "But I have all that leftover roast. We were going to have hot and cold sandwiches with my macaroni salad."

"Which sounds delicious, Maise," Dab said quickly, "but you deserve a night off, too. What do you say?"

Into the short silence, Eleanor ventured, "I do believe I could eat pizza."

"I heard good things at the hair salon about that new Papa Razzi's place. The one near the Walmart out toward Magnolia." Sherry tilted her head at me. "Didn't you and Eric eat there?"

"Twice. Goofy name, but they serve some of the best pies I've ever had."

"I'm in if it's good old-fashioned American pizza. None of them fancy ingredients for me," Fred barked.

"What do you say, Maise?" Aster asked her sister. "Can you handle a cook-and-KP-free night?"

Maise turned a stern gaze on me. "Does this place make Hawaiian pizza?"

"Ma'am, yes, ma'am," I said smartly.

"With ham or Canadian bacon?"

"Ham, pineapple, and whatever else you want."

She grinned. "Let's go!"

I FELT SECURE THAT AMBER AND T.C. WOULDN'T chew, rip, or otherwise damage anything in the apartment for the short time I'd be gone, so I fed them, left on some lights and Animal Planet, and loaded Sherry, Maise, and Eleanor into my Camry. Dab drove Fred and Eleanor in his Caddy. There was more room in the trunk for Fred's walker (sans the tool belt), and more room for Eleanor to stretch her long legs.

We arrived at Papa Razzi's before the big dinner rush, which meant Fred didn't have to wait too long for his sausage, pepperoni, and black olive pie, and Maise soon drooled over her ham, pineapple, cheese, and yellow peppers.

I glimpsed a side of the Silver Six I'd not only never seen, but never imagined. Not only did they chow down on the three pizzas we'd ordered, they bopped to the oldies music, tunes from the 1950s to the 1970s. Okay, the women got into the music more because they chair-danced and sang along. The menfolk snapped their fingers, tapped their toes, and kept eating. After Aster belted out Steppenwolf's "Born to Be Wild," all the ladies joined in on every song they knew from "Rock around the Clock" to "The Little Old Lady from Pasadena." They even got me to sing "We Are Family," though they switched up the lyrics to "I got brothers, sisters with me."

I didn't know if I'd ever get to see Sherry and the gang cut loose like that again, but I'd never hear music from those eras without having an extra wide smile on my face.

We were walking to our cars when my cell played the whistling of Eric's ringtone. I was almost in too good a mood to answer, but I did anyway.

"Nixy, where are you?" he demanded. "Fred's car is in the parking lot, and so is Sherry's Corolla, but they aren't at home and neither are you."

The urgency in his voice made my stomach clench. I beeped open the car locks but stepped away to talk.

"What's wrong? Did something happen at the farmhouse? The store? Oh, please tell me T.C. and Amber are okay."

"It's nothing like that, but where are you?"

"We're just leaving Papa Razzi's Pizza."

"You weren't supposed to leave town," he snapped.

"Eric, we're twenty minutes away, not on a plane to R— Oh, wait. What's happened?"

I listened as he huffed a breath. "Detective Vogelman wants to see the Silver Six. Right now. Come to the station."

"Not until you tell me why."

"We found Dexter Hamlin. Dead."

"Don't tell me he had a peanut allergy, too."

"No. A bullet allergy. Get over here as soon as you can."

Chapter Fourteen

AUNT SHERRY MIGHT HAVE HAD MACULAR DEGENeration, but she read my flare of anger like a book. So did the rest of the gang, so I broke Eric's news as gently as I could. Fred and Dab didn't curse around women, and the ladies reciprocated, but I was certain we all bit back strings of phrases more colorful than "Tarnation," "Consarn," and the ever-popular "Dadgummit."

Fortunately, it was only eight o'clock, not too late to phone Dinah Souse. She promised to meet us at the station and warned us to keep mum if we arrived before she did.

I don't know how things went in Dab's car, but a grim atmosphere descended in mine. I'd worked myself into a fine fury by the time I wheeled into the station's small parking lot and spotted Eric waiting out front.

He stood away from the station door under the night security lights, and seeing him didn't improve my disposition. It didn't even make my pulse leap. I slammed the car door and stomped toward him ahead of the Six.

"Thank you for coming," he said formally as I stepped into circle of light.

"Like we had a choice?" I snarled.

Aunt Sherry had caught up with me and grasped my arm. "Now, Nixy. The detectives are only doing their jobs."

"Not very dang well if they're pulling us in for questioning," I shot back. I gave Eric my version of the evil eye and had the satisfaction of seeing him gulp. "On Monday night when we were together, did you know Vogelman had search warrants for the farmhouse and emporium?"

He cleared his throat. "I knew she was applying for them, but you know good and well I couldn't tell you. I'm a law officer. You don't warn the subjects of a search that you're coming."

I knew he was right, but I was too angry to care. "You're a detective. You should be working with your new sidekick to find the truth. Instead she's taking the easy road and harassing my family."

Eric pursed his lips and turned toward the station door, where Aster and Maise stood with Sherry. Fanned out just behind them were Dab, Eleanor, and Fred, sans his walker and steadying himself on Dab's arm. And behind them stood Charlene Vogelman.

"I am doing my best to find the truth," she said evenly. "As for your charge of harassment, file a complaint."

"Believe me, I will," I growled.

She ignored me and turned to Aster. "Ladies and gentlemen, will you please come with me?"

"All of us?" I asked.

"Everyone except you."

"Why do I get a pass?"

"You don't, but there isn't enough room to separate all of you. I'll see you in forty-five minutes."

"I can't sit long in a hard chair, you know," Fred grumped. "And I need my walker."

Dab nodded and returned to his car while I ground my teeth to keep from saying something I'd regret. Not tonight. Not tomorrow. But eventually.

"When Fred is ready," Aster drawled with perfect calm and courtesy, "we'll be happy to join you just as soon as our lawyer arrives."

"Did you call Dinah Souse?" Eric put in.

I could tell by his tone of voice he was attempting to smooth the waters, but I wasn't having it.

"Bet your b—"

"Nixy!" Sherry scolded.

"—badge we did."

Did the corners of his lips twitch? He'd better not be amused.

"Good to hear, but there's no point in standing outside while you wait for her."

Headlights hit our little group, and I breathed a relieved sigh as a compact car slid into the parking space next to Dab's Caddy. As he closed the trunk of his car, Dinah emerged from hers with her briefcase, perfectly coifed and professionally dressed. How did she and Eleanor always manage to look immaculate?

"Detectives Shoar and Vogelman," Dinah said, extending her hand to each of them in turn. "Care to tell me what this is all about?"

"Ms. Souse," Vogelman said, "I'll give you a few minutes to consult with your clients before we question them."

"Thank you," Dinah said, as if the detective was doing her a favor instead of obeying the law.

Vogelman held the door as everyone traipsed in, first through the reception area, then disappearing through the door to the inner sanctum.

Everyone but me, because Eric blocked the front door.

"You can't go in now. You know that."

"What is that horse hockey about separating them?"

"It's procedure, and don't worry. I'll take care of your family."

"Is she dragging us in here just because Dex Hamlin is dead?"

Regret etched his features. "Nixy, go check on T.C. and Amber. This door locks at nine, so just be back before then."

I WALKED BACK TO MY PLACE INSTEAD OF DRIVING to blow off some steam and to kill a little time. My darling critters greeted me with the kind of enthusiasm pets are famous for giving their errant owners. Amber pranced around me while T.C. wove in and out of my legs. I swore my blood pressure dropped just seeing them. I patted and praised them for being good and got licks and purrs in return. If I'd had time, I would've curled up on the couch for some serious snuggle therapy, but I was on a mission.

"Want to walk, girls?"

As Amber dashed for her leash, I dropped my purse on the counter and extracted my license and a little cash to tuck in my pocket. Next, I got T.C. into her harness and Amber on her leash, then clipped my set of keys to the leash handle with a D-ring. Good thing I was wearing cargo pants. I grabbed a handful of cat and dog treats and dropped them in one leg pocket, then added a handful of peppermints for my sour stomach in the other.

Less than ten minutes later, my buddies had done their business, and I'd dropped the bagged remains in the small Dumpster behind the police station. Yes, it was a childish bit of "Take that, Vogelman" defiance, and not as calming as Aster's lavender water, but I smiled as I walked back around the building.

That made me wonder if Aster had lavender water spray in her purse. As far as I knew, she didn't leave home without it, but she hadn't spritzed it on the way to the station, and we could've used it. That alone spoke to how shocked we'd been.

Hopefully, she'd made liberal use of it before Vogelman began the rounds of questioning. Even Fred might not have objected to being doused.

Staring at the door to the station's inner sanctum, I willed all six members of my family to walk through it. Or even for Dinah to come give me an update. Nothing happened. Mind control was obviously not in my skill set.

I pictured the area behind the door as I'd last seen it. The décor wasn't special in the short hallway or in the open space beyond it. Wall plaques and cheaply framed group photos of Lilyvale's finest hung in the hall. In the main room, seven desks and four times as many mismatched filing cabinets lined the perimeter. There were rolling desk chairs for the officers and stationary chairs for visitors. Eric better have corralled the nicest chairs for the Six. The restrooms were in the back near a battered counter accessorized with a coffeemaker and a single sink. There was a private office for the chief of police, another office for special use, and doors to two interview rooms.

Eric had allowed me to observe an interview in June. Was he now standing in the tiny space where I'd watched him question a suspect back then? I shuddered. The Six could hold their own with Vogelman, especially with Dinah by their sides, but just picturing the scene made me reach in my pocket for a peppermint.

I tried to settle in the torture-chamber chair with T.C. in my lap and Amber stretched across my shoes. Petting the cat soothed me some but didn't distract me enough. I played two games on my phone but couldn't focus. I kept checking the time. Eight forty-five was in the rearview mirror. Nine o'clock came and went. The six had been in there for over an hour. How long could it possibly take Vogelman to understand that none of them had a thing to do with either death?

At nine twenty, footsteps approached. I held my breath as the door opened and let it whoosh out when Aster, Maise, Dab, Eleanor, and Fred tromped in.

I rushed to hug each of them, words spilling out as I did. "Are y'all okay? What happened? Has she been questioning you all this time?"

"We're fine, just tired," Aster said on a sigh.

"I ain't fine," Fred humphed, and rubbed a hand over his girth. "Best pizza I've ever ate is soured in my stomach."

I handed him a peppermint as Eleanor explained. "We were waiting for each other, but the detective called Sherry last. She insisted we go on home."

"We all fit in my Caddy," Dab said.

"No problem. I'll bring Sherry back, if she's willing to wait until I have my turn with Vogelman."

"That woman is a danged lunatic," Fred charged. "Might as well be buildin' her case on air."

"As for what happened, we'll tell you later. Right now, we need to rest and regroup," Maise said.

"And get me some antacids."

ALONE AGAIN, I BIT THE END OF MY FINGERNAIL AND paced. I'd about worn a rut in the linoleum when Sherry shuffled into the reception room. Followed by Vogelman.

I heard a growl. Was that Amber or me?

"Sherry!" I threw my arms around her while Amber happily panted *unh-unh* noises and T.C. repeatedly meowed.

Over Aster's shoulder, I caught the detective scowling at my pets.

"Only service animals are allowed in the station," she said.

I bared my teeth. "These are emotional support animals. Can't you see how they're comforting Sherry?"

"Looks like they're more likely to trip her," she said. "They'll have to stay out here while you and I have a talk."

I turned to my aunt. "Sherry, can you wait a few more minutes for me?"

"Did everyone else go home as I asked?"

"Yes, and I'll take you back. Here, have a seat, and take my phone to call the house."

"I have Eleanor's phone," Sherry said, waving mine away.

"Great. Tell the gang we'll be on our way in fifteen minutes."

"I'd make that thirty," Vogelman said.

I turned to face her, slowly and deliberately. "Make it ten, Detective."

As I moved to follow her, I saw Amber cock her head at Sherry, then put a paw on her knee.

"Yes, Amber," Sherry said, giving the dog a scratch under her chin. "Thank you for your sympathy."

I managed not to gape, but that was the first time I'd seen Sherry pay much attention to Amber. Bernice Gilroy had told me that Sherry's dog had died shortly after her husband had, and she probably lacked the heart to get another pet. She'd never shunned the critters, but she'd never played with them the way Fred and Dab had from the start.

Knowing my furry friends would be good company, I strode into the heart of the station.

Dinah waited at the table in the interrogation room and gave me an encouraging smile. I took my place beside her and gave Vogelman my stinkiest stink-eye. She gave me the cop stare back, but it didn't faze me.

"Aren't I getting the chance to consult privately with Ms. Souse?"

"Do you need to?"

My gaze cut to Dinah's. "If she asks a question I don't think it's in your best interests to answer, I'll nudge you."

"Okay, your ten minutes starts now, Detective. Get to it."

"You've lived in Lilyvale since May?"

"I have."

"And did you know that Fred Fishner owns a pistol?"

"I understand he owns an antique gun, but I've never seen it."

"Where does he keep the pistol?"

"I don't know."

"Would you have reason to believe he keeps it handy?"

I snorted. "If Fred wanted to keep it handy, he'd pack it in the tool belt he straps to his walker."

Her eyes narrowed. "He didn't have anything attached to the walker tonight."

"That's because he takes his tool belt off when it will be in the way or create too much noise. We went out to eat, so he dispensed with it tonight."

"What does he keep in the tool belt?"

"Besides tools? A small paintbrush and a sample-size jar of paint for touch-ups. A little bottle of lubricant, white lithium spray, and a rag to un-squeak hinges. Work gloves." I shrugged. "What he carries varies with the jobs he's doing."

"Did you know Cornell Lewis and Dexter Hamlin?"

"In passing, yes."

"Did you kill either of them?"

"I briefly fantasized about offing Dex Hamlin, but I felt sorry for Cornell. And before you ask why, you already know. He said he'd changed and I believed him."

"When did you last see Mr. Hamlin?"

"Sunday morning when Officer Bryant marched him away in handcuffs. I saw his truck—or rather Eric told me it was his truck—on Sunday evening. He blew through a stop sign when we were walking T.C. and Amber."

She looked down at the open file before her, and I glanced at the time display on my phone. Seven minutes to go.

"Ms. Nix, did you tell us everything you knew about finding Mr. Lewis's body?"

I opened my mouth to say I had, but the cookies in the car popped to mind. Specifically, the number of cookies I thought I'd seen.

"I did, but this seems a good time to ask you something."

"Nixy," Dinah warned with one word.

I turned to her. "Don't worry. I'll behave as long as the detective doesn't go all *Dragnet* on me again."

A beat passed, and then Dinah cracked a grin. Vogelman didn't.

She slapped a hand on her papers. "Excuse me? What does that mean?"

"You were stiff and officious, but that's beside the point."

"Well, then, enlighten me. What is your point?" Her tone carried sarcasm, but her gaze was sharp and expectant.

"How many cookies were on the plate in the car? I saw whole ones and some pieces, but I didn't carefully count them."

Vogelman hesitated, then shrugged. "There were six unbroken ones and two in pieces. Why is that important?"

"Let me refresh your memory. On Saturday Cornell had a plate of snickerdoodles. Aster's label was on the cover. There were four whole cookies then. He said he'd need to ration them to make them last the day."

"I have that in my notes," Vogelman admitted.

"So he either ate all of Aster and Maise's cookies and bought another plate at the bake sale—"

"Stop right there," the detective interrupted. "I checked with the sale organizers. Mrs. Parsons and Mrs. Holcomb made the only plate of snickerdoodles donated."

"Then a person unknown gave Cornell more. Maybe it was innocent. Maybe the other cookies were unintentionally tainted. Or maybe introducing peanuts to the cookies was intentional. The result is that Cornell ate them and had an allergic reaction."

"Mrs. Parsons or Mrs. Holcomb could easily have given Mr. Lewis more cookies. They admitted the recipe makes four dozen, yet they donated only one dozen."

"I'll bet they kept two of those dozen, one to freeze and one to eat, and the last twelve went to Mrs. Gilroy, their next-door neighbor. They feed her all the time, and she has a fierce sweet tooth. In addition, if all the peanutty cookies came from the same batch, then Cornell would've reacted to the one he'd already eaten on Saturday."

She frowned and glanced down at her notes, and then back at me. "Ms. Nix, do you own a handgun?"

I blinked at the radical change in topic. "I do not."

"Do you know how to fire a handgun?"

"I dated a guy who took me to a firing range once. That was four or five years ago." I shook my head. "Poor guy. He shot himself in the foot, and that was the last I saw of Glock Gary."

Dinah made a choking noise. I didn't dare look at her. I checked the time on my phone.

"You have three minutes left, Detective, so let me summarize. I didn't kill Mr. Lewis or Mr. Hamlin. No one in my family killed either man."

"Then why did we find him on your aunt's land?"

I sat back in my chair, reeling from that bit of news. "You found him at the farmhouse?"

"On another piece of property."

"Another piece? As in undeveloped land? One with a forest of pine trees?"

"Yes. Out of all the places in the country, Mr. Hamlin was found on Ms. Cutler's land. Do you know where it is?"

I frowned. "Aunt Sherry owns eight parcels or whatever they're called. I don't know where they all are, but I know they're fenced, and the access roads are gated and padlocked."

"Have you seen that for yourself?"

"I drove by them in April when Aunt Sherry showed me around Lilyvale and the surrounding areas." I started to add that Sherry had told me about the logging company harvesting trees because I'd been concerned about her finances. But Vogelman didn't need to know that, and I was out of patience.

"Listen, I know you want to solve these murders. I know there are signs that point to Maise and Aster. From your questions, I'm guessing you have suspicions about Sherry, Fred, and maybe all of my family."

She didn't bat an eye, and I pressed on.

"Whatever evidence you think you have, consider this. It would be stupid to give a man cookies you know will kill him and leave a plate cover with your name on it. To kill a second guy and leave his body on your own property? That's not stupid, Detective. That's completely brain-dead."

"I can appreciate you defending your aunt and her housemates, but I will do my job whether you like it or not."

"We're done, then. Good-bye, Detective."

I hadn't seen Eric on the way into my interview, and I didn't see him on the way out. He might've been in the observation room or he might've gone home. I didn't care. My priority was getting Aunt Sherry home.

T.C. was sprawled across Sherry's lap when Dinah walked out with me. I smiled at the sight, collected my critters' leashes, and followed Dinah and Sherry outside.

As we crossed the parking lot to our cars, I was about to ask Dinah for the highlights of the other interviews. She must've read my mind, though, because she held up a hand.

"I know you want a briefing, but Sherry Mae is tired, and so am I. I'll come by the emporium tomorrow to discuss the situation in detail."

"Okay, Dinah. Thank you for coming so quickly and for staying until the bitter end. You're a lifesaver."

She flashed a smile. "Let's hope not literally."

While she got in her car, I beeped the Camry unlocked and opened the passenger door for Sherry. The animals jumped into the backseat.

When I started the car a few seconds later, Sherry said, "Step on it, Nixy. The gang is on pins and needles waiting for us, and, um, we have something to confess, child."

I did a double take. "You're keeping me in suspense."

"It's best if you hear from all of us at once."

On that ominous note, I took off.

Chapter Fifteen

ASTER, MAISE, DAB, ELEANOR, AND FRED MUST'VE heard my tires on the gravel driveway because they spilled onto the wide, wraparound farmhouse porch before I had the car in park. Maise shot down the porch steps to hug Sherry as soon as she planted her feet on the ground.

The family must've been more worried than I'd imagined because as they ushered us into the parlor, I noticed cordial glasses on the coffee table and a half-empty bottle of Aster's honeysuckle wine. The open bag of pretzels reinforced how distressed they'd been. I'd rarely seen the seniors snack at all, and never this late at night.

Dab and Fred took the two wingback chairs at the far end of the long couch, and Amber headed straight for Fred to lie beside his feet. Aster dropped cross-legged to the floor close to the coffee table, while Eleanor and Maise led Sherry to the couch, where all three sank into the comfy cushions. I should know they were comfy. I'd spent a good number of nights sleeping on that couch before I moved into my apartment.

That left the upholstered chair closest to the entry for me, and I sat with my stomach in knots. I rather expected T.C. to come sit with me, but she leaped to the sofa, padded to Sherry's lap, and lay with her tail curled around her paws.

Eleanor poured Sherry a glass of wine. When I declined, she picked up her own glass, but no one spoke. Now that I saw my aunt in bright light, I was concerned about her pallor. I broke the silence.

"Can you talk about what happened in your interviews, or did Vogelman tell you to keep mum?"

"I went first," Dab said, but with a sly grin instead of a scowl. "She said she knew I'd worked as a chemical engineer and asked me how I'd make peanut oil. I told her I wouldn't make it. If I ever wanted such a thing, I'd go buy it at the store. She scribbled notes like there was no tomorrow."

Maise cleared her throat. "I was second. She asked me about peanut oil, too. I told her I use all-vegetable shortening all the way." Now she cracked a smile. "I thought she was going to turn green when I told our mother used lard, but shortening was healthier."

Aster scooted back from the coffee table with a handful of pretzels so she could see us all. "I went in third. The detective kept harping on the plate of snickerdoodles, and how they ended up in Cornell's car. Well! I finally told her I might still be a hippie at heart, but not a psychic. You went next, Eleanor. What did she yammer at you about?"

"The time I lived in Ozark Arms, and what Cornell had done to me. He was rude, insulting, incompetent, and thoroughly unpleasant every time I saw him, but I learned to avoid him. And after the first time he supposedly fixed my oven, I never called on him again."

"That's right," Fred chimed in. "She called on me, and when I couldn't help her, I referred her to specialists. They never could fix that oven and stovetop, though. Just like I couldn't stop that rattle in your old car, Maise. I swear that clunker laughed at me."

"It wasn't that bad, Fred."

To keep us on track, I said, "Fred, Vogelman asked me about your pistol. Did she grill you about it, too?"

"The stupid idjit woman has lost her mind if that's all she's got on me. Gun ain't loaded, and I ain't shot it in years. She sent Eric over to get it so she could see if it had been fired."

"What do you mean by 'sent him over'? You didn't give him a key to the house, did you?"

"He followed us home, but there'll be nothin' to find. It's a family piece, just for show, even if I do bluster about it from time to time."

I turned to Sherry. "How about you?"

"She hassled me about the pieces of forested land I own and what a great place it was to hide Dex's body. As if."

I nodded. "She asked me about your land, too. And the cookies. And about Fred's Colt .45."

"And there's more." Sherry paused and took a gulp of wine. "Remember that confession we have to make to you? Brace yourself, child."

"For heaven's sake, what could be so bad?" I demanded, anxiety eating at my gut.

"My arrest record."

My jaw went slack, but after a silent moment, the others chuckled and chortled. Fred laughed so hard, he slapped his knee and momentarily startled the dog.

"What on earth is so funny about having an arrest record?"

Eleanor waved a hand. "Nixy, I do believe we've all been arrested at least once."

"At—at least?" I stammered.

"At one time or t'other we've been in the pokey for disturbin' the peace, resistin' arrest—"

"Unlawful assembly," Dab put in.

Aster giggled. "Nixy, you do realize how old we are, don't you?"

I blinked.

Maise shook her head as if I were the class dunce. "If you did the math, you'd get it, but I'll save you the trouble. We belonged to the generation of activism. Sit-ins."

"Protest marches," Sherry added.

"And pro-marches, too," Eleanor said. "We each marched for civil rights, although not together. We hadn't met back then."

"I protested the Vietnam War, but my dear sister never held it against me even though she was already in the Navy."

That bit of Maise's and Aster's history I remembered hearing from Sherry, but I was still stunned.

"Apartheid, dolphin-safe fishing, save the whales," Dab said. "We've all taken up causes now and then."

I shook my head. "I'm speechless."

"Too bad Vogelman wasn't," Sherry said tartly. "How she could think a charge of civil disobedience years ago has any bearing on these murders, I don't know."

"She's grasping at straws," Dab said.

Maise turned to me. "Can't Eric talk some sense into her?"

I shrugged. "Y'all saw how he acted tonight. I don't think he'll tell me squat even if I do talk to him."

We chatted another five minutes before Fred stretched and swung his walker around from the side of his chair.

"Don't know 'bout the rest of you, but I'm for bed."

That was my cue to leave with the critters, but I reminded the gang to call me immediately if they needed anything.

As I settled the animals in the backseat, I glanced at Bernice's house. I didn't see any lights on, so I presumed she was in bed. I also presumed she'd have the scoop on the Six being questioned before the sun went up. If she didn't already.

I'd backed out of the driveway and pointed the car toward home when my cell played Eric's ringtone. I glanced at the passenger seat where the phone rested. Answer the call or give him the silent treatment? Who was I kidding? I wasn't the silent-treatment type.

"Are you at the farmhouse?" he asked when I answered the call.

"I am. Are you calling to tell me Inspector Clouseau is on her way over to arrest every last one of the Silver Six?"

"No, and, Nixy, Vogelman is not incompetent."

"Agree to disagree. So, are you still at the station?"

"I'm in the parking lot behind the emporium. I wanted to see you," he said, his dreamy voice deepening.

Okay, I had to admit that got to me. I wanted to see him, too, in spite of my frustration and ire. I sighed.

"All right, I'll be home in about five minutes."

"I'll be waiting."

THE FUR BABIES WENT NUTS WHEN THEY SAW ERIC, but they didn't seem interested in walking. Up in my apartment, they lapped up his attention right after they lapped some water.

"How are the Six holding up?" he asked from his end of the sofa. I sat on the other end. This was not a snuggle-time talk.

"They're tired and ticked, and so am I. Sherry told me Vogelman made a big deal about her arrest for some protest march."

"Did you know about her record?"

"Eric, that's not a record. That's an isolated incident forty to fifty years ago. Besides, every one of the Six has been arrested for supporting some cause or another, but that didn't keep them from clearing the background checks to volunteer at the technical college."

He rubbed the back of his neck. "I know bringing that up may have been a little extreme—"

"A little?" I snorted. "Eric, Vogelman pulled that bit of ancient history out of her hat to intimidate Sherry. It didn't work. And the peanut oil thing? Maise wouldn't be caught dead cooking with olive oil, much less peanut oil."

He shrugged and extended his hand, palm up, across the divide of cushions. "Nixy, I don't want this to come between us."

I hesitated only a second before I put my hand in his. "I don't either, and I understand your position. I really do. I just don't have to like it."

With our fingers loosely linked, he offered a smile. "We've butted heads over my cases before. Like when Sherry was a suspect back in April."

"Yes, but you gave her the benefit of the doubt. You didn't take the easy way out. You kept digging, and you listened to me when I brought you information."

"I had the advantage of knowing Sherry from the time I was a teenager," he said, his voice carefully neutral.

"I remember. She was one of your favorite teachers."

"Right, and I also wasn't under the same kind of pressure Charlene is."

"You mean she's bent on impressing your chief."

"To a point, you're right. I had to placate him while I continued investigating, but not necessarily impress him."

"Making a false arrest isn't going to win her points, is it?"

He opened, then closed his mouth.

I squeezed his warm hand and scooted marginally closer. "Eric, I get that this is her case. I get that she has to do what she thinks best. She's way off base, though, and as long as she's focused on my family, how hard will she look for the real killer?"

"Or killers plural. Lewis was essentially poisoned, but Hamlin was shot."

"Can you tell what caliber of gun was used?"

"No, and the bullet lodged in the body. Whoever did it policed his brass."

"So you have to wait for the autopsy," I groused.

"Yes, but you don't." His lips quirked. "I know you're

snooping with the Six. Charlene told me about the flip chart in Fred's workroom."

"She poked fun about it, right?"

"Yep."

"At least she didn't tell me to butt out of the case."

"I won't either. I'll only say be careful, and if you have anything you think we should know, tell me. Okay?"

I gazed into his bedroom brown eyes. "Okay."

He scooched close enough to put his arm around my shoulders. "Good, now will you please kiss me?"

THURSDAY MORNING, I WAS STILL UNHAPPY WITH the whole situation of Vogelman questioning the Six. In contrast, I was happy to have seen Eric last night and settled some of the tension between us. I smiled through my routine: get dressed, feed myself and the critters, take our walk, and get ready to open the store.

Then I found the list of names Eleanor had prepared, compared them to those on the flip chart, and made a plan.

So had the Silver Six, because as they burst through the back door with the huge tray of cookies they always had on hand for customers, Maise announced, "We have a plan!"

Since they were in better moods than I expected, I laughed. "Tell me."

Maise marched to our customary confab worktable and slapped a legal pad on it. "Fred and Dab need supplies from Big George's hardware store."

"For them holiday metal-art things you want," Fred put in.

"They'll do recon for scuttlebutt there on both Cornell's and Dex's enemies." Maise stabbed her finger on the pad and continued. "Sherry needs her hair trimmed, so she's headed to Helen's salon in fifteen minutes. Aster and I will hold down the fort while you go with Eleanor to talk to more people on her list. Any questions?"

"Just one," I said.

"Speak."

"What on earth did y'all have for breakfast?"

Fred barked a laugh, and Maise swatted my arm. "Move out."

"Aye-aye."

SINCE IT WASN'T YET TEN IN THE MORNING, I LEFT Eleanor making phone calls to locate our quarries while I ran two errands. First, I stopped at Gaskin's Business Center to pick up the photos I'd e-mailed to Kay requesting 5 × 7 prints. After a short chat with her, I left with the pictures in a manila envelope Kay had provided and popped down to Great Buns to see what Judy had heard lately.

She was alone in the bakery but madly boxing cookies at the stainless-steel counter. When she saw me, though, she stopped and rushed to hug me.

"Oh, Nixy, I heard about that new detective questioning the Six. How are they doing?"

"They're fighting mad," I said as Judy pulled away. "Please tell me you've heard some gossip that could be a lead."

She returned to the counter, changed her plastic gloves for a fresh pair, and resumed filling the cookie box. "I heard Dex Hamlin was found dead somewhere out around the Pines Motor Court. The truck was parked on an access road back in the trees."

"Yeah, on a piece of Sherry's land on a road her logging company uses."

"Sherry has a logging company?"

"I said that wrong. The company she hires uses those access roads."

"Ah, those access roads are all over the place. Maybe a logger bumped Dex off."

"Why?"

"No idea, but you and the Six are in full investigation mode, right?"

I gave her a weak smile. "As of today, yes. Please keep your ears open for us, will you?"

"You've got it, but check out that company. And don't get yourself in trouble again, or you'll wear me thin."

SHERRY HAD LEFT FOR HER HAIR APPOINTMENT BY the time I returned, but Dinah Souse was in the store. There were no customers at the moment, and she repeated the briefing she'd given to the seniors.

"Every scrap of evidence is circumstantial, but I fear Vogelman will present it to the county's deputy prosecuting attorney."

"Dinah, I've watched my share of cop shows, but dumb this down for me. Do you think Aster and Maise will be arrested?"

"If the detective has her way, that might happen. If it does, I'll push for the arraignment to be held as quickly as possible. After the ruckus y'all's friends made when Sherry was questioned last spring, I don't think the judge will want to keep them in custody for long."

"Do you really think the circumstantial evidence is compelling enough to sway Judge James?" Eleanor asked.

Dinah sighed. "Given the chance, I'd argue against it, but I can't take action at this point. I know how worrying this is, but strive for calm."

"I'll break out the lavender oil and make more spray."

"Whatever it takes, get on with life as usual. You have nothing to hide, so don't."

I'd get on with life by getting on with the investigation.

ELEANOR AND I DECIDED TO TRACK DOWN MARshall Gibson, the goateed hospital volunteer, before keeping our lunch appointment with the Darbys and Lorraine

Chandler. When she couldn't reach him at home, she called the hospital. I was a bit surprised that whoever she talked with gave out the information, but she was told he was working.

After checking at the main desk, then the ER, we ran him to ground in the compact but relatively comfortable surgery waiting room making new pots of regular and decaf coffee. The hospital only had twenty beds, so I was surprised to see ten people waiting for word on their loved ones.

We had no privacy for the talk we needed to have.

When Marshall turned from the beverage counter with its bar sink, his face lit with pleasure when he recognized Eleanor.

"My dear Mrs. Wainwright," he said as he quick-stepped to her. "How are you? Not here for surgery, I hope."

"No, Marshall, I'm fine, and you know I asked you to call me Eleanor."

"Yes, but that was several years ago." The phone on his desk trilled, and he hurried to answer it. All eyes in the room turned to him, waiting. "O'Malley family," he said when he replaced the receiver.

"Here, here," a young woman said as she rushed to the desk. Four others I took to also be O'Malleys anxiously crowded behind her.

"All is well. Your mother is in recovery, and the doctor will be here in a jiffy to talk to you. There's a private room next door if you'd like to meet him there."

After distracted thank-yous, the family headed out. At least that was five fewer people listening. If Marshall would even talk to us.

He made a tick mark on a printout, laid the pen precisely beside the paper, and straightened. Then he narrowed his gaze on me.

"I know you. You came looking for that scoundrel—" He must've realized he was talking too loudly because he broke off and then motioned us into the hall. Once there, he rounded on me.

"You were looking for Cornell Lewis in the ER," he snapped.

"Yes, but not because he's a friend. Or rather was a friend."

"Then why?"

"I do believe we need to start over. Marshall, let me present Leslee Nix, Sherry Mae Cutler's niece. She goes by Nixy, and we're looking into Cornell's death."

"And now Dex Hamlin's, too."

Marshall shook his head. "Eleanor, Lewis was a scourge. Why do you care that he's dead?"

"Because my dear housemates and I are suspects in his murder," Eleanor said baldly.

"That's preposterous!" he exclaimed. "You still live at Sherry Mae Cutler's farmhouse, don't you?"

"That's right, and Aster Parsons and Maise Holcomb live with us, too."

"Maise was a nurse here in town," he said as he stroked his goatee with a thin index finger that looked like it had been broken. I noticed his hand trembled slightly as well. Was he nervous?

He peered into the waiting room, then sighed as he turned back to us. "I don't know what I can tell you, but I'll help if I can."

"We appreciate that, Mr. Gibson."

"Marshall."

I jumped right in. "On Sunday when I saw you in the ER, you said you hadn't seen Cornell Lewis and he hadn't come in for treatment."

"That's right."

"You also seemed surprised he was in town. You hadn't heard rumors he was here?"

"Actually, Barbara Linden—you remember Barbara, Eleanor?" She nodded, and he continued. "I was watching football and cooking on Saturday, but I saw her when I went out to get my mail during halftime. She told me she'd seen him at the folk art festival."

Huh. So Marshall did know Cornell was in town. "Did Barbara mention if she saw him with anyone in particular? Did you want to confront him?"

"No, she didn't mention anyone," he said, and looked at Eleanor, "but, yes, I did want to have a few choice words with him. I wanted to warn him away from bothering any of us. I even drove downtown, but when I saw how far away I'd have to park, I went home. He wasn't worth that much trouble."

I couldn't decide whether I believed him, but I changed gears. "How long have you volunteered here?"

He hesitated as if I'd thrown him off stride, then answered proudly, "I'll get my five-year volunteer pin next month."

"This is a delicate question, but do you remember Dennis Moreno from the apartment complex?"

His expression closed ever so subtly. "He worked at the library."

"I heard he was bullied, too."

"He was. He was gay, and Cornell was merciless to him."

"*Was* gay?" I echoed. "Is he deceased?"

"Not as far as I know. He moved home. His mother was ill, I think."

"Do you know of anyone who would kill Cornell Lewis?"

"The residents would've loved for him to keel over, but he was fired, and that was good enough for us."

"Okay, thank you for your help," I said as the waiting room phone rang.

Marshall said a quick good-bye and strode off to answer it.

"What now, Eleanor? Can we drop in on anyone else on your list?"

"There will be no dropping in on anyone," she said firmly. "We have thirty minutes before we meet the group for lunch. I do believe I'm in the mood for a strong cup of coffee, so drive to the Dairy Queen. And then, Nixy, you will tell me why you keep asking my friends about Dennis Moreno."

LILYVALE WAS SMALL ENOUGH TO COVER A LOT OF ground in a short time, so we were at the DQ drive-through in minutes. With a black coffee for Eleanor, and a coffee with sugar for me, I explained myself.

"It feels important, Eleanor. I heard a rumor that someone Cornell bullied ended up dead. Judy thought she heard it from Debbie Nicole from the library, but none of you who were there at Ozark Arms seems to remember a death. Doesn't that strike you as odd?"

"Nixy, as I told you before, talk with Debbie Nicole about it. If anyone can answer your questions about Dennis, she's your best bet. Truly, I don't believe most of the residents knew him well."

"He wasn't unfriendly if he saw Minnie regularly and ran books back and forth to her."

"He wasn't unfriendly at all," she said. "He simply kept more to himself than not."

I sighed and wheeled into the parking lot behind the emporium. The CPA that Barbara worked for was across the street, so we'd walk.

"Okay, I'll call the library this afternoon to see if Debbie Nicole will talk to me."

"Good. Let's go meet our lunch dates. I've already told them we're investigating and why. I certainly hope they know more than everyone else we've spoken with."

"Keep the faith, Eleanor," I advised, and tried to keep my own.

Chapter Sixteen

LORNA HAD SAVED US A ROUND TABLE FOR SIX SET back near the stairway that led up to the Inn on the Square. There was an after-café-hours covered staircase built into the back of the building. Guests came and went that way via their individual codes punched into the weatherproof box.

Eleanor and I had just taken chairs facing the door when Randy and Billie Jo Darby entered the restaurant. Both were slender, looked fit, and were in their early sixties by my estimate. They wore sneakers, jeans, and Arkansas Razorbacks polo shirts. Theirs were white shirts with a red logo, but it reminded me that the photos of Lee Durley and Cornell Lewis were in the manila envelope in Fred's workroom.

Eleanor stood and waved to them, and the three exchanged warm greetings before I was introduced.

"Good to meet you," Billie Jo said as she shook my hand. "I've heard a bit about you around town."

Randy smiled and it made his eyes crinkle. "What she's too polite to say is that we heard you've been in on solving a few murders."

"Guilty as charged," I said, "but Eleanor, my aunt, and the rest of the gang helped a lot."

"I hope we can help, too, although I don't know quite how since we've been touring California for a month," Billie Jo warned as she took the chair beside mine.

Randy sat next to her and added, "Great trip. We saw the coastal redwoods, the giant sequoias, Yosemite."

Billie Jo patted his hand. "Randy was an executive with a logging company, but the man loves his trees. We saw other sites, too. The wine country, San Francisco. Randy even took me to Disneyland and the San Diego Zoo and Coronado Island."

"But I drew the line at Tijuana," Randy declared.

"That sounds like a wonderful vacation," I said.

Billie Jo laughed. "Oh, it wasn't a vacation. Not in the strictest sense. Randy and I love to travel, and now that he's retired, we can pick up and go whenever we like."

"I do believe I'd forgotten how often you two are on the go, Billie Jo."

"Well, you've been gone from Ozark Arms for years, Eleanor. No reason you should remember. Did I understand that Lorraine Chandler was joining us?"

"Yes, and she just came in."

Eleanor rose and waved, and this time all the residents and former residents of Ozark Arms greeted one another, and I had a moment to observe Lorraine. Of average height with short brown hair and a maternal figure, she was also in her late fifties or early sixties. She'd dressed in slacks and a lightweight sweater and wore chunky gold earrings.

Eleanor introduced us, and Lorraine sat beside her just as Lorna came to take our orders. Since all of us ordered one kind of salad or another, our beverages and lunches were soon on the table. We visited for a few minutes, during which time I learned that Billie Jo and Lorraine had taught together at the elementary school.

"Why exactly did you want to talk with us?" Billie Jo asked.

I cut my gaze to Eleanor, who blotted her lips before she spoke.

"We're attempting to learn who might have seen Cornell Lewis during the few days he was back in town."

Lorraine's expression sharpened. "You mean you're looking for his killer."

"We aren't accusing anyone," Eleanor said hastily. "But he came to our store, apologized for his past behavior, and said he was making amends where he could."

"We're hoping that if he went around apologizing to other people, one of them might have seen something."

"Or some*one*. Namely the killer, correct?" Randy asked.

"That's the size of it."

"I moved out of the Arms before he was fired. I highly doubt he'd know where I live now, and I certainly didn't see the worm," Lorraine stated flatly.

"So you didn't come to the folk art festival?" I asked.

"I didn't. I was in Little Rock visiting my grandchildren all weekend."

Billie Jo shrugged. "We didn't get home until yesterday, and that's when we heard Rotten to the Core had been murdered."

"So you don't know of anyone who saw him?" Eleanor asked.

Randy shook his head. "Rumor does have it that Dexter Hamlin was found dead somewhere out in the country. Is that true?"

"It is, and we were all questioned about it."

"Hah! Good riddance to bad rubbish."

I blinked. "You knew Hamlin?"

"To my disgust. The man tried to blackmail me, and Cornell Lewis had to have been in on it."

"What?" Eleanor and I said in unison.

"The short version," Billie Jo supplied, "is that Hamlin said Randy had suggestive photos of young girls in our apartment. He demanded to be paid five thousand dollars."

Randy banged the table with his fist. "Those young girls were our granddaughter and her friends. They were taking modeling classes in Dallas. Not that they were wearing anything scandalous, but the only way Hamlin could have known about the photos is if Cornell went through our things and found them."

"Or I suppose Hamlin could have been with Cornell when he was supposedly fixing something or other in our apartment. They used to drink together as I recall, so one or both of them could easily have done the snooping."

My mouth hung open, and I when I glanced at Eleanor, she wore the same stunned expression. "I never heard about this outrage," she exclaimed. "You didn't pay him, of course."

"I told Hamlin to stuff it, but he went to my company. I was called on the carpet and had to explain the situation."

"And I," Lorraine said, "marched into that CEO's office and told them Billie Jo had shown those photos to the other teachers, just like the proud grandparent she is."

"My company backed down, but I was plenty angry enough at the time to have shot both of them like the vermin they were."

"Goodness!" Eleanor breathed.

"It turned out well in the end," Billie Jo said with a wave of her hand. "Randy had the option to take early retirement a year and half later, and I still think the company sweetened his package because they had doubted his integrity."

"I got the package because I earned it, dear," Randy countered.

I smiled at the comment, but my thoughts tumbled over one another. If Hamlin had tried to blackmail the Darbys, how many other people had he done the same to and succeeded? How many had he still been sucking dry? It sure gave a host of people a reason to kill him, but how did I begin to investigate that angle?

I didn't. Unless the Six knew a heck of a lot more about Hamlin than they'd told me, we were up a creek. We didn't have the resources to snoop into bank accounts or whatever might hold leads to the killer. Eric did, and I believed he'd pass the information on to Vogelman, but would she act on it?

LUNCH BROKE UP AT TWELVE FORTY-FIVE. ELEANOR insisted on paying the check, but Randy insisted the rest of us contribute to the tip. Another round of hugs among the friends, and Eleanor and I headed straight across the square to see Barbara Linden. Her office, or rather the office of Brad Brady, CPA, was a stone's throw from the emporium facing Stanton Drive.

Barbara proved to be a tall blonde in her forties with a ready smile, and I was sure we'd been introduced sometime in the summer, though I hadn't had the chance to visit with her.

"Oh, my goodness, Eleanor!" She popped out of her desk chair and embraced my friend. "How are you?"

"I'm fine, and you look the same. How is your mother?"

Barbara chuckled. "That crazy woman moved to California to do commercials, and she's actually had roles in some local ones. Can you believe it?"

"That's wonderful!"

"You know, it really is. She's having the time of her life, and I admit I'm just a little envious that she had the nerve to go for it. Just like you and your friends opening the Handcraft Emporium." She beamed at me. "You're Nixy, and I'm Barbara. We met in passing this summer."

"I remembered you as soon as I saw you," I said.

"I'm just sorry I don't stop in more often. Now then, what can I do for you? Are you looking for a CPA?"

I let Eleanor take the lead again.

"We're visiting with people who live at Ozark Arms, or used to live there," she said.

"You want to know about Cornell Lewis? Oh, no need to be startled. That new female detective talked to me yesterday."

"Was this here or at your apartment?"

"The apartment, and she asked to take a look around. I thought that sounded odd, so I asked what she was looking for. When she told me peanut products, I laughed because I'm allergic to nuts."

"You are?" Eleanor said. "I never knew that."

"No reason you should know."

"Barbara, did you see Cornell Lewis this weekend?"

"I did! I saw him at the festival, over at the hot dog stand. I swear my heart stopped."

"What did you do?" Eleanor asked.

"I turned right around and left, which was all right. I'd already spent what I budgeted for the festival. I just wanted out of there."

"Do you think he saw you?" I asked.

"No, he was helping customers." She visibly shuddered. "I heard he came into the emporium to talk to you, Eleanor. Is that true?"

"Yes, on Friday afternoon. He said he was making amends, but I didn't believe it for a moment."

"The thing is, we're trying to find out who might have seen or talked to him before he was killed." When she suddenly looked affronted, I quickly added, "We're not out to accuse anyone of murder, but to find out if anyone else was seen with Cornell. That person could be the killer."

Barbara shook her head. "Aside from customers, I didn't see anyone else but that Dex Hamlin creature. I understand he's dead, too."

Eleanor nodded. "Barbara, I can't tell you exactly why, but the detective thinks my housemates killed one or both of them."

"Are you joking?" We shook our heads, and Barbara

grasped Eleanor's hand. "Oh, my friend, I am sorry to hear this. I had a feeling one of you was under the gun, just from the questions that woman asked. I told her I was relieved when Lewis was fired but didn't know a soul who'd kill him."

An alarm went off on Barbara's desk, and she hustled to turn it off. "I'm sorry, ladies, but Brad is due back and has a client coming shortly. I need to pull files."

"If you think of or hear of anything else that might help us—"

"I'll call immediately."

"Thank you," Eleanor said just as my phone rang.

A glance showed that someone was calling from the shop's landline.

"Mayday, mayday," I heard before I could say hello.

"Maise? What's wrong?"

"Get over here pronto. Detective Vogelman is arresting Aster and me, and Fred's about to have a coronary."

ELEANOR AND I RUSHED OUT OF THE CPA'S OFFICE in time to see a plain sedan taking up two of the diagonal parking spaces in front of the emporium. A patrol car took another space.

Aster stood by the sedan, one hand braced on its roof, the other on the open back door, chin raised in defiance. Maise exited the shop, escorted by Officer Bryant. Sherry, Fred, and Dab spilled out the door behind them.

Maise moved to stand by her sister, her eyes shooting sparks, looking ready to storm a beach and take no prisoners. Doug Bryant planted himself on the sidewalk as if to take care of crowd control. Vogelman guarded the ladies until they were both in the backseat, and then she shut the door. At least she hadn't put them in handcuffs.

Vogelman ignored Fred, Dab, Sherry, and everyone who'd stopped to stare. Which was dang near everyone who happened to be shopping or owned a business in the square. She got in the sedan with the ladies, backed up, and drove off toward the police station.

Eleanor had already crossed the street when I unfroze and followed. Fred's face was so flushed, I was tempted to call an ambulance. Sherry blotted her eyes with a white handkerchief, the kind Dab always carried. Dab stood stiffly, arms at his sides, fists clenched.

A couple of bystanders looked militant, too. They were the business owners who knew us all well. Some crowded around the five of us where we stood on the sidewalk, and others milled about nearby.

"Ridiculous!" one angry voice shouted.

"Ludicrous!" another agreed.

"This is an outrage," said a voice I recognized as Lilyvale's mayor, Patrick Paulson.

Then there were a few plaintive voices asking what was happening.

"Eleanor, we need to get into the store," I said.

She nodded and took Sherry's elbow while I motioned to Dab and Fred. When we were inside, I stopped at the door and turned to those who'd trailed after us.

"Everyone, thank you for your support. We need some time right now."

I saw heads nod, but Mayor Paulson pushed his way through the throng. He'd been joined by B.G. Huff, councilman and owner of the furniture store down the block where I'd bought just about everything for my apartment.

"I can't interfere with police business, but B.G. and I can sure see to Maise's and Aster's comfort." Mayor Paulson patted my arm. "Try not to worry overmuch."

I didn't know what he meant by seeing to their comfort, or how he expected us not to worry, but I thanked him and ducked inside. Then I locked the door and flipped the OPEN sign to CLOSED.

Jasmine hovered behind the counter, her eyes huge. I hadn't expected to see our work-study clerk here today, then recalled it was yesterday she'd had several major tests.

I looked around for Sherry and found her sitting in a decorative chair. It wasn't really made to sit in, but it held her weight, and I wasn't about to tell her to move. My poor aunt was pale and trembling, clearly in shock.

I took command and turned to Jasmine. "Will you man the landline, please? I have a feeling that phone is about to ring nonstop."

"Yes, ma'am, but what should I say?"

"If people want to bring food, ask them to take their dishes to the house. If they ask what else they can do—"

"Tell them to pray," Eleanor said from behind me.

"Yes, ma'am," Jasmine answered as the shop phone rang.

I caught sight of movement outside and went to peer out the display window to see if the crowd had dispersed. Those who'd been bunched at our door were gone, but others streamed by on the sidewalk. I thought they disappeared into Gaskin's Business Center. Odd, but not a mystery on my priority list.

I refocused on Sherry's white face. "You've called Dinah, I'm sure."

"Immediately. She'll be over as soon as she can."

"Were Maise and Aster arrested because of those stupid cookies?"

Sherry threw up her hands. "We don't know. All Vogelman would say is that the police have new evidence."

"Do you think Dinah will find out what it is?"

"Maybe, but I'm more worried about how long Aster and Maise will have to stay in jail."

I clasped her hands in mine. "You were at the salon this morning when Dinah came by, but she told us that if it came to this, she'd push for a speedy arraignment."

"But it's Thursday. What if they have to spend the whole weekend there?"

"Knowing Aster, she'll meditate after she spritzes them both with lavender water."

"She can't use the spray," Dab said. "The detective wouldn't let her take her purse."

"Woulda confiscated it at the station anyway," Fred put in. "Idjit woman."

I knew he meant Vogelman, not Aster, and patted his arm. "Then we'll smuggle in the spray bottle just as soon as we can see her."

"What do we do until then?" Dab asked.

"We do what Maise would. Fall back and regroup."

JASMINE SAID SHE COULD RUN THE STORE WITHOUT us and reminded me that Kathy was supposed to come in for more training that afternoon when she finished with her classes. Reassured Jasmine had us covered, I flipped the sign back to OPEN but told Jasmine to tactfully stonewall any gossip seekers.

Dab, Fred, Sherry, Eleanor, and I went to the workroom to confab. Amber parked herself between Dab and Fred, and T.C. leaped to the table. She purred like a finely tuned engine, and the sound alone was calming.

With a roll of tape from Fred's stash in hand, I slipped the photos of Cornell with my pets and the accidental shot of Durley from the envelope.

"Who's that young guy? He important?" Fred asked as I taped the prints to the flip chart.

"His name is Lee Durley and I'm not sure he belongs on the board, but I don't want to overlook any detail." Photos secure, I took the marker in hand, labeled them, and turned to the seniors. "First, let's pool our information. Did you gentlemen learn anything new at the hardware store?"

Fred snorted. "The short of it is, t'ain't one solitary person had dealin's with Cornell who liked him."

"And everyone we talked with hated Dex Hamlin," Dab said.

"Did anyone at all stand out as a possible suspect in either murder?"

"Not one more than t'other." Fred looked at Sherry. "You hear gossip at the beauty shop?"

"It isn't much, but Helen takes on some of the newly graduated cosmetology students from the technical school. Well, one of them, Carmel Williams, used to live at the Arms, and she both feared and hated Cornell because he'd leer at her and make suggestive comments. Carmel told Helen she hoped he went over to Bog's Barber Shop for haircuts because she'd be sorely tempted to sink a pair of scissors in his neck."

"Is it too much to hope that she's still with Helen?" I was relieved Sherry was regaining some color in her face.

"She moved to Texarkana before he was fired, but Helen has another hairdresser who still lives at the Arms. Annie Byrd. She came in while I was there, and she told me she'd seen Cornell at the bake sale on her way to work Saturday. Cornell saw her, too, but didn't recognize her. She's lost a lot of weight since he was fired and cleared out of town, but she scooted right on out of there."

I madly wrote names and comments beside each one on the flip chart. When I'd caught up, Eleanor relayed what she and I had learned in our interviews during the past two days. Again I recorded the highlights, but for all the people we'd talked with, we were still woefully short on suspects. As in we pretty much had none.

"What if we go at this another way?" I mused aloud. "What if we look at Dex's murder first?"

"If Dex attempted to blackmail Randy Darby, then he must've blackmailed other people. Successfully or unsuccessfully," Dab said.

"That'd surely be reason enough to kill 'im, but how're we gonna find out who he had under his thumb?"

"Look at the people he pressured to get him into the festival?" I asked.

"I do believe you'd be stirring up a hornet's nest there."

"Eleanor is correct," Dab said. "Dex was connected to a councilwoman, a Chamber of Commerce director, and even a clergyman. Now, some of those connections may be cousins by marriage, twice removed, and possibly on the wrong side of the blanket, but—"

"The what?" I asked.

"That's a euphemism for illegitimate, child," Sherry said.

"My point is who in their right mind would admit to being blackmailed?"

My shoulders sagged. "You're right. We have information about Cornell being a bully, maybe a drunkard, and a general sleaze. We know Hamlin was universally disliked, but tolerated perhaps because he was a blackmailer."

"Nixy," Aunt Sherry said, "what about that young man who moved out in a hurry before his lease was up? Minnie said he worked at the library, correct?"

"Yes, and I need to go talk with Debbie Nicole. I just haven't had the chance."

"Before you go a-harin' off doin' that, what about the fella up there? If he's nobody, he don't need to clutter up the board."

"We should look him up on the Internet. Nixy, where is your tablet?" Sherry asked.

"In the apartment."

"Well, run up and get it, child. While you do that, Eleanor and I will check in on Jasmine."

Dab stood and stretched. "I need a little exercise. I'll take Amber and T.C. for a short stroll."

That's all he had to say for T.C. and Amber to be on their feet, both spare leashes in Amber's mouth. Good thing she didn't slobber.

I popped up to my place, snagged my tablet from the kitchen counter where I'd forgotten to take it off the charger, and fired it up as I returned to the workroom. Fred had an electric can opener on the table that belonged to Ida Bollings. Surrounding the appliance were a handful of Phillips and flat-head screwdrivers in various sizes, and another one in his hand.

I didn't have high expectations of finding Lee Durley. People I'd think would have at least Facebook pages sometimes didn't, but looking couldn't hurt, and might help.

I waited a few minutes, thinking Sherry and Eleanor would come back. When they didn't I forged ahead with the search.

"Whoa!" I said when his name popped up immediately, and with multiple listings no less.

"What?" Fred asked, abandoning his project to come stand beside me and peer at the screen.

"Looks like this guy is a private investigator," I answered, pointing to the first entry under Arkansas Private Investigators, Durley Investigations.

"Well, click on that, missy," Fred commanded.

I did, and up came a page, a photo of piney woods as the background. There was a small photo—a lean guy with a shelf of books behind him—overlaid on the background, and sure enough, it was the Lee Durley I had met. I scrolled down, scanning a short bio as I went.

"Can't see that clear 'nough," Fred complained. "Read it aloud."

"How about I summarize?" I countered. "He's licensed, bonded, and insured. Experienced in law enforcement, has twelve years working as a private investigator, and located in El Dorado. That's odd."

"What's odd?"

I gave Fred the highlights of seeing Durley, from our first meeting, to seeing him toting shopping bags and walking with his sister, and ending with spotting him the morning I found Cornell's body.

"You say he was shoppin' with his sister?"

"He told me it was his sister. I never saw her up close. Maybe it's the sister who lives in the house where I saw him after I found Cornell."

"Maybe he was here investigatin' somethin'. Does he operate in this area?"

"All over southern Arkansas. Nothing about his marital status or family. I guess that wouldn't be appropriate on a professional website."

"What else does it say?"

I clicked on *About Us* and found a slightly longer bio. "Okay, Durley is an Arkansas native, raised in the same city he now works. Huh. He has a female partner, Sally Maynard." She didn't look like the woman I'd seen with him. She'd been thinner. The partner was much younger, and she looked nothing like him. So not related, I presumed.

"Makes sense to have a woman in the firm. She can go places and do things that he can't." Fred humphed and went back to Ida's can opener.

"But he didn't say, 'Go, Razorbacks,'" I murmured.

"What's that?"

I told him of my exchange with Durley, and he only laughed. "You're makin' a mountain from a molehill, missy. For a practical woman, you sure 'nough have a good imagination."

Fred was right. Even if the woman who'd been with Durley was his PI partner and not his sister, I wouldn't recognize the woman from the website photo unless I'd collided with her at the festival.

For grins, I clicked back to the main search page. Lee Durley had a Better Business Bureau listing, reviews on a find-a-local-business site, and a LinkedIn account. Nothing on Facebook, but the man certainly appeared to be on the up-and-up.

The way things were going, maybe it was good to know

of a reputable private investigator. The Six and I were getting nowhere fast.

I went to our murder board and checked off Durley's name, but before I could take down the photo, Sherry burst in.

"Dinah is here and she has news!"

Chapter Seventeen

DAB WALKED INTO THE WORKROOM FROM THE alley just as Eleanor and Dinah followed Sherry through the door from the store. We gathered at the workbench as usual, but the questions flew before we were all settled.

"How are Aster and Maise?"

"What in tarnation made that idjit arrest them?"

"Are they at the police station?"

"When will they be released?"

Dinah held up a hand. "First things first. Maise and Aster have been booked and are in a county holding cell. They aren't happy, but they are doing well under the circumstances."

I rephrased Fred's question. "Aunt Sherry said Vogelman had new evidence? What is it?"

"The police traced the car Cornell died in, and it used to belong to Aster and Maise. Vogelman had the crime scene technicians do some routine fingerprinting, and both ladies' prints were found."

"But they donated that car a few months after they moved into the farmhouse," Sherry said.

"Seven months after," Fred muttered. "I recollect the last time I worked on that confounded vehicle. Hard to believe that old junker's still runnin'."

Dinah cracked a brief smile. "Aster and Maise told Detective Vogelman about the donation to the church, but she wants the paperwork, and that paperwork may have disappeared."

"Not from their tax files, it hasn't," Sherry said stoutly.

"I do believe I know where to find those, too," Eleanor said.

"Unless the detective can compare their personal records with the church's and verify the facts, she's going to remain skeptical about how the car ended up in Camden. The previous reverend retired, and the key church ladies who were there at the time have left as well."

"Are you saying," Dab asked, "that our friends have to stay in jail until someone at the church finds the donation records?"

"Or until the church in Camden can produce proof regarding how they came to have the car. The preacher and his small staff are on a spiritual retreat until Saturday."

"Oh, no!" Sherry cried. "That means a weekend in jail."

"Not necessarily," Dinah said calmly. "Their arraignments will be held tomorrow morning at nine. I'll be arguing that they aren't flight risks, and I'm pushing for them to be released on their own recognizance."

Eleanor nodded. "You believe the judge will support you?"

"It will be Leo James, and he has no reason not to, especially if Vogelman can reach the preacher in Camden on Sunday."

"Back up a minute, Dinah. Where were their fingerprints found? On a door handle? Steering wheel?"

Sherry vigorously shook her head, making her bangs flop

wildly. "No, no. They detailed it themselves before they gave it away."

"Then their prints must've been found in an out-of-the-way place."

"I haven't discovered that detail yet, but I agree. Still, we don't have the resources locally to do a detailed analysis, and you must see it doesn't look good, even if the prints being in the car is circumstantial."

We were quiet a moment, and then I asked, "Can we see them? Aster needs her lavender spray."

Dinah chuckled. "Oh, you haven't heard the best part yet."

"Well, tell us, woman," Fred growled.

"Mayor Paulson has arranged for Mr. Huff to provide two new therapeutic mattress toppers for the ladies, as well as fresh pillows and nice sheets."

My mouth fell open. "Vogelman went for that?"

"She didn't have much choice when the sheriff and the other Hendrix County powers-that-be agreed."

"So, *can* we go see them?" Sherry asked.

"Very likely, but I'm still working on it," she said as she stood. "When I know, you'll know."

IT WAS NEARLY TWO IN THE AFTERNOON WHEN DInah left. Kathy Baker was due in about three, but Jasmine had been stuck greeting customers and gossip seekers for too long. We all had tasks to catch up on, and we needed something constructive to do. We wouldn't stop thinking about Aster and Maise, but busy hands made the time go faster.

Eleanor and Sherry worked the floor with Jasmine while I e-mailed and called artists to see how soon they could deliver more of their pieces. Last I saw, Fred was putting the can opener back together and Dab was sketching designs for holiday-themed metal art.

The store had emptied at three, and I had looked up the

library phone number to call Debbie Nicole when Kathy rushed into the shop panting for breath, her brown eyes huge in her face.

"Y'all have to come see this!" she exclaimed. "Outside. On the courthouse grounds."

"What's wrong?" Eleanor said, moving to comfort the apparently distraught girl.

"It's not wrong," Kathy said, and grasped Eleanor's hand. "It's wonderful and—just come see. Get Dab and Fred, too."

Jasmine flew to the workroom, and when they'd joined us, we trooped out the front door with Kathy in the lead and Fred with his walker *clank-clunk*ing to bring up the rear.

As one, we stopped and stared at the spectacle.

Twenty-plus Lilyvale citizens marched around the courthouse carrying poster board signs fastened to yard stakes and chanting, "Free Maise now! Free Aster now!"

Kay Gaskin joined us on the sidewalk with a huge grin. "Isn't it great? So many people came in, we ran out of poster and foam board, and so did Big George at the hardware store. John and Jane Lambert made an emergency run to the Walmart in Magnolia for more."

John and his wife, Jane, dressed in matching colors and were friends and neighbors of the Silver Six. I spotted them coming around the far corner of the courthouse marching together. She wore a blue skirt with a khaki blouse, and he wore khaki slacks with a blue shirt. Other longtime friends of the Six I'd met in April also marched. Duke Richards, Dairy Queen owner, carried a FREE ASTER & MAISE sign, and he'd fortunately left Barker the Shotgun at home. Pauletta Williamson, known for her permed gray hair and always wearing squash blossom necklaces, walked ahead of petite Marie Dunn, who wore one of her many denim dresses. Bob Newton from the subdivision across the road from Sherry's farmhouse exited a car with four others, all in jeans, short-sleeved shirts, and tennis shoes. They trotted up to the lawn, without signs, but they took up the chant. As

I watched, bald Bog Turner, the barbershop owner, and Big George Heath of the hardware store joined the protest.

When Cindy Price, the peppy forty-something reporter-photographer from the *Lilyvale Legend*, showed up, I cringed. Not that I'd given thought to keeping Maise's and Aster's arrests out of the paper, but there was no chance of that now.

"This'll teach that idjit detective to mess with the Silver Six," Fred crowed.

"Unless it gets our protesting friends arrested," Sherry breathed, her tone clearly awed.

"I doubt that will happen, Sherry Mae," Dab said. "The local jail isn't large enough to house so many people at once."

"Dab is correct."

I whirled to find that Dinah Souse had come up behind us. She flashed a full-on grin.

"Did you know about the demonstration?" Eleanor asked.

"I saw the group gathering when I came back from the sheriff's office, so I knew something was up, but not what. Impressive show of support, isn't it? Rather like in April when your friends thought Sherry Mae would be arrested for murder and rushed to confess to the crime themselves."

I recalled that well, and with a smile. The police had shooed Sherry's friends into the parking lot to take statements and even called in patrol units to help with crowd control. The confession marathon hadn't lasted long, but it made a statement. After Eric had questioned Sherry for a few hours, Dinah with her, they'd walked out of the station to a cheering section of townspeople.

This, though, was a whole other level of friendship.

Dinah's cell phone dinged, and she stepped away to answer it. As she did, I noticed Eric's pickup and a patrol car. Uh-oh.

Eric pulled into the diagonal parking slot a few doors down from the emporium, and the patrol unit parked in one of the far slots facing the courthouse. Officer Bryant was back. He unfolded himself from the car, shut the door, and then stood with hands on his hips watching the marchers.

Eric descended from his truck and slammed the door. He gave a nod to Sherry, Eleanor, Dab, and Fred, but strode straight for me. I couldn't tell for sure if he was angry, amused, or a bit of both.

"What's Doug Bryant doing?" I called, to preempt whatever he'd planned to say.

"Watching to be sure everything stays calm." He stopped before me within arm's reach. "Please tell me you had nothing to do with organizing this march."

"I had nothing to do with organizing this march, but hey—" I did a fist pump. "Power to the people."

He tried to level me with his cop stare, but his lips twitched. "Chief Randall is fit to be tied."

"I don't imagine your new partner is happy either," I said and arched a brow. "So, Detective Shoar, did you know about the arrest warrant?"

"Not until Detective Vogelman was on her way over. The demonstration gave me a good excuse to come talk to you."

"You needed an excuse?"

"I need to maintain some semblance of impartiality where you're concerned, especially in public. Even if it's an illusion."

"He's right."

Again Dinah had come up behind us, and I turned to her along with my family. The heat of Eric's body warmed my back, and in spite of everything, having him close warmed my heart.

"Was that a good-news phone call?" Sherry asked.

"Not the best news, but you'll be pleased. The jail visit is a go."

"Will we be allowed to take the lavender water?"

"With caveats, yes. You'll be allowed to take a new spray bottle and a sealed, never-opened vial of lavender oil. You'll have to prepare the lavender water on the spot with a deputy observing. Aster won't be able to keep the mixture, but she can spray herself to her heart's content until you leave."

"When do we go, and can we all go together?" I asked as Eric moved to stand at my side.

Dinah chuckled. "Since Sheriff Brooks has also heard about the march for freedom, give it an hour, and I think the deputies will be happy to let you in."

"We should take cookies for the deputies," Sherry mused.

"Just don't be offended if they refuse the treats," Dinah cautioned. "Also I'd advise that only you ladies visit today."

"But won't Maise and Aster be out tomorrow?" Sherry cried.

"They should be, but I won't promise it. Now, if you get to the jail around dinnertime, you'll have to wait until after six and before seven."

I lightly touched Dinah's arm. "Thank you for going to bat for the family."

"My pleasure, Nixy." She leaned in closer. "The Silver Six are always entertaining."

Eric snorted but covered it with a cough when I glared at him.

"We'd best get crackin'." Fred punctuated his declaration with a shake of his walker. "I've got a brand-new spray bottle in back with the price sticker on it. It's bigger'n the bottles Aster uses, but it'll do."

"And I do believe Aster received a new shipment of oil this week," Eleanor said, her eyes shining.

"She did, and I know where she stashed that box," Dab said. "Eleanor, let's go get that oil, pronto."

"While you're home," Sherry said, "take those extra cookies out of the freezer. I'll take what's left of our morning supply over to the marchers. Nixy, will you help me? We'll take the sweet tea and bottled water over, too."

"Of course, Aunt Sherry. We'll all meet back in the workroom in half an hour?"

"Done."

The seniors streamed back into the emporium with Jasmine and Kathy in tow. Dinah told me to call if we had further questions, and she headed back to her office across the street.

Eric moved closer and discreetly took my hand. "It's all going to work out, Nixy. And, if it's any comfort, Aster and Maise were in good spirits when I saw them at the station."

"How good?"

"They were singing 'We Shall Overcome.'"

I grinned and squeezed his hand. "No wonder Dinah said the Six were entertaining."

"They can hold their own, and we'll find the real killer or killers."

"I know you will— Oh, wait. I have scoop to share. I found out that Dex Hamlin had attempted to blackmail Randy Darby."

Eric's posture stiffened, and he let go of my hand. "Where did you hear this?"

"From the man himself, and he believes Cornell was involved in gathering extortion-worthy information. Or what he thought was worthy." I waved a hand. "Randy and his wife, Billie Jo, still live at Ozark Arms, but they've been on an extended vacation. Vogelman should talk with them."

"If she won't, I will. Anything else you want to share, Nixy Drew?"

"I wish. Eleanor and I have talked to a number of past and present Arms residents, but I can't see a single one of them as a likely suspect."

"Now maybe you understand why Vogelman's investigation keeps circling back to Aster and Maise."

"Actually, I don't, but I can't do squat about it."

The wind chimes tinkled, and Sherry stuck her head out. "I hate to rush you, but I'm doing it anyway. Refreshments for the marchers now, talk later."

* * *

JUST OVER AN HOUR LATER, WE LEFT THE MEN AT the emporium, Fred in his workroom, Dab helping Jasmine and Kathy in the store. I drove Sherry and Eleanor the few miles out to the county jail on pins and needles, and I wasn't the only one suffering from a case of nerves.

Deputy Megan Paulson, Mayor Paulson's niece, accepted the paper plate of cookies, then ushered us through a checkpoint, where we went through a metal detector. We surrendered our purses but kept the spray bottle and oil. Next Deputy Paulson showed us into a break room, where she set the plate of cookies.

"Ladies, you can make the lavender water here at the sink."

We'd just begun when Detective Vogelman walked into the room sour-faced and steely-eyed. Eleanor's composure slipped, and so did the vial she held. I caught it, and without a word, she let me take over.

"Do you want a step-by-step?" I asked with a quick glance at Paulson and Vogelman.

"Depends. Do you know what you're doing?" Vogelman asked.

I didn't rise to the bait. "I haven't mixed the essential oil and water myself, but I've seen Aster do it. It isn't rocket science."

Okay, so I did get a snark in.

"Keep your hands visible at all times," Vogelman snapped.

"You know, Detective, this isn't fairy dust. Aster and Maise won't disappear."

"Nixy, play nice," Sherry said mildly. "Aster needs this calming boost."

I merely nodded, and completed mixing ten drops of lavender oil with a few ounces of water. When the smell was too strong, I added a bit more water, sealed the spray top onto the bottle, and shook it side to side to mix it.

"You want a test spritz?" I asked Vogelman.

She declined but Deputy Paulson spoke up. "I'll try it."

I lightly sprayed the mixture over her head, and after a moment, she smiled. "That's nice."

"I was skeptical the first time Aster used it on me, but it really is soothing and calming."

"Yes, it is," Sherry said, and took the bottle from me.

She and Eleanor spritzed themselves, and then Sherry gave me a few squirts. "Better add a little more water, Nixy, and a drop or two more of oil. Aster is going to need a good dousing, and Maise will use it, too."

"Ms. Holcomb uses lavender water?" Deputy Paulson asked.

Sherry chuckled. "She will to make Aster happy."

Megan Paulson smiled, and after I added more water and oil, I turned the spray bottle over to her. We were then led to a stereotypical visitation room like those I'd seen on TV and in films. A wall interspersed with Plexiglas panels separated visitors from the incarcerated. Blue counters ran the length of both sides of the spaces, and chairs and phones were positioned on each side of each panel. Our lavender-induced calm proved temporary, because Sherry paced and Eleanor fidgeted in one of the chairs as we waited.

At last, Maise and Aster entered their side of the room. The sound was muffled, but the Plexiglas didn't completely cancel noises. No shackles or handcuffs, and they still wore their street clothes—both in blue jeans, with a dark green button-up blouse for Maise and a flowing tie-dyed blouse for Aster. Deputy Paulson followed them and presented Aster with the lavender water.

"Oh, thank you, Megan!" Aster exclaimed, and immediately held the bottle over her head and pressed the pump lever several times. Next she aimed behind her head and spritzed at her back, followed by more misting all down the front of her body.

I'd thought both Aster and Maise had looked a little gray when they came in, but as Aster took three deep, slow breaths, her complexion seemed to return to its normal tan color.

"You want me to spray you now, Maise?"

"Later, Aster," Maise said, using her in-command tone. She pulled a second chair to the window and sat across from Eleanor. "We don't have much time, and right now I want a sitrep from the girls."

Aster took the other seat but accidentally-on-purpose gave Maise a light lavender water misting as her sister lifted the phone receiver and positioned it with the earpiece and mouthpiece facing upward. A crude speakerphone, but Eleanor did the same with ours, and it worked.

Aster continued to spray herself every few moments, and I had to hide a grin because Maise's color had also improved. Their side of the visitation room would certainly smell divine for the next group of, uh, detainees. I couldn't bring myself to think of Maise and Aster as prisoners.

"I'm so glad you didn't have to change into jail clothes!" Sherry exclaimed.

"Not since we expect to be out tomorrow," Maise said. "Is Dinah making that happen?"

"Your arraignments are tomorrow at nine," Eleanor confirmed.

"Did Dinah mention a bail amount?"

"We have savings," Aster added as she gave herself another misting.

"We'll handle whatever comes," Sherry assured them, "but don't worry. Dinah is angling to have you both released on your own recognizance. I'm sure the charges will be dropped entirely before long."

"If they aren't, the townspeople may storm the jail," I joked to lighten the mood.

Eleanor laughed. "Nixy is correct. Our friends are holding a protest rally in the square. Marching around the courthouse, chanting, the works."

Aster sighed. "Sounds like the old days. Activism isn't dead."

I grinned at her wistful expression. "Not by a long shot, especially when it concerns you and the rest of the Silver Six."

Maise rapped her knuckle on the counter. "What's the status of the investigation? Have you narrowed down a suspect list?"

Eleanor and Sherry looked to me to answer, and I grimaced. "I'm sorry, but no. Eleanor and I talked with the Darbys, Lorraine Chandler, and Barbara Linden today—"

"Don't forget Marshall Gibson," Eleanor added.

"Yes, and Mr. Gibson. Anyone could have killed Cornell, and Randy Darby might've gone after Dex, but the Darbys have been out of town."

"Randy Darby had a beef with Hamlin?" Maise barked. "What was it?"

"Attempted blackmail."

Her jaw dropped. "Are you serious?"

Eleanor nodded. "If the man tried pulling that on Randy, he was probably doing the same to others."

"Which is a good motive to murder Hamlin, but what does that have to do with Cornell Lewis's death? No, never mind. The guard will be here in a minute."

"We'll fill you in tomorrow when you're out of here," I promised, "and I do have one more lead. I need to talk with Debbie Nicole."

"She worked with that librarian, Dennis Moreno, who up and moved so suddenly," Sherry said.

"I'm hoping she'll have information about why Dennis left town and be willing to tell me."

"Whether she gives you another lead or not, it will be good to have answers," Aster said as the door at the back side of the room opened.

A woman I didn't recognize entered the room but didn't say a word. She didn't have to. Maise stood and said it for her.

"Time's up, but we'll see you in the courtroom."

"We'll all be there," Sherry assured her.

Aster glanced at the guard. "Just a few more sprays, all right?"

The guard nodded, and Aster went to town with that lavender water. She misted herself, then Maise, then the phone receiver before she replaced it on the hook. Then she spritzed herself and Maise once more for good measure.

On the other side of the wall, we waved and smiled as the ladies looked back at us. Aster surrendered the plastic bottle, and they walked out. As soon as they did, Eleanor and Sherry choked back sobs. I replaced the receiver on our side of the Plexiglas and hugged them both.

"It really will be okay," I murmured. "Let's go fill Dab and Fred in on the visit."

Chapter Eighteen

BY THE TIME SHERRY, ELEANOR, AND I ARRIVED back at the emporium twenty minutes before our five o'clock closing time, the marchers had dispersed. I didn't know if they'd show up the next day, but it was fine if they didn't. I was grateful for the show of support.

It didn't take long to bring Dab and Fred up to speed, and didn't take long for me to convince the seniors to call it a day either. Jasmine also left to get ready for a date, but Kathy offered to stay to help me ready the store for the next morning.

"Kathy, I have a question for you," I said as we counted the register receipts. Which were lower than usual, but no surprise considering the chaotic day.

"If you're going to ask if I want to work here, the answer is yes."

"Even after all the craziness of this week?"

She smiled. "Jasmine told me it's usually a calm, easy job, but I kind of enjoyed the excitement."

I leaned my hip against the wooden counter. "I wish I could

say the same, but Jasmine is right. We keep the working environment friendly and light. Probably to the point of boring. And business may be considerably slower after the holidays."

"I don't mind, Ms. Nixy," she said as she handed me the tally. "Even the few days I've been here, I've learned a lot of practical things I don't get in my business classes."

"Good, and call me Nixy. I'll check with the Silver Six, but I know they're pleased with your work." I paused. "There is something else, Kathy."

"What's that?"

"Do you remember much about living at Ozark Arms? About the people there who might've wanted Cornell Lewis dead?"

"First off, I saw my name on the flip chart. Jasmine told me it was y'all's murder board."

"It is, and your name is there because I thought you might remember seeing or hearing things that the older people might not have paid attention to. Maybe seen that someone had a deeper hatred of Cornell than the others."

"Well, I can tell you straight up that I wanted him dead, but that was after he all but pushed my mom down the stairs. Once we were gone, I didn't think about him much, although I admit it set me back to see him last week." She shook her head. "I got over it, though. It helped to talk it out with my boyfriend."

"I'm glad, but any details you can recall might be a big help. For instance, did Cornell give any particular residents a harder time than others?"

She snorted. "He was an equal-opportunity bully as far as I remember."

"Did you and your mom ever notice things missing or disturbed after he'd been in your apartment? Did you ever see Cornell sneaking into other apartments, or sneaking anything out of them?"

"If he did that, it was in the daytime when people were at work." She paused and frowned. "There was one time I was home sick while my mom was at work. He came in while I was in the kitchen, and I caught him poking around in a two-drawer file cabinet where Mama kept her receipts."

"What did he do?"

"He blustered. Asked me if I was playing hooky, and threatened to call the police. I told him I had a fever and he'd better get out before I threw up on him."

I couldn't help but laugh. "Bet he got out of there fast."

She gave me a gamine grin. "He sure did."

"Thanks, Kathy. If you think of anything else, remember anyone threatening Cornell, let me know."

"Sure thing."

"By the way, Kathy," I said as she went to get her purse, "who are you seeing? Has he been into the store?"

"Derek Goodson, and man, was he angry when I told him about Cornell. He offered to beat him up for me, but I told him to forget it. All that happened a long time ago, and the man wasn't worth getting into trouble over."

"It's a good thing he listened to you. Have a good night."

Or had Derek listened to Kathy? I considered putting his name on the suspect list, but no and no. Men didn't generally go bake cookies to kill someone. Especially young men with a lot more on their minds than tracking down Cornell. Way too much trouble.

After locking the front door behind her and setting the alarm, I checked the workroom door lock with Amber and T.C. looking on. When I opened the door leading from the workroom to the apartment, they scampered upstairs. Only as I trudged up behind them did I remember I'd never phoned Debbie Nicole. Was the library open late on Thursday? I couldn't remember, and I was too tired to ask one more murder-related question today. I wanted some comfort food, a soak in the claw-foot tub instead of my usual shower, and maybe a little reading in bed.

I fed the critters and realized I'd need to take them out again before I called it a night. Maybe I'd just let them out back to do their thing in the parking lot. There was a strip of grass back there, and I could do poop patrol in the morning if needed. Plus, they'd never once tried to run off, and animal control wouldn't be looking for strays after dark.

As Amber and T.C. crunched their munchies, I searched the fridge for my own meal. The leftovers from Tuesday's dinner at the farmhouse were front and center. Roast with carrots, potatoes, and small sweet onions, a dab of green bean casserole, and chocolate cake. I could work with that.

I could've heated my dinner on the stove, but I didn't want to deal with washing pans. My microwave warming trick was to cook a bit longer at a lower temperature setting, so I plated the roast and veggies, covered them with a paper towel, and let 'er rip. While the aromas of comfort food permeated the room, I flipped through TV channels. I scrolled past HGTV, something about World War I on the History Channel, and several sitcom reruns. The *Thursday Night Football* game wasn't on yet, so I settled on Animal Planet as the timer dinged.

I'd just finished the last bite of cake when Eric's ringtone sounded.

"Hey, Nixy, how did your visit with Maise and Aster go?"

"Other than the location, it was good. Did Detective Vogelman complain about the lavender water?"

"She didn't say a word to me, but I haven't seen her in a few hours. She may have gone on home to her dad." He paused a beat. "I was thinking about taking T.C. and Aster to the park for a quick visit. Are you game?"

"They will be, and they'd appreciate the attention, but I'm beat."

"I'll be happy to take them by myself if you aren't too tired to bring them downstairs."

I thought about the steep steps for a minute, but I'd have to go down them and come back up at some point. If Eric took them out, they might be able to settle down for the night.

"You're on, and if you don't mind, let me give you a key to bring them back upstairs."

The connection was silent for a moment. "Are you okay?"

"My nerves are fried to a crisp," I said, using a Sherry phrase. "I'm considering a long soaking bath."

He chuckled. "I could help with that, too."

"I'm sure you could, but maybe another time."

"Like on our getaway to Eureka Springs?"

His voice had deepened, and my skin tingled, but I kept my voice light. "Let's catch the killer, and we'll see."

AMBER AND T.C. WERE ECSTATIC TO SEE ERIC AND would've smacked into the door in their eagerness to jump into the truck if he hadn't already opened it. He kissed me on the cheek and told me he'd be back in an hour, and I hightailed it upstairs to begin my indulgence.

I left my few dishes in the sink and ran a not-quite-scalding-hot bath, liberally sprinkling the water with the scented Epsom salts Aster had given me. Lemon to lift the spirits, rosemary to stimulate mental alertness. Rosemary was as calming to me as lavender, and I let myself sink into the water and absorb all the mojo the essential oils and salts could deliver.

I might've fallen asleep with my head cushioned on the cushy bath pillow. Thoughts scrolled through my mind, but I didn't attempt to focus on any of them. My sense of time and place grew fuzzy as I drifted, and only the cooling water roused me. Time to get moving.

I dried with one of my most decadently fluffy towels, pulled on black yoga pants that had only seen a yoga mat once, and topped them with a Dallas Cowboys football jersey. When I opened the bedroom door, I about jumped out of my skin. Eric sat on the couch with a mostly eaten burger and a small mound of fries on a paper plate. He'd tuned into the football game, but the volume was set so low, it was barely audible.

"Feel better?" he asked with a lazy grin.

"Much, thank you. I take it T.C. and Amber were good for you?"

"So much so that I accidentally dropped a few fries and they scarfed them up."

"After you wiped the salt off the fries, I hope."

"I might've done that," he said with a shrug. "I also got you a banana shake. It's in the freezer."

Ahh, more comfort food. I loved that he remembered my favorites, even if it was just from the Dairy Queen. I headed straight to the kitchen to grab the shake and a spoon. When I did, I noticed that he'd washed the plate, fork, and glass I'd left in the sink and had them drying on my stainless rack on the counter. Eric really was a keeper.

I warred with myself about posing questions about the murders, but I was so tired, my thoughts so jumbled, I wasn't sure I could string a coherent sentence together. In the end we sat on the sofa in companionable silence watching the game as he finished his dinner and I worked on my shake. Two of my favorite teams were playing tonight, so I didn't care who won. I was feeling relaxed and serene for the first time since before the folk art festival, and I intended to stay there.

THE BOUNCY MUSIC OF MY CELL PHONE ALARM awoke me Friday morning at seven. I vaguely remembered setting my alarm but had no memory of moving from the sofa to my bed.

Eric had obviously tucked me in, leaving me in my yoga pants and jersey. I gave myself half a minute to be embarrassed, and a full one to grin like a lovesick lunatic. That done, I sprang out of bed to get my morning under way. I had a court date to keep.

* * *

JUDGE LEO JAMES WAS IN HIS LATE FIFTIES WITH short salt-and-pepper hair and laugh lines around his eyes and mouth that contrasted with his solemn, distinguished demeanor.

Or rather he was solemn until the bail-setting part of the arraignment, when the prosecutor argued against releasing Maise and Aster on their own recognizance by bringing up their arrest records. When Judge James heard that the arrests had been over forty years ago and involved protest marches, he looked right at them and said, "Right on, sisters." That was when I knew we were out of the woods, however temporarily.

The ladies had to return to the county jail to be processed out, and Dinah warned us that could take a few hours. They would call when they were ready to rock out of there. Still, word that they'd soon be home had raced through the square, because Sherry, Eleanor, Dab, Fred, and I exited the courthouse to cheers from friends and business owners.

We opened the emporium only a few minutes past our regular time, and minutes later well-wishers began coming by. Kay Baskin from the Business Center was first in the door, but Lorna Tyler, Helen from the beauty shop, B.G. Huff from the furniture store, and many others streamed in and out. Sherry and Eleanor had been prepared for the onslaught. They'd brought a fresh batch of chocolate chip cookies from home that morning. As I greeted each person, thanked them for their support, and helped pass out cookies, I also asked them to call if they heard any little thing about Cornell's whereabouts from Sunday morning until Monday morning, and about Dex's from Sunday night to Wednesday. They all promised, but I had little hope of any new leads. The people who knew something would've spoken up by now.

Except for the killer. Or killers.

I wished we knew if we were dealing with more than one.

* * *

AT ELEVEN FORTY-FIVE, ELEANOR WENT TO PICK UP Maise and Aster. The goal was for them to go home for a shower and a rest. Thanks to Mayor Paulson and B.G. Huff, they'd been made as comfortable as possible in jail, but a nap couldn't hurt.

Not that I thought they'd rest for long.

Sherry and I were manning the store front when Dab called me to the workroom to see his holiday-themed metal-art sketches. My favorite for Halloween was a grouping of a pumpkin, a broom, and a cat. For Thanksgiving, Dab had drawn a footed cornucopia. He explained the plan was to weave metal strips to resemble a basket and said Sherry had agreed to supervise the weaving. The result would be gorgeous, and I knew he, Fred, and Sherry would pull it off in spades. Then Dab showed me the two pieces he'd designed for Christmas. I loved both the silver bells with holly leaves hanging from a curved stand and the simple silhouette of the Holy Family.

"Will these be easy enough to produce in time for each holiday?" I asked.

"We've decided to do limited editions every year," Dab said.

Fred nodded. "Ain't no use in floodin' the market, now is there? A'sides, we can make 'em collector's items."

"Brilliant, gentlemen!" I enthused. "The bells can be a table or mantel decoration, or be hung on a wreath hook on a door."

"Hmm. You're right," Dab mused as he peered at his sketch again.

"Speakin' of hooks," Fred said, "you know Aster 'n' Maise ain't entirely in the clear for Cornell's murder. You ever call Debbie Nicole over at the library?"

"No, it went right out of my mind, but I'll do it now."

When I reached her, Debbie Nicole's tone of voice made

it obvious that she was surprised to hear from me, much less get my offer to take her to lunch. She couldn't leave the library due to a rescheduled book club meeting, so I arranged to bring a meal to her at one o'clock. Chicken-cranberry-pecan salads from the Lilies Café, and classic chocolate éclairs from Great Buns.

I called Lorna to put in my order, then Judy.

"I have three eclairs left," Judy said, "and I'll throw in the extra to celebrate Aster and Maise being free women again."

"You're the best, Judy."

"And don't you forget it," she quipped. "See you soon."

THE LIBRARY WAS LOCATED A BLOCK FROM THE hospital on the opposite side of Magnolia Road. Since both Judy and Lorna had put my orders in a sack with carrying handles, I decided to walk.

The building was more or less in the Georgian style, two stories, red brick with white columns anchoring a wide porch set with double doors. Concrete stairs led to the porch in the front, and a ramp had been added along one side for handicapped accessibility.

A large foyer funneled patrons to the checkout desk, and various spacious rooms held orderly bookshelves and comfy-looking club chairs. The upstairs held more books but also boasted three meeting areas. I'd attended a mystery book club in one of them in August.

Debbie Nicole Samp and I hadn't kicked off our acquaintanceship under the best of circumstances, but she'd been more cordial each time I'd seen her. Yes, I made it a point to get a library card when I'd moved to Lilyvale in mid-May. Although she was in her early thirties, only a few years older than I was, I had doubts we'd ever be best buds. I hoped that she wouldn't take offense to my questions about her former colleague.

After I asked for Debbie Nicole at the desk, I stood aside to soak in the special ambiance all libraries have. I spotted a few people I recognized from town, but they all had their heads in books. I also saw Lee Durley in the fiction section. He stood peering at a top row of books, scanning the titles. Though he was in profile to me, I started to wave, but then he pulled out a book and turned away. I wondered why he was in town again but figured he was visiting his sister. Maybe he was here with her, though I didn't see a brown-haired woman near him. I didn't see anyone near him.

"Nixy." Debbie Nicole greeted me, pulling me out of idle speculation. Her blonde hair was cut in a breezy style, and she wore a black pencil skirt with a silky blue blouse and black pumps. Professional but approachable, especially when she smiled and held out her hand.

"Hi, Debbie Nicole." I smiled and, holding both bags in one hand, extended my hand to her.

She took it briefly and nodded at the food bags. "You're very kind to bring lunch."

"No problem. I appreciate your time."

"Let's go upstairs to the staff break room. We have a gallon of sweet tea and one of cherry lemonade in the fridge, and we should have some privacy right now."

"That would be great," I said as I followed her to an elegantly curving staircase. She led me to a long room with a slightly battered table, mismatched chairs, and a three-seater sofa along the back wall. The front wall held an L-shaped kitchenette with a full-sized fridge, microwave and toaster ovens, and a twelve-cup coffeepot.

"We store supplies for ourselves, and for the various events our Friends of the Library group sponsors," she explained as she opened several upper and lower cabinets. They held paper plates, napkins, coffee filters, mugs, and disposable cups for hot and cold beverages. She took flatware from a drawer flanking the double sink.

"Do you want tea or lemonade?"

"Sweet tea, please. This is a great setup. The entire library is laid out nicely."

"We're proud of it," she said with a proprietary glance around the room as she carried paper plates, napkins, and forks to the table. "The elevator is too industrial for some of our patrons' tastes, but it was originally a service elevator, meant only to move books and library furnishings between the two floors."

I took the two containers of Lorna's chicken salad from the sack and set them on the table, then brought out the eclairs. "At least the elevator is original to the building. Retrofitting one would take a chunk of change."

"That's the truth."

We sat, ate, and drank, and all the while I had to bite my tongue to keep from blurting out questions. I refrained, knowing Eleanor would tell me this was the time to make nice. Besides, Lorna's chicken salad was too tasty to rush.

We'd nearly finished with the divine eclairs when Debbie Nicole raised the reason for my visit.

"I heard through the grapevine that your aunt's friends have been released from jail. That must've been a nightmare for them."

"It's been a challenging week for all of us," I replied. "I've been meaning to contact you with some questions for days but was always sidetracked."

She nodded. "Is this about Cornell Lewis's murder?"

"And Dexter Hamlin's, though I can't figure out how they're related."

"Ask away," she said with a wave of her hand.

"Let me tell you what I've heard, and you can tell me what's true. Does that work for you?"

"Go ahead."

"All right." I took a deep breath and took the plunge. "Eleanor Wainwright and I have been visiting current and former residents of Ozark Arms who knew Mr. Lewis to see if they know who might've killed him. Because I heard a rumor that a former resident died or almost died, I've been asking people about that."

Her eyes narrowed and her lips thinned, but she kept silent. I pressed on.

"Not a soul we've talked with knows a thing about it, but several said a library employee named Dennis Moreno suddenly moved out of his apartment maybe fourteen months ago or so. It was before Cornell was fired. Anyway, the young man moved before his lease was up, and without telling some of the residents who had regular interaction with him."

I paused again, eyeing the librarian's stony expression.

"Uh, one or two of the residents mentioned seeing a man cleaning out the apartment a few days later. It was nighttime, so no one can identify him."

I stopped talking when I noticed that Debbie Nicole's fists were clenched and her entire body had grown rigid. Any moment I expected her to blow up at me. To tell me to get out of her library and never darken the double doors again.

Instead, she heaved a deep breath and let it out on a shaky sigh.

"It's true," she said.

"What is?"

"To an extent, all of it."

Debbie Nicole played with her unfinished glass of cherry lemonade, sighed, and then met my gaze. "I'll tell you what I know, but I don't want it to come back to me as gossip. Deal?"

"Absolutely. If what you have to say gives me a lead to clear Aster and Maise, the only person I'll tell is Eric Shoar."

"Okay, then, Dennis Moreno did work here, and he was an amazing employee. He was also a friend, although we seldom saw each other after hours. He told me the apartment manager was a supreme jerk. He said the residents called the guy Rotten to the Core."

"I heard the same nickname from Eleanor."

She inclined her head and sipped her lemonade. "Cornell hassled Dennis about being gay, and with all the hate crimes you hear about, it worried me. Dennis assured me the man belittled and bullied everyone except maybe his drinking buddies. Dennis chalked it up to plain old ignorance and meanness, and made a game of telling me new Rotten to the Core stories every few days."

She smiled in reminiscence.

"Sounds like he was an exceptionally tolerant guy."

"He was that and more, but he began coming to work increasingly upset. When I asked what was wrong, he said it was personal and blew me off. A week later he came to work with his back killing him."

"What happened?" I prompted when she didn't immediately continue.

"He'd been in a car accident nine months earlier, and at first he only told me he'd fallen and reinjured himself. A few days later I overheard a patron ranting about the way Cornell treated Dennis, and that Dennis should sue the man for nearly running him over."

"Who was the patron?"

She shook her head. "He'd left by the time I came to the desk, but I made Dennis tell me about the incident. He brushed it off again. Said he still had pain meds and muscle relaxants from the accident."

"He wasn't willing to make waves," I murmured in sympathy.

"No, and it would've been far better if he had," she said, her voice growing brittle. "He kept all that bottled up inside, and not a week later, he called me at night to tell me he was sick and wouldn't be in the next day. I couldn't shake the feeling something was seriously wrong, so I went to his apartment. The door was unlocked, and I found him half conscious on the couch."

"Oh, no," I murmured.

"I took him to the hospital."

"Lilyvale's?" I interrupted.

"I started to take him there, but he begged me to take him to another town. Actually, he begged me to let him die." Her voice broke, and I kept quiet while she composed herself. "I took him to the medical center in Camden and told them he'd merely lost track of how many pain pills he'd taken. He had the legitimate prescriptions, and I'd taken the bottles with me.

"They treated him, kept him overnight, and didn't report the overdose to the police. I stayed with him until he was moved to a room. When I called the next morning, he was still there, but when I went back to Camden after work, I was told he'd been released and a male relative had taken him home."

"Home where?"

"Well, I thought it would be to his apartment, but he went to his mother's house in El Dorado."

"You're certain?"

"I am. I had his mother's number as an emergency contact and called her. She said he was resting. I called several more times over the course of the next week, and she always told me he'd call back."

"But he didn't," I said.

"No, and after four or five calls, I let it go. I sent his last paycheck to his mother's address, but I still wish Dennis had told me if the set-to with Cornell is what triggered the suicide attempt. He just wasn't the type, you know?"

I didn't know firsthand, thankfully, but I nodded. "Debbie Nicole, did you ever meet his mother or any of his other relatives?"

She glanced at her bracelet-style watch before focusing on me. "I didn't. I think his mother had been treated for cancer, so he went home to see her instead of her coming here. He only worked at this library for a few years, and he didn't talk all that much about his family or friends. At least not that I can remember off the top of my head."

"Do you still have his employment files or other papers where there might be more information?"

"I can look, but even if I find something, I don't know how out of date it will be."

"Okay, this is the last question, and it's the most difficult to ask. Would Dennis have held enough of a grudge to kill Cornell?"

"No and no," she said as she stood and began gathering our lunch trash. "Dennis was a private person, but he was a kind, cheerful guy who let most things roll off his back. If he was ever capable of killing, it would've been to strike back in self-defense."

She stopped fussing with the trash and held my gaze with her steady blue eyes. "In spite of the proverbial revenge being a dish best served cold, I don't know of anyone who'd have the patience to plan Cornell Lewis's murder, especially when he'd been gone from town this long. If anyone here knew where he was, I never heard of it."

"If someone *had* known, I'm sure it would've been an item of gossip."

"The grapevine is the blessing and curse of small-town living," she agreed with a smile. "I've got to go, but thank you for lunch."

"Thank *you* for answering my questions. I saw how difficult it was for you, and I appreciate your help."

"If anything else comes to mind, I'll call."

I strolled back to the emporium, turning over the information Debbie Nicole had given me. She seemed certain Dennis Moreno would not have killed Cornell, but what if she was wrong about him? If he was still in the area, he'd have opportunity, in the general way of things at least. Motive had to be retaliation or revenge. Six of one, half a dozen of the other, as Fred would say. I put it on my mental list to look him up on the Internet this afternoon.

If not Dennis himself, perhaps a relative or friend had schemed to murder Cornell. Since poison in general was traditionally a woman's weapon, perhaps Dennis's mother had plotted the killing. But that presupposed that she knew he had a peanut allergy. None of the past or current residents admitted to being privy to that critical nugget. The only way his mother could have known was if Dennis knew and told her.

Or Dennis did the deed. Or another relative or friend had sought and got revenge. Too bad Debbie Nicole had so little information about the family, because if we struck out with the Moreno connection, we were up the creek on suspects.

HALFWAY BACK TO THE EMPORIUM, MY CELL chirped, and I pulled it from my cargo pocket. The screen read *Unavailable* with no number. Probably a telemarketer, but on the chance it could be Debbie Nicole, I answered. If she'd remembered something, I didn't want the call to go to voice mail.

"This is Nixy," I said.

I heard a scratchy breath, and then a menacing "Stop asking questions."

Chapter Nineteen

I HALTED IN MIDSTEP, MY HEART POUNDING. "WHAT? My connection is bad."

Another breath, and the voice spoke again. "You heard me. Stop asking questions."

"Why? Who are you?"

There was no answer. The line was dead.

I don't know how long I stood rooted to the sidewalk staring at the screen. I thought the caller had been a man because his voice was guttural, as if he'd disguised it. Or had it sounded more mechanical?

I waited for the shakes to start, but anger surged instead. Stop asking questions? My Aunt Fanny, as Sherry would say. I had to be on the right track, or this yahoo wouldn't have called me. Never mind how he got my number. The guy either was the killer or was protecting the killer, and he didn't know squat about me if he expected a call to make me back down.

I considered phoning Eric immediately. Or Vogelman. But I hadn't recorded the call, and I doubted the new detective in town would take my word on faith. Eric would, but what could he do when she was lead investigator?

The call had come after I talked to Debbie Nicole. Not after talking with any of the other seven people Eleanor and I had interviewed. Was that significant? Instinct said a big ol' yes! So did the caller fear that the librarian had already told me something that threatened the killer? Or fear she'd remember something more? Wait. Was Debbie Nicole at risk?

I'd call Eric at some point soon. Maybe call the librarian with a word of caution, too. No matter what other actions I took, I marched on to the emporium, a new layer of steel in my spine, determined to solve these murders come hell or high water.

I WASN'T HAPPY THAT MAISE AND ASTER WERE IN the shop when I returned, but I wasn't surprised either. Jasmine and Kathy had come in, too, so the Six and I left running the store to them and had a confab.

"What'd you get outta Debbie Nicole?" Fred asked right away.

"Did she spill the beans about the guy who up and moved?" Aster asked.

I wasn't about to mention the phone call, and I'd rehearsed how much of what the librarian told me to divulge. I trusted the Six not to blab, but I'd promised Debbie Nicole I wouldn't reveal the whole story to anyone but Eric. And only then if it provided a lead.

"The man was Dennis Moreno, and he did work at the library. He had a bad back, and then had an accident that made it worse. That's when he moved. He went home to El Dorado."

"When?" Sherry asked.

"I didn't remember to get specific with Debbie Nicole, but the other people Eleanor and I spoke with said it was shortly before Cornell was fired."

"Are you saying we're shot down in flames again?" Maise barked.

"I need to do a little more research, but we might be. We have motive in spades, but opportunity and even means are iffy."

"The means was the cookies," Dab put in.

"That's our operating theory, but to our knowledge, there were no actual peanuts in the cookies. We have to figure out how that ingredient could've been introduced, and in a high enough amount to trigger a reaction without Cornell tasting the nuts."

"I do believe you might have a word with Judy at Great Buns. As a baker, she may have ideas we've overlooked."

"That is brilliant, Eleanor. I'll pop down there this afternoon."

"Nixy, explain why opportunity is iffy," Aunt Sherry said.

"No one seems to have known or cared where Cornell was for the past fourteen months, give or take. Word that he was here in town had time to spread between Friday afternoon when he was helping set up Gone to the Dogs and Sunday morning when he left the square, but the people who are the most likely suspects either didn't know he was back, or weren't interested in tracking him down."

"And the Darbys were out of town. I'd forgotten how much they travel," Aster said.

"What you need is to have another gander at what all them people told you and Eleanor. Might be it could jog loose somethin' you didn't see before."

I shrugged. "Couldn't hurt, but let's not do it today. I want to talk to Judy, and then why don't all of you call it a day. Jasmine and Kathy can help me the rest of the afternoon."

"You got no reason to mollycoddle us," Fred objected.

"I'm not, but we've had a rough week, and we need to be as sharp as we can be. Remember, if Vogelman can't get in touch with that pastor in Camden, or the church didn't keep a record of getting Aster and Maise's old car, they may have to stand trial for murder."

And that stopped all objections in their tracks.

I CAUGHT JUDY IN AN AFTERNOON CUSTOMER LULL.

"You here for a maple donut for Fred, cake for Mrs. Gilroy, or a chocolate croissant for yourself? I have a few servings of banana icebox cake left."

I perked up. "The specialty dessert at Adam Daniel's restaurant? I heard Daniel might've given you the recipe."

"You heard right. Daniel and I were in culinary school together in Little Rock. He decided it was too labor intensive to have on the menu all the time, so he'll serve it in the summer, and I get to offer it the rest of the year." She tapped her chin. "Although I don't know if he gave me the exact recipe. His tastes different. Oh, well, you want a piece?"

"Judy, I just stuffed myself on one of your eclairs."

"And your point is?"

"I wouldn't say no to coffee and an oatmeal cookie. And I need your help."

"Two coffees and one cookie coming up. Have a seat."

I took a chair at our usual table nearest the store phone, planted my elbows on the table, and rubbed my forehead.

"How are Maise and Aster?" she asked as she whirled from the coffee station to the bakery case.

"They're fine. They came back to the store this afternoon, and I'm sending the entire crew home when I get back. They need downtime."

"And you need to solve this murder?"

"With any luck, both murders."

She plunked the huge cups, my plated cookie, and herself at the table. "So what can I do to break the case?"

"I've exhausted the possibilities of how a peanut product got into the snickerdoodles. That is, without Cornell noticing the smell or taste when he was snarfing them down."

"Got it," Judy said with a decisive nod. "So let's analyze the issue. Peanut dust on the cookies. *NCIS* did an episode that had the baddie putting peanut dust on the cover of an airplane pillow. The victim didn't smell it, but Ziva did. That was a stretch for me. I mean that the woman with the allergy didn't detect the smell, but that's one explanation if the dusting wasn't heavy handed."

"Light dusting, check. How else could the snickerdoodles have gotten peanutty?"

"Using peanut oil in the recipe," Judy offered, "but everything I've ever tasted that was cooked in or baked with peanut oil had a distinct flavor."

"Vogelman questioned Maise about using that. Do you think the flavor is strong enough for an allergy-prone person to detect?"

"That's too subjective a question for me to answer, Nixy."

"Okay, so dusting and using oil. How else could peanuts have gotten into those snickerdoodles?"

"Peanut flour."

I blinked. "There's such a thing as peanut flour?"

"Sure, but again I think someone with an allergy to the nuts would be able to smell and taste it." Judy frowned, stared into space a minute, and then continued slowly, "Unless the cookies were made with a smaller amount of peanut flour mixed with standard white flour. I wonder if that would do it?"

"Is peanut flour easy to get?"

"I doubt the local groceries carry it, but a store in a bigger town like Texarkana probably would. I can get it from my supplier. In fact," she continued, eyes shining eagerly, "I'll put in the order this afternoon. When I get it, I'll try it in my own recipe. Mine makes sixty cookies and calls for three and a half cups of flour, I think. Anyway, I'll use different proportions of regular flour to peanut flour, and we'll do a taste test."

"That's brilliant except we aren't allergic to peanuts."

She blinked and slapped the palm of her hand on her

forehead. "Well, duh on me. You're right. Tasting peanut flavor is one thing. Reacting to it is the true test."

"Just having the peanut flour possibility helps more than you know. You're the best, Judy."

"Yes, I am, and I'll expect a suitable reward if my theory breaks the case."

I LEFT JUDY WITH THE INSTINCT THAT SHE'D NAILED it with the peanut flour angle. Eager as she was to be on the case, though, I hated for her to take the time and trouble of making multiple batches of cookies. Would Eric answer a few questions that might confirm we were on the right track? The worst he could do was stonewall me. Besides, I needed to tell him about that phone call. I stopped on the sidewalk in front of the Be Sweet ice cream store and entered his number.

"I need some answers," I said when I heard his voice.

"Can this wait?"

"Is Vogelman in earshot?"

"Yes."

"Then just say yes or no. Were there peanuts in the snickerdoodles you found in Cornell's car? I mean actual pieces of them."

"No."

"Did anyone detect the smell of peanuts on the cookies?"

"No."

"Did anyone at the scene have a peanut allergy or a sensitivity to them?"

"Yes."

"But that person didn't smell the peanuts?"

"No."

"That's all I need, but I have something to tell you."

"What's that?"

I opened my mouth to fill him in on Judy's theory but decided it could wait. "I'll call you later."

* * *

THE SIX REFUSED TO LEAVE RIGHT AWAY. THE women visited with well-wishers—a few of them who'd brought food. The men discussed materials for their holiday metal-art pieces.

At four I rounded up the seniors and sent them home, but only after I promised to come to the farmhouse for dinner. Sherry said they had enough food to serve Cox's army, and needed me to take a load of leftovers to Mrs. Gilroy. This worked out fine since I'd broken down and scored a hunk of banana icebox cake for Mrs. Gilroy. Which was part cake, part mousse, and all awesome.

Kathy left early for her Friday night date with Derek to the high school football game, so Jasmine stayed until just after five to help me close. Then she and Lamar were off to a movie in El Dorado. I thought about calling Eric, inviting him to the farmhouse feast and having the talk with him, but if he needed to keep his distance, I wasn't closing it more than absolutely necessary.

Although that hadn't stopped him from coming to my place the other night. I shrugged. If he wanted to see me, he knew where to find me. Otherwise, I'd simply tell him about the call when I got home.

I did remember to put in a quick call to Debbie Nicole. The library was still open, but she wasn't available and I didn't leave a message. Really, what could I say? *Let me know if you get any weird calls? Watch your back?* No point in alarming her.

I crossed through Fred's workroom with Amber and T.C. scampering ahead as I headed for my apartment, and noticed that the flip chart was gone. So was the easel it had been propped on, and the markers, too. Looked like the Six were determined to review the few facts we'd gathered with or without me.

Upstairs, I fed my critters, changed out of my emporium

polo shirt, and removed the clear plastic container holding the banana icebox cake. Even catching a whiff of the dessert made me gain ten pounds. The sooner I got this to Bernice Gilroy, the better.

Fifteen minutes later, I parked in the farmhouse's gravel drive and opened the car door for T.C. and Amber, and they shot out to bound around the yard, first chasing birds and squirrels, then chasing each other. I knew they wouldn't run off, so I went in the back door to the hall. The kitchen was to my left, and as always, Maise was at the stove.

"Good, you're here." Maise started to shove a bowl of lima beans at me but saw the clear plastic cake container. "Didn't I mention we have dessert for everyone?"

"This is for Bernice Gilroy," I said, and took the few steps to the fridge to stow the container.

"Since when does Old Lady Gilroy like that stuff?"

"I don't know that she does, but it's rich enough to satisfy her sweet tooth for days."

"Fine, take this on in before the beans get cold."

I did as commanded, grinning to myself. Our chief cook got her nose out of joint when I bought something from Judy that she could make just as well, but Maise understood supporting our fellow businesses on the square.

I pushed through the swinging door from the kitchen to the dining room, and stumbled when I saw Herkimer Jones pulling out a chair for Aunt Sherry. The rest of the Six were either pouring sweet tea and water or settling into their seats, so I set the bowl on the table amid a chorus of greetings.

"Hello again, Dr. Jones," I said, as I took my customary seat at the far end of the table. Fred had scooted down to squeeze in beside me.

"Call me Herk," the doctor replied.

Sherry sent him a shy smile. "Herk came by to check on us, so we invited him to stay."

"That's great." And it was, but it was certainly odd to see him making eyes at my aunt.

Perhaps because of our guest, the dinner conversation focused on the upcoming classes we'd scheduled. We'd begun the tradition for our grand opening in June with a gourd art class, and had since sponsored sessions in both folk art and glass painting, wreath making, and a messy sand art program for children. Fun, yes, but the shop vacuum got a workout after that. Fred even grouched his way through a class on simple home repairs and maintenance.

Then it hit me. Next week Aster was to give a class in making body scrubs with essential oils, and it had been booked solid for a month. I didn't want her under a cloud for that. I didn't want her under a cloud at all. That strengthened my resolve. We had to redouble our efforts to find out who killed Cornell Lewis and Dexter Hamlin, and get answers fast.

By six fifteen we'd eaten our fill and done the dishes, with Herk pitching in to help. I didn't think we'd be having our confab about the case, but I was wrong. Sherry asked if he'd like to stay and give his opinions, and he accepted. Huh.

We trooped into the parlor-cum-living-room-cum-craft-room, where a trifold display board sat on the easel from the store. The photo we'd had of Cornell was posted with his name written beneath it. One of the seniors had found a fuzzy picture of Dex Hamlin and labeled it, too. It appeared to have been printed from an online article. At the bottom, on the right panel of the trifold board, was the shot of Lee Durley with his name duly noted. Obviously, the seniors didn't think him important but kept his picture for reference.

"Isn't it great?" Sherry gushed. "This way we don't have to flip pages, and Fred rigged the broken broomstick in back so the fold-out sides don't flop."

"Ingenious as always, Fred," I answered.

"Thankee kindly," he replied, milking his country drawl. "Get on with it now."

Since the doctor was here, I wanted to pick his brain. "Herk, I know you mentioned anaphylaxis when you looked over Cornell's body. Any chance the victim reacted to an insect sting?"

Herk shrugged. "There's always a chance, but I didn't see indication of that. Besides, not to be indelicate, particularly after such a wonderful meal, but I noted emesis on the victim's shirt. That's more often a by-product of ingesting an allergen than a sting."

"Okay, for simplicity, let's agree Cornell died as a result of eating snickerdoodles tainted with peanuts. That's our means."

Eleanor raised her hand to get our attention. "I do believe there is one small problem here. The people we visited didn't seem to know Cornell had a peanut allergy, or that that he had a fondness for snickerdoodles."

"Any one of these here people could be lyin' 'bout that," Fred grumped. "Could be lyin' 'bout any manner of things."

"True, but we have to work with what we know."

Maise pointed at the board. "Start from scratch. Review the facts in the order you got them. You talked with Minnie Berry at Pines Breeze first."

With that suggestion, we launched into recapping who'd said what, who'd reacted with any hint of guilt, and who'd had anything to gain by Cornell's death. Of course, a whole host of people might benefit from Hamlin's death, particularly blackmail victims. After a lively discussion, I summarized.

"So, we're agreed Hamlin's and Cornell's deaths are connected, but how? Everyone we talked with had motive to kill Cornell to some degree or other. Most likely revenge or retaliation. Marshall Gibson and Debbie Nicole seemed to be holding on to the most anger toward Cornell. Randy Darby and Billie Jo are still hot about Hamlin's attempted blackmail, but they were out of town when he was killed."

"Oh! Did you remember to tell Eric about all that, child?"

"Yes, Aunt Sherry. He said he'd pass on the information, but who knows if Vogelman will take it seriously."

Herk cleared his throat. "It sounds like only Barbara Linden, Marshall Gibson, and Jim Diller knew Cornell was in town."

"Well, there's Annie Byrd, the young lady at Helen's salon," Sherry corrected, "but she didn't make it to the suspect list."

"Why not?" Herk asked.

The Six and I exchanged startled looks. "Good question. Sherry, could you go speak with her tomorrow?"

"Of course, child."

"Back to Herk's comment, he's right. Our current top three suspects knew Cornell was in town on Saturday. Any of them would have time to bake up a deadly batch of cookies, but I can't see Marshall or Jim going to that much trouble."

"That don't track for me either," Fred put in. "If Jim did the killin', he'd'a whomped the guy with a wrench and been done with it."

"And I do believe Marshall would come up with a means other than cookies," Eleanor said.

"So that leaves us with Barbara Linden?"

Uneasy glances and shrugs rippled through the parlor, so I moved on.

"Last we have opportunity, and this is the sticky one. Cornell was living in his car, so how did the killer find him to give him the cookies?"

"Minnie's only transportation is the Pines Breeze van," Aster said.

Dab nodded. "The rest have cars, but I can't see any of them driving all over town looking for Cornell."

"And yet whoever did this had to keep track of him somehow. Maybe the killer even knew in advance that Cornell would be in town working for Hamlin."

Sherry snapped her fingers. "Wait a moment. Cornell would have to see to his, uh, needs. He'd have to use the facilities somewhere, most likely at a convenience store. Someone could've seen him there and followed him."

"I do believe Sherry is onto something," Eleanor said, grinning. "Our suspect follows Cornell until he parks, seeming to settle in for the night."

"Then goes home and bakes cookies?" Maise snorted.

"They could've been store-bought," Aster offered. "Every store I know of sells peanuts, too, even if they're in those small snack packages. Poke little pieces of peanuts into the cookies, and that's that."

"A good theory, except Eric told me there weren't any peanut pieces in the cookies."

"He shared that?" Sherry asked, brows raised.

"I called him after I saw Judy and put him on the spot."

"Well, don't leave us in suspense. What else did he say?"

"Keep this in confidence, but he said that though no one on the scene detected the smell of peanuts, someone there was sensitive to them. He didn't say who."

"Goodness, that didn't occur to me," Herk said, eyes wide.

"What didn't?"

He looked a little uncomfortable but answered me. "There were other odors on the body but not peanuts. They have a distinctive scent."

"Hmm. I don't suppose the state lab reports have come back," Aster said.

"Not that Eric confided in me."

"What about your talk with Judy?" Eleanor asked. "Did she have any insights?"

"Yes, but this needs to stay on the down-low, too."

When every member of the group nodded, I relayed the highlights of my visit with Judy to exclamations of "Oh, my" and "Bless my soul."

"I've heard of peanut flour but would never have thought of using it and white flour together," Maise said.

"Herk, Cornell told me he went through snickerdoodles fast. Let's say one cookie with a limited amount of peanut flour in it might not bother him. Eating one at a time over several hours might not cause much of a problem. But what about half a dozen in, say, thirty minutes to an hour?"

Herk shook his head. "My considered opinion is yes. If each cookie contained enough peanut flour, that well may have triggered the allergy. Of course, the more peanut flour used, the more likely the reaction was to occur."

"But it's possible for him to have received small doses in each cookie?"

"I'd say probable. In addition, depending on the cinnamon content, the spice could potentially mask the peanut taste."

"Great, thank you, Herk. Okay, we've discussed Cornell. What about Hamlin? Any ideas how to ask questions about him and who to approach?"

Dab shook his head. "I don't think we should go there. If we have too few suspects in Cornell's case, we might end up with half a phone book in Hamlin's."

"And we don't want to rile anyone with city or county power," Aster added. "As Dab said before, who would admit to being blackmailed?"

We all fell silent until Fred spoke up.

"You got one more name up there," he pointed out. "That Durley guy. You ever fill everybody in on him?"

"Did I?" I scanned blank faces. "Okay, here's the scoop on Lee Durley."

After I told them what I knew of the private investigator from his website, Fred scratched his jaw. "El Dorado sure comes up a fair amount. Kathy's mother, that fella who up and moved from his apartment, and this guy."

"You think it's significant they all live in El Dorado?" Sherry asked.

"Don't know, but it bears some thinkin' on." He pushed up from the armchair and pulled his walker to him. "I ain't seen your critters lately. Are they still outside?"

"Probably. They went back out after you fed them scraps."

"What makes you think I did that?" he blustered.

"Oh, please, Fred," Sherry said with a grin. "We all know about it."

"Humph. Well, then, I'll round 'em up so they'll be ready to go on home."

Translation, it was time to leave. As soon as I made a flying visit to Bernice Gilroy's to give Fred time to play with Amber and T.C.

Chapter Twenty

MAISE PACKED THE BERNICE BASKET WITH GENERous servings of every dish friends had brought to the Six. I added the banana icebox cake and went down Sherry's gravel drive, out to the street, and then up Bernice's sidewalk. It was later than I usually visited, and I didn't know what programs she watched on Friday night, but I was pretty certain she'd open the door. She knew how to pause a live broadcast.

"Took you long enough, Sissy," she snapped as she hauled me in the door by my arm. "You been at the farmstead for hours."

"An hour and a half, Bernice," I corrected, knowing I'd see her binoculars on the retro kitchen table.

"Don't sass, and get that food on into the kitchen. I'm half starved."

I raised a brow as I followed her and plunked the basket on the table. "Don't you have any food in the house?"

"Nothing I want to eat." Bernice scrunched her face, making her look like a pruned elf. "Show me what you brought."

I named them for her as I handed over each container of the most perishable foods and she stowed them in the fridge. Sliced ham and half a loaf of bread, baked chicken, tuna-noodle casserole, potato salad, mac and cheese, shrimp creole and rice, a container with sweet green peas and another with green beans and bits of bacon. From the peek I got inside the fridge, she *had* been slim on dining choices, but these supplies should last her at least a few days.

She set the cookies, brownies, and lemon bars on her always spotless counter, and I saw that she'd stacked empty plastic containers near the sink. Wonder of wonders! Was she sending those back to the farmhouse? I hoped so. The Six kept supplying containers for the leftovers, and that wasn't a cheap proposition.

"What's this?" she asked as I lifted the icebox cake in its clear plastic container from the basket.

"Banana icebox cake. It has chocolate and white chocolate mousse in it."

She narrowed her eyes. "Who made it?"

"My friend Judy at Great Buns Bakery, but it's a recipe from the Adam Daniel's restaurant. Very rich, very good. I ate it when Eric took me there in June."

She nodded. "Guess that's enough endorsement for me. Now put these containers in your basket, and tell me why your detective arrested Maise and Aster. He ought to know better."

"He's not working the case. The new detective is. Charlene Vogelman."

"Is that Chris Kiddner's girl?"

"You know him?"

"I met him years ago. He moved here from Oklahoma. Worked for the forest people, and then his wife died. Always was a grumpy old guy."

I hid a grin at that. Bernice must have thirty years on Charlene's dad. And grumpy? A bit of the pot calling the kettle black, but I loved her anyway.

"Are you working the case?" she demanded.

"Yes, but we're not making progress narrowing the suspect field. It's making me a little crazy."

"It would. Sissy never liked to be stymied. She forged ahead no matter what."

"If I knew where to forge, I'd do it."

"You looking for one killer or two?"

"We have no clue, but we have more information about Cornell, so we're focusing on his murder." I cocked my head at Bernice. "Was Cornell's love of snickerdoodles common knowledge?"

"Anybody who recalled him at that picnic might remember he gave himself a bellyache on them. It wasn't the first thing folks came to associate with him."

"A bully with a weakness for snickerdoodles? I guess he wouldn't talk about that." I paused. "So what would Mark Harmon do, Bernice?"

"Tell the writers to fix the script, but this is real life. Maybe you ought to hire one of those Magnum guys." At my blank look, she added, "Get with the program, Sissy. *Magnum, P.I.* Tom Selleck's old show. The hunky guy with all the chest hair."

I choked, thankful that I didn't have anything in my mouth. If I had, I would've spewed it across the room.

"Bernice Gilroy!" I exclaimed when I could speak again. "You are a raunchy old lady."

"It's what keeps me young," she said, and made shooing motions. "Take my advice or don't, it's time for my show."

"What are you watching tonight?"

"The news channel. I'm catching up on current events."

The door shut behind me with a distinct click, but I swore I heard her cackling as she went back to the kitchen.

I RETURNED TO THE FARMHOUSE TO FIND HERK HAD taken his leave. The Six had loaded the flip chart, trifold display board, and easel into my trunk along with the leftovers Maise insisted I take home. And though Amber and T.C. were happy enough to jump into the Camry, they looked out the back window at Fred as we headed down the drive. Sometimes I wondered if they'd be happier living with him, having the run of the yard and Fred to dote on them. But they soon scampered into the passenger seat, where I knew they really shouldn't ride, but I hadn't bought them pet car seats yet.

Who was I kidding? I loved their company. I owed them a trip to the dog park, too, where we could play until we were exhausted. Usually I was the one to collapse on a bench first, but I loved romping with them. Maybe we'd go this weekend.

"Okay, girls, about that phone call this afternoon. I need to tell Eric about it, but should I wait till tomorrow?"

Amber sniffed. T.C. just stared at me.

"Tell him tonight?"

T.C. meowed. Amber barked.

"You sure? I bet you just want to see him, don't you?"

A streetlight caught the gleam in their eyes.

"Tell you what, I'll flip a coin when we get home. And don't shake your heads at me. If he's still keeping his distance, he won't come over anyway."

They flopped on the seat, for all intents like kids denied a treat. But when I wheeled into the empty parking lot behind the emporium, they both came alert. A moment later, I thought I knew why. Something white, fastened to the gray alley door, fluttered in the slight breeze.

What on earth?

Maybe it was from Judy telling me she wanted to try the cookie experiment just for fun. But, no. Judy had my cell number. She would've called or texted.

A note from Debbie Nicole? Maybe she'd remembered something and wanted me to call. She didn't have my number. Not unless she'd retrieved it from the library's Caller ID system.

I parked and stared at the piece of paper. I could make out large letters on it, but not large enough to read from so far away. Then I shrugged and opened my car door. It was only a hair past eight o'clock. If the note asked me to call, I would.

I'd scarcely stood when T.C. and Amber shot out of the car right behind me. They sniffed the air and stiffened, their fur standing on end.

"What's wrong, girls?" I asked as I pressed the key fob and heard the trunk unlatch.

Amber answered with a low growl. T.C. hissed.

Just then, my cell rang. I grabbed it without checking the Caller ID.

"Read my note," said the same guttural and partly garbled voice I'd heard this afternoon. "Last warning."

The red phone symbol appeared on the screen, and I stood stock-still, gripping the phone until my fingers cramped. When it rang again, I didn't look at the display.

I answered with, "Stop bothering me, buster."

"What's wrong?" Eric asked. "Where are you, Nixy?"

"In the parking lot. There's a piece of paper taped to the alley door, the animals are acting weird, and I just got a threatening phone call."

"Get back in the car and lock the doors. Now."

I called to T.C. and Amber, but they were pacing the alley.

"Forget them. They'll run if they have to. I'm on the way."

I didn't see anyone lurking nearby, but I slammed the trunk, got in the car, and hit the door locks. In under two minutes, a police car with light bar blazing whipped into the alley at one end, and Eric's truck screeched around the turn at the other. I couldn't see the officer in the squad car, but whoever it was turned on the spotlight and played it over the lot.

Eric jumped out of his truck and slammed the door, a heavy-duty LED flashlight in hand. He swept it over the

Dumpster as he paced around the area, then aimed the light toward the building on the corner.

"Cut the spotlight," he called.

It went dark, but Officer Bryant exited the cruiser and turned on a similar flashlight. He stood by, watching Eric. Presumably waiting for direction.

Amber and T.C. had cowered at the alley door but now bounded over to Eric. "Hello, ladies," I heard him say through the window I'd cracked when the cavalry arrived. "Nixy, you okay?"

"Fine," I hollered, opening the car door. I climbed out, my heart still racing but my knees not the least bit wobbly.

Eric crossed the space between us and tugged me into his arms for a quick hard hug. "Hey."

"Hey yourself."

"Stay here for a minute, will you? We're going to look around."

I nodded and called T.C and Amber to me. This time they came immediately, and sat at my feet as though guarding me.

Eric motioned to Doug Bryant, and they converged on the alley door, flashlight beams aimed at the note.

"Call the techs, Doug," I heard Eric say. "It's a long shot, but we might get lucky and find prints."

Bryant headed to his patrol car, and Eric joined me. He took my hands, leaned against the car, and tugged me closer.

I swallowed the lump of nerves in my throat. "What's on the note?"

He squeezed my fingers gently. "It reads, *Stop asking questions*."

I gulped. "In letters cut out of a magazine? Handwritten?"

"Nothing so dramatic as magazine letters. It looks to be a computer printout. I'll have the crime scene techs confirm it."

"Really? The note won't have to go to the state lab?"

"Oh, it will. All evidence has to be officially processed,

but the tech can give me a simple opinion. Now tell me about the phone call."

"There have been two of them today," I said, and went on to give the few details I could.

As I spoke, Eric's mouth grew tighter, his expression stony, and his grip on my hands near crushing. When an SUV pulled into the parking lot, he released me. I guessed the crime scene techs were on call, because that was who climbed out just as a dark sedan cruised in before they unloaded their equipment.

"Why is Vogelman here?"

"Nixy, the threats are related to her case." He quirked a brow at me. "Unless you're asking questions about something else."

"Nope, just the one," I said, and put on the happiest face I could manage.

"Then be nice," he said so only I could hear him. "She's doing her job."

Since Vogelman wore a ferocious scowl along with her dark green pantsuit, keeping my happy face in place took some effort.

"Ms. Nix." She greeted me as she reached us.

"Detective."

"What's going on?" she asked Eric.

"Threatening note on the emporium's back door, and Nixy's received two similar phone calls since this afternoon," Eric summarized.

Vogelman glanced at Jan Blair and the second crime scene tech, both busy taking photos of the note, the door, and the alley.

"What's the note say?"

"Stop asking questions."

"That's a threat? Sounds more like good advice."

"Detective," I said sharply, "I am not amused."

She gave me a long look, easy to see in the ambient light cast by lamp posts and the officers' flashlights. When she finally sighed, she said, "Neither am I. Will you please come to the station so I can take your statement?"

"When?"

"Now."

I looked over at Eric, then back at Vogelman. "I'll need to put my pets upstairs."

"Not until I go through the building, you won't," Eric said.

"Did this creep try to break in?"

"There are no scratches around the door or deadbolt, but I want to be certain he didn't leave any surprises."

"And here I thought I couldn't get any angrier," I said through clenched teeth. "This guy is going down."

Amber rose to her feet and pawed the side of my leg with a sympathetic whine. T.C. looked as if she wanted to leap into my arms but settled for rubbing her cheek on my tennis shoe.

Vogelman cleared her throat. "Ms. Nix, why don't you bring your pets to the station with you, and we'll get the formalities taken care of so you can get home."

I didn't gape, though I wanted to. I smiled. "Thank you, Detective. I appreciate it."

She inclined her head. "I'll meet you there."

She strolled back to her car, and I admit I was speechless for all of ten seconds.

"Wow, that's some concession," I said quietly to Eric.

"Will you be able to hold your temper with her? Count to ten or something?"

"I'm good. I can count way above ten."

"Give me your key, Nixy Drew, and be careful."

VOGELMAN SAT IN A CUSHIONED SWIVEL CHAIR, A lined white pad on the gray metal desk in front of her, a pen in hand. I settled in the unpadded metal seat opposite her. Amber stretched herself across my feet, and T.C. softly purred in my lap. I felt my tension drain away even as Vogelman cleared her throat.

She told me to start at the beginning, so I did. I related that Eleanor and I had been questioning people, and I told her who when she asked. She'd talked to most of them before we had, and it wasn't a state secret anyway.

"Wait, did you ever talk to the Darbys?" I asked.

"The couple who'd been out of town? I interviewed them yesterday."

I waited for her to elaborate, but she only urged me to continue. Rats!

"Today I talked with Debbie Nicole at the library."

"Why her?"

I hesitated, then picked my way through what to say. "I'd heard about a man she worked with who suddenly moved out of Ozark Arms. There was some mystery around that, so I asked her for the down-low."

"And?"

"I also promised her I wouldn't tell the story to anyone but Eric."

"Are you trying to annoy me?" she asked mildly, but I heard the ire in her tone.

"I'm keeping my word," I said. "Oh, and I called the library this evening to alert her about the weird call I got, but she wasn't in."

"You think she might be in danger?"

"I don't know, but I didn't want her to freak out."

"Like you did?"

"I was shaken and concerned, Detective. Not freaked out."

"Uh-huh."

She palmed her cell phone and tapped the screen. "Eric? Are you finished with the walk-through at Ms. Nix's?"

She listened. "Right, I do want to see the note, but I don't need to sign off on the chain-of-evidence form. Ask one of the techs to come to the station with it and you."

She disconnected the call, drummed her fingers on the

desktop, and then opened several screechy drawers. The noise made Amber lift her head and perk her ears, but when Vogelman fished some stapled papers from the last drawer and closed it, Amber settled again. I wasn't a master at reading upside down, but the printed list looked like a roster. Vogelman flipped to the second page and made another call.

"Betty, this is Detective Vogelman. I hope I'm not calling too late." She paused. "Nothing to watch out for, but I need Debbie Nicole Samp's number."

The woman across from me chuckled, and I marveled at it. Oh, sure, she'd been friendly with me initially, but lately I'd seen nothing but her cop face. Well, except when she allowed me to bring the critters here.

Vogelman jotted down a number. "Thanks, Betty. I'll check in with you soon."

The detective disconnected and caught me staring, so I cleared my throat. "Friends in high places?"

"Neighborhood watch connection. Do you want to phone Debbie Nicole, or do you want me to do it?"

"I'll call," I said, and tapped in the number as Vogelman recited it.

After apologizing for calling her home number, I told Debbie Nicole about the warning calls but not about the note. She said she hadn't received a call, but thanked me for the heads-up.

"I found some memos to myself in an old file," she told me before she disconnected. "I haven't had a chance to look through them all, but I'll let you know if I get more information about Dennis's family."

As I disconnected, Eric came in along with Jan Blair, who handed the suitably sealed note to Vogelman.

"It's computer generated on standard printer paper," Jan said. "I can't see a single fingerprint on the tape, so there may not be any on the paper."

Vogelman nodded. "Thanks. Did you find anything else?"

"We bagged some cigarette butts, and candy and gum wrappers, but nothing of particular interest."

"I figured. Go on home after you finish packing this with the rest."

Eric had hung back but pulled up a chair and sat at the end of the desk between me and Vogelman. I figured he was positioning himself to intercept me if I launched myself over the desk at the detective. Which I would never do. Still, it gave him the perfect spot to watch.

"Ms. Nix, tell Eric what you wouldn't tell me."

"Hmm. I suppose I can't be faulted if you happen to overhear. Plus, Eric won't have to repeat the information to you and risk getting it wrong."

"Hey, I'm right here."

I shot him a smile. "Okay, here's the deal, but please don't bring this up with Debbie Nicole unless it's absolutely necessary."

I relayed the librarian's story about Dennis, his injured back, Cornell's harassing him for being gay, and reinjuring his back when Cornell supposedly tried to run Dennis down. I also stressed that the overdose could've been an accident, only leaving out that Dennis had told Debbie Nicole to let him die.

"I find it extra odd that the caller didn't see fit to threaten me until after I left the library."

Vogelman clicked her pen three times. "What you got is more a warning than a threat, but I agree the timing is interesting. Are you certain the caller was a man?"

"The voice was part garbled and part mechanical sounding, so no, I'm not certain. What I am sure of was the menace in the voice."

Chapter Twenty-one

ERIC ESCORTED ME HOME, ALTHOUGH I DROVE BEcause he'd sprinted to the station when he got Vogelman's call. How he ran in boots, I didn't know. I could barely trot in tennis shoes. I just didn't have a runner's build.

That was my story, and I was sticking to it.

The crime scene techs were gone, of course, but I could see the black fingerprint powder against the light gray alley door. The door and jamb weren't coated in dust, but it was enough to be noticeable, even in the ambient light.

"I need to clean off the door before the Six see it."

"Let's take Amber and T.C. around the block, and then I'll help you."

Loving Eric the way they did, my pets did their prancing, sniffing, and bug-batting thing. This wasn't unusual behavior, but they looked to him after every other "trick," like a child who wanted to know a parent was watching with approval. On the way back, Amber found a plush spot of grass near a corner streetlight and flopped over to have a roll, her body twisting to get a good doggie Nirvana scratch. T.C.

followed suit, and I had to wonder just what they were rolling in. T.C. sprang up first, then pounced onto Amber's belly, which made Amber scramble to her feet with a paw to T.C.'s face. When Eric burst out laughing, both critters stopped to look up at him, and I swear they preened.

Upstairs in my place, I refreshed their water bowls, then grabbed a couple of clean dust rags and spray bottles of both plain water and bathroom cleaner. Eric rechecked the apartment, which wasn't necessary but was touching.

We went to work cleaning the outer door first. Eric trained his truck's high beams on the back of the building and used his police-issue flashlight to be sure we did a thorough job. Then he turned off his headlights and locked the truck, and we shifted to the inside. The workroom overhead lights didn't pick up as much dust, but we wiped down the areas with another clean rag before spritzing water and cleaner.

Amber barked her approval when we finished, and T.C. just looked up from licking her paw.

"Will you help me grab some stuff from my trunk?"

He arched a brow. "The murder board?"

"How did you know?"

"It's not in the workroom or your apartment."

"All things considered, I'm glad the Six hauled it all to the farmhouse."

"Let's go, and then we'll head upstairs for the night."

We'll go up for the night? My heartbeat kicked up, but he probably hadn't meant what I thought. Probably that was my wistful thinking.

Back upstairs, Amber fetched her soft disk for Eric to throw. He did, then got out T.C.'s fuzzy snake toy. Meantime, I made coffee. I wouldn't be sleeping for a while, and Eric said he'd have a mug, too.

"I wonder if the Silver Six have already heard there was action here tonight," I mused.

"If they had, they'd be on the phone right now."

"Or come tearing over here. Since neither of those happened, I can wait to tell them tomorrow."

The coffeemaker sputtered to mark ending its cycle, and I brought our mugs to the living room. The critters must've worn out fast because Amber had curled up at Eric's hip, and T.C. had stretched out on the middle cushion behind him on the sofa back. I sat cross-legged next to Eric. Time to ask him some pertinent questions.

He preempted me, though. "Are you feeling calmer?"

"I'm feeling frustrated. I want to know who made those calls and left the note. I wish Lilyvale were wealthy enough to have a super crime lab of its own."

"Believe me, so do I, but that might not help us find your 'unavailable caller.'"

"At least Charlene Vogelman is taking me seriously." I paused. "This *does* prove to her that someone else is behind the murders, doesn't it?"

"It's certainly given her doubts about Aster and Maise." He took my hand and held my gaze with those sexy brown eyes of his. "Nixy, you need to be extra alert to your surroundings and stop asking questions."

"Done and done. Eleanor and I had run out of people to talk to anyway. What I don't get is how this guy knows that we've been asking questions."

"People talk. You know that. It's possible that someone you interviewed gabbed to others, and the killer somehow heard about it."

"Gossip Central at its best," I agreed, though I had the nagging thought it was more than that. "It's still weird that this guy waited until after I talked to Debbie Nicole to start up with me. Do you suppose he could've bugged me or the shop?"

His eyes widened, but he didn't scoff at the possibility. "Let's think about that. You don't carry your purse all the time, and it wouldn't do much good to put a tracker on your car."

He was right, of course. I didn't carry my brown suede hobo bag often now that my commute was a flight of stairs. I could always pop up and snag whatever I needed, and my trifold wallet and the red cowhide flat wallet I'd inherited from my mother could have cobwebs on them for all the use they got. I kept some tens and twenties in a kitchen drawer under the utensil tray. If I planned to stop at Great Buns or at Lilies Café, I stuck a bill in the pocket of whatever cargo pants or jeans I was wearing that day. As for tracking my car, that would be a snore fest. I never went far.

I smiled. "I see your point. Bugging the shop wouldn't make for interesting tidbits either. The Six and I don't generally talk about cases in the store. We meet in Fred's workroom."

"How many cases are you working on?"

"Just Cornell's murder. We gave up on Dex Hamlin's. If he was the big bad blackmailer we've heard he was, the suspect list is too long to imagine."

"Yeah, that's what we're finding. Motive in spades, and plenty of the suspects own firearms, but there's no one we can nail with opportunity."

I leaned my back against the sofa's armrest. "You know, Hamlin might've killed Cornell. If they were buds in the past, Dex might've known about the peanut allergy. He might also have known Cornell was living in his car and where he would park overnight."

"And just happened to feed him deadly cookies?"

"The cookies could have nothing to do with any of this. Hamlin could've forced Cornell to eat a handful of peanuts. Or forced him to inhale peanut dust."

"Except we didn't find a package of nuts in the car, empty or not. I don't suppose it will hurt to tell you this now, but Jan Blair is sensitive to peanuts. She never smelled a thing, never had so much as a tickle in her nose or throat. Which reminds me, what were all your questions about this afternoon?"

"I was fishing, but you'll love this!"

"Tell me."

I wiggled into a more comfortable position. "On the theory that the cookies contained peanut something-or-other, we're stumped on why Cornell didn't detect the smell or taste before he'd eaten too many. Eleanor suggested I brainstorm the issue with Judy, and she came up with a brilliantly simple possible solution."

"How brilliant, how simple, and how possible?"

"Substituting some peanut flour for regular white flour. And Herk, Dr. Jones, thinks we're right on target."

"That's ingenious, Nixy. I never would've thought of it, but I'll mention it to Charlene." Eric took my hand and scooched a little closer. "I've got your back, you know. In spite of how Charlene has handled the investigation, she's been doing her job to the best of her ability."

"By arresting Maise and Aster?"

"Granted, the arrest seemed extreme."

"Extreme on steroids, Eric, but I know you couldn't interfere."

"So you and I are okay?"

"We're good."

He cupped my jaw with his warm hand, and the sizzle shot from my head to my toes.

"Want to seal it with a kiss?"

I put a dash of sauce in my smile. "That can be arranged."

As our lips met, T.C. chirped at our shoulders, and Amber sighed.

Or that could've been me.

SOMETIME IN THE NIGHT, MY SUBCONSCIOUS URGED me to a decision. I'd call Lee Durley and ask about his services and fees. Bernice Gilroy's comment about Magnum had planted the seed, I was sure, but what could it hurt? Eric couldn't actively investigate Charlene's case, so I had no help in that quarter. He *had* promised to let me know when lab reports came in, but I was tired of spinning my wheels.

I rushed through my morning tasks. I didn't know if Durley's office was open on Saturday, and leaving a voice-mail message wasn't ideal, but I wanted to call before I lost my resolve. And before the Six arrived at the store. I didn't want to share my suggestion with them until I had more information.

I hadn't bothered to set up the trifold board on the easel the night before, so I did it now. I'd been over the lists and possibilities until my eyes crossed, but it wouldn't hurt to make a few notes for the meeting. If there was to be a meeting.

I pulled up the PI's website on my tablet and called the number. On the third ring, a man answered. I recognized his voice and spoke before I chickened out.

"Mr. Durley, this is Leslee Nix. Nixy. I met you at the folk art festival last weekend. With my dog and cat," I added, to jog his memory.

"Your dog saved my cell phone, right?"

"She did. I'm sorry to bother you on a Saturday, but I need to ask about hiring you."

A momentary silence, and then, "What seems to be the trouble?"

I explained as succinctly as I could. "I'm not sure this would go to trial, but I'm worried about my family being under a cloud. They're elderly, in case I didn't mention that. Is this the kind of case you'd take, and what are your fees?"

Again there was a short pause, and I heard papers shuffle at his end. "I'm not sure what I can do for you in this instance, but I'd be happy to meet with you. The consultation is free, and we can go from there."

"That works," I said, releasing a relieved breath. "Is there any chance you can meet with us today about one? Our work-study girls will be in by then and can watch the store for a few hours."

"I can see you at two," he countered.

"Great, thank you! Is your office address the same as the one on your website?"

"Sure is. Do you need directions?"

I didn't. I could navigate with my trusty tablet app, but I jotted them down anyway. After thanking him again, I disconnected and felt better for having done *some*thing to forge ahead. I really did hate to be stymied.

THE SIX WEREN'T HAPPY WITH MY EXECUTIVE DECIsion to consult with Durley, but they grudgingly agreed to the meeting at two. All but Fred, that is. He said Ida Bollings was coming to pick up her can opener, and he didn't want to miss her.

We opened the shop to a group of early birds, and I minded the checkout counter while Aster, Sherry, and Eleanor restocked their wares. When I asked where they'd found the time to craft, they told me they'd put finishing touches on partly completed projects. It was good to see more lotions, balms, painted gourds, and whittled figures on display, and some of the goods were snapped up as soon as they hit the shelves.

At eleven thirty we took a delivery of items from our artists. Ten pieces of semiprecious stone jewelry from Diane Grindall, an 8 × 10 framed mosaic with an autumn theme and colors from Mags Deets, and two large stained-glass pieces from Sarah Swanson packed individually. I'd let Jasmine and Kathy put out the jewelry and mosaic, but I'd need to rearrange the window display to handle the stained glass.

The girls came in early for their afternoon shift, so at eleven fifty the Six and I stopped for lunch. The sandwiches were made with the last of the lunch meat friends had dropped off at the house, Maise told me. Slaw and corn chips weren't her idea of healthy side dishes, but we happily munched away. T.C. and Amber sat under the worktable at

Fred's feet, and I pretended not to notice when he slipped the critters a bite or three.

At five after twelve, the door between the workshop and store opened, and I jumped up to hold it for Ida Bollings as she came through with her walker. My pets didn't scamper over to greet her. They knew to stay out of the way of canes and walkers.

"I come bearing pear bread, but don't let me interrupt your lunch," she said as she handed me the loaf. "I just came by to get my can opener."

"Got it right here," Fred called. "Come sit a minute."

Dab pulled out a bar stool, and Ida pushed her walker to the worktable where we were seated. Then she paused to eye the trifold display board. After all of two seconds, she pointed at each photo.

"Knew of him, knew of him, saw him last weekend."

I gaped at her. "You saw who, Ida?"

"The fella right there in the corner picture."

The air in the room stilled, none of us spoke, and the Six looked as shocked as I felt. When the pulse in my throat slowed enough for me to speak, I said, "Ida, that's Lee Durley. He was at the folk art festival."

"Humph. Not when I saw him, he wasn't."

Could Ida have the information we needed? Torn between excitement and dread, I asked, "Ida, where did you see Durley? And when?"

She scooted her walker and herself to the seat Dab had pulled out for her. "It was Sunday night at the convenience store. I got out of my church ladies meeting late and went home but decided I wanted a root beer."

It was all I could do not to drag information from her, but I swallowed my impatience. "Ida, this is important. Are you sure Lee Durley was the man you saw?"

"He was in the parking lot under the pole light they put up near the Dumpster, and he was with the murdered man.

Cornell Lewis, I mean, since that obnoxious Dexter Hamlin was murdered, too."

"So Lee Durley was actually with Cornell on Sunday night?" I pressed, completely shell-shocked.

"Yes, and come to think of it, I think I saw the Hamlin man buying beer that night. The store was busy, though. I might be wrong." She cocked her head at me. "You know what he drives?"

"He has a white pickup."

"Could've been him, then. A white pickup left about the same time I did."

"Good Lord," Sherry breathed.

I sat hard on my own bar stool, gathered my thoughts, and looked at Ida. "When you saw the two men, what were they doing?"

"Just talking far as I could tell. The younger man, Durley, was in some sort of a white jumpsuit and was holding a small sack. He opened it, and Cornell looked inside."

"Did you hear them say anything?"

"I heard their voices, but nothing I could make out. I got in my car, and as I drove off, they both got into another car."

"They were in the same car? Together?"

"Girl, that's what I said. What is the fuss about?"

Fred chuckled. "Ida, you may just'a blown a murder case wide open."

Chapter Twenty-two

I WENT HALF CRAZY WAITING FOR IDA TO LEAVE SO the Six and I could talk freely. Not that we ran her off. She was headed to Virginia's Jewelers two doors up the street from us, then on to Great Buns, and hadn't meant to linger as long as she had.

"We have an appointment to meet with a killer?" Aster asked when it was only the seven of us.

Maise huffed. "We can't be certain of that, can we?"

"I do believe Ida seeing Cornell and Durley together is beyond suspicious."

"And to see Dex Hamlin in the same place?" Dab shook his head. "That isn't coincidence."

Sherry flapped her hands at me. "For heaven's sake, child, call Eric."

I stepped away while the Six cleaned up the paper plates from lunch and refilled their mugs with sweet tea. Amber and T.C. must've sensed my agitation, because they paced alongside me as I muttered, "Pick up. Come on, pick up."

Eric didn't. I left a message for him to call me, and

punched in Charlene Vogelman's cell number. The one I'd had since I first met her but never had the occasion to use. No luck there either. Dang! Should I leave what was bound to be a complicated message? Would she give the least bit of credence to our new information? In spite of Eric's assurance, I wasn't convinced she believed the harassing calls and note were from the real culprit. I wouldn't be until she dropped the charges against Aster and Maise.

"Eric isn't answering, and neither is Vogelman," I reported, and saw six eager expressions fall.

"Figures that idjit detective ain't on the job when we need her."

"I left messages to call, and I'll try again. In fact, I can call the sheriff's office. The nonemergency number. Maybe Megan Paulson is on duty."

Just as I turned on the screen, my cell rang and displayed the library's number.

"Nixy," Debbie Nicole said when I answered. "I was looking through those papers I told you about and found something. We talked about having some speakers talk about their unusual jobs, and Dennis suggested a private investigator. Specifically, his stepbrother."

"Did that happen to be Lee Durley?"

"You know him?"

"After a fashion."

"Well, Dennis was very proud of him and told me they were close. That all the stepsiblings were. I'll bet Lee picked Dennis up from the hospital and cleaned out his apartment, too."

"I think you'd win that bet, Debbie Nicole. Thanks for letting me know."

"Out with it, child," Sherry commanded when I'd disconnected and looked up.

I relayed the highlights of the call, and Dab nodded.

"He'd certainly have motive to go after Cornell. But why wait so long?"

"Too busy helping his brother and the family deal with the overdose trauma?" Aster offered.

"Then Cornell was fired and left town," I added as I sank onto my seat. "It'd be easy for Durley to lose track of him. At least for a while."

I patted my lap expecting T.C. to hop up, but both she and Amber sat on their haunches beneath the easel and murder board, heads turning to each of us as they listened to our conversation.

"I do believe a PI would have the skills and tools to find him again, even if that took time."

"Right, Eleanor, and when he knew Cornell would be in Lilyvale, Durley showed up to take revenge," Sherry concluded.

"I wonder if he knew about the allergy and the snickerdoodle fetish?" Maise mused.

"We're losing sight of one thing," Dab said. "We have a consultation with a killer. What do we do? Cancel?"

I opened my mouth, but Fred spoke first.

"I say we storm the varmint's office."

"And do what? Hang him from the yardarm?" Maise asked.

"I'd sure like to give him a taste of his own medicine," Aster snapped. "Imagine setting us up to be charged with murder!"

"You know," Aunt Sherry said slowly, "I'll bet Dex Hamlin knew Durley killed Cornell and was blackmailing him. There could be evidence in his house."

"Now wait a minute," I said, but the Six were on a roll. They were blowing off steam, I assured myself, so I shut my mouth and let the conversation flow fast and furious.

"How do you propose we get in?"

"Fred can pick the lock."

"Where will the rest of us be?"

"Nixy goes with Fred, and we five will keep the appointment at his office. Surely we can keep him busy for thirty or forty-five minutes."

"I do believe that might work."

"You in, missy?"

All eyes turned to me, and I shook my head. "Have you lost your collective minds? We can't break into Durley's house."

"Why not?" Maise asked. "Aster and I can't get into more trouble than we're already in."

"Charlene Vogelman changed her mind about you," I said, stretching the truth only a tad. "Besides, we don't know where Durley lives."

"Eleanor can do a property search."

"And if she can't find the information, Lamar can. He's a genius with search engines," Aster said earnestly.

"Forget it. We'll all be in the slammer if we get caught, and—"

"Not if'n we can get the goods on this skunk," Fred interrupted.

"Y'all, we absolutely, positively cannot do this. For heaven's sake, if Durley is really guilty, he's already killed two people. He won't think twice about adding us to the list."

"Now, missy, he cain't kill all of us. Dumpin' our bodies would keep him hoppin' for a week."

Growing desperate to convince them this was lunacy, I said, "Y'all, the man has a gun. We can't protect ourselves."

"He'll be meeting with us," Sherry said. "He won't have a reason to hurt perfectly harmless seniors."

"'Asides, I learnt to throw knives as a boy. I can do the same with a screwdriver, and I'm deadly at twenty paces."

I wanted to laugh, but the urge to cry was stronger. Oh, so very much stronger. I tried another tack to end this crazy scheme. "Durley is going to wonder why we didn't all show up."

"Did you tell him how many of us were coming?" Sherry asked.

"Well, no."

"If he asks, we simply tell him Fred had a fix-it emergency."

"What about me?"

"We'll tell him Amber got sick," Maise said.

Amber cocked her head. *"Ur?"* I took that as dog for *Say what?*

Aster clapped her hands. "Oh, that's good. We'll say she threw up all over you just as we were leaving."

Now Amber lowered her head and growled. I was right there with her. Growl, howl. Either would do.

"I do believe you'd best give in, Nixy," Eleanor said gently.

"You're on board with this?"

Maise crossed her arms over her chest. "We're doing it whether you go along or not. Damn the torpedoes and full speed ahead."

I gave up and let my head *thunk* on the table.

I HELD OUT HOPE THAT ELEANOR WOULDN'T FIND Lee Durley's residence, but Jasmine's boyfriend had stopped in to see her, and Lamar helped search for and locate the property. Was it a legal search? I didn't want to know.

I also held hope that Eric or Charlene would call me back. I hadn't wanted to explain the whys and wherefores of our accidental discovery in a voice mail, but I was growing desperate. We had to leave in ten minutes to make it to El Dorado on time.

I placed calls to both Eric and Charlene again as I trudged upstairs. Again no luck, but this time I left messages as clear and concise as I could. In the apartment, I grabbed my hobo bag. It showed its age and wear, but it held my pepper spray. Except when it didn't. Dang. Checkbook and extra cash. A pen and a small spiral notebook with little pockets for receipts. Sunglasses case. Travel pack of tissues. Three battered Band-Aids. No pepper spray, and I had no clue where I'd put it, no time to search. Maybe I'd pick up a broken chunk of concrete curbing from the alley. Any weapon was better than none.

All the lavender spray in Aster's arsenal couldn't make me feel good about breaking and entering.

DAB DROVE THE LADIES TO DURLEY'S OFFICE, AND I drove my white Camry to the address we had for Lee Durley. Not to insult Fred's ride, but his truck was more likely to attract a neighbor's attention.

I'd programmed Durley's office address into my tablet's navigation app and gave Maise the written directions, too. I plugged his house address into my phone's nav app and gave the cell to Fred. I'd never traveled far with him, and he proved to be a backseat driver. He talked, lectured, and told me how to drive all the way to El Dorado, but had grown quieter as we got closer to our destination. When we turned onto Durley's street, the silence in the car was thick. He might be having an attack of conscience. He might be having an attack of nerves. He might be having a heart attack. He still wouldn't back out, so I didn't bother to offer the option.

We cruised around the block to get the lay of the land. Durley's 1960s-era ranch-style house didn't have a garage. Just a carport, and there were no vehicles in his driveway or in front of his house. In a stroke of luck, the house next door to Durley's was for sale, *and* a high evergreen hedge ran down the driveway, separating the properties. Instinct and watching crime shows told me I should park on another block, but I didn't want Fred to walk that far. Besides, after I backed into the for-sale house drive and parked, I hopped out to peer through a gap in the front room drapes. No furniture, and several flyers were strewn on the front porch. I took both clues to mean the house was empty and trotted back to my partner in crime.

"Remember the plan?"

"I ain't senile, missy. Course I remember. If'n a neighbor stops us or somebody's at Durley's house, you turn on the charm and use your gift of gab."

I made sure my cell was muted as we headed to Durley's, then dropped it in my cargo pocket. The fist-sized chunk of concrete in my hobo bag bounced against my ribs, but it was a reassuring weight. Thankfully, the sidewalks and walkways to the houses were relatively flat and in good repair and didn't slow Fred down. He *clank-clunk*ed his walker along at a good clip, and we soon stood on Durley's small porch. Since we had no clue if Durley had a wife, girlfriend, roommate, or heck, a cleaning lady, I rang the doorbell and then knocked. Twice. No sounds of movement from inside, and no dogs barking.

"Are you good to go?" I asked quietly.

"Bet your nuts 'n' bolts."

We both donned white exam gloves that I'd stuck in my bag, the kind we used when we cleaned the store. Fred slipped a long brown case from the tool belt on his walker, and I held it for him as he extracted several gadgets. How long he'd owned a professional lockpick kit, I didn't want to know. He certainly was proficient with it, though, because in a minute flat, he gave me a broad smile.

"Got it."

"You're a man of many talents, Fred. Now, remember, we only have about twenty minutes to search."

"Then let's get 'er done."

He opened the door, and we froze waiting for an alarm to sound. Nothing.

"It might be a silent alarm." Maybe it was silly to whisper, but who yells when they're breaking and entering?

Fred clomped over the threshold and peered at the wall beside the door, where a security box was mounted. No red light, no green light, no lights at all.

"Maybe he forgot to set it," Fred murmured.

A private investigator who forgot to set his alarm? I shrugged. It could happen, but we needed to move fast just in case.

"Where'd you want to search first, missy? Where'd a guy like this keep the gun he used on Hamlin?"

"On his person?"

Fred rolled his eyes at me. "How 'bout a backup weapon?"

"Let's look for an office."

The house retained its original layout, so it wasn't difficult to find our way through the living-dining room, past the opening to the kitchen, and on to the hall, where we found a bathroom and three small bedrooms. The wood floors creaked now and then, but the whole place was neat as a pin, almost as if no one lived there.

In the last bedroom facing the front of the house, we found an executive-sized gray metal desk, a two-drawer lateral file cabinet made of cheap laminate that had seen better days, and a black desk chair. The file cabinet was locked, and the shallow middle drawer held nothing but pens, pencils, and paper clips. Fred started searching the four deeper drawers marching down one end of the desk, and I took the ones on the other side.

In the last drawer, I hit pay dirt. A manila file labeled simply CORNELL. I yanked it out, opened it, and quickly leafed through page after page.

"Whatcha got there?" Fred asked.

"A lot of notes about Cornell. Where he was, what he was doing."

"Anything 'bout Durley killin' him?"

"No, but we don't have time for me to read the whole thing. This should be enough for Vogelman to act on. Let's go."

"What about the gun? Could be in the closet."

I itched to get the heck out of there but stuffed the folder in my bag and opened the closet door. No rack of rifles and pistols, knives and swords. Nothing but a three-tier bookshelf loaded with printer paper, envelopes of every size, and a stack of business cards.

I shut the door, made sure the desk drawers were properly closed, and put the chair back in the position we'd found it. We made tracks for the front door but paused where the hall emptied into the living-dining room. I peered out, scanning the space. Why, I don't know. If the coast wasn't clear, we were sunk.

"Hold up, missy," Fred said when I was halfway to freedom.

"What's wrong?"

"I been thinking 'bout that peanut flour brainstorm Judy had. Maybe there's some in Durley's kitchen. Let's look."

"We have the file, and that's incriminating enough. We need to get out of here."

"But findin' that ingredient would be like findin' the smokin' gun. Bound to seal the deal for that idjit detective."

Fred headed toward the kitchen. I had no choice other than to follow, but my itching-to-get-out feeling tripled. This room was done in bachelor brown and tan with large ceramic floor tiles. I plopped my bag on the Corian counter to help Fred search the cabinets. We found a tiny pantry with baking soda, baking powder, sugar, and white flour, but no peanut flour.

I pulled my phone from my cropped pants pocket to check the time. We'd been inside the house eighteen minutes, and I had eight new messages. Some texts, some voice mails. I read the first text from Eleanor.

BUG OUT!

For a second, I couldn't breathe, and then I exhaled in a whoosh.

"Fred, we have to go right now."

I dropped the phone into my pocket and snatched my bag by its top with a suddenly sweaty hand. The file added to the weight of the concrete lump hidden there as I whirled to leave.

Except Lee Durley's frame blocked the entire doorway.

Chapter Twenty-three

MY HEARTBEAT STUTTERED, THEN RACED. MY GAZE locked on the shoulder holster strapped across his chest, a gun nestled inside it. My stomach plummeted.

I met Durley's steady gaze, and oddly, his eyes weren't brimming with malice and evil. He didn't even look particularly angry. Instead an amused half smile curved his lips, and that frightened me more.

I knew this plot had been a bad idea.

Durley held up a small tan sack with PEANUT FLOUR in red letters and swung it side to side tauntingly.

"Looking for this?"

"Matter a' fact, we are," Fred said from behind me. "Hand it over, and we'll be on our way."

Durley laughed and shook his head. "Nice try, old man. You aren't going anywhere but where I tell you."

"Who you callin' old?" Fred grumbled.

Frightened as I was, Fred's bravado helped me quell my head-to-toe trembling so I could think.

Durley drew his gun and gestured toward the living room. "Come on out here."

If I could swing my bag at his head fast and hard—

"Move!"

Durley stepped back, out of the doorway, and I eyed the distance between us. I'd have to lunge at him in order to land a hit anywhere on his body. Should I pretend to trip? If I smacked him hard enough to disable him, I might be able to kick his gun away and we could escape.

"Ms. Nix, give it up."

I blinked. "What?"

"I see the wheels turning. You won't get the best of me, so move it."

The part of me that hated being bullied rebelled. "Or what? You'll shoot us where we stand?"

Surprise crossed his face. "I'm not a monster, Ms. Nix, and I don't want to shoot you. I'm taking you hostage."

"Right, like you won't shoot a hostage. Bad guys don't let witnesses live, and you've already killed two men."

"They deserved it. You don't. Not if you cooperate," he ended with a scowl. "Living room. Now."

I didn't trust him, but I was short on options at the moment. I edged toward the doorway with Fred's walker *clank-clunk*ing behind me.

"What about Fred? Will you let him go?" I asked, again judging the distance between Durley and me. Too far. Whacking him was a no-go.

"I'll tie him up and leave him here."

Fred humphed. "You and what army, varmint?"

"Actually, Ms. Nix will tie you. I'll check her work."

I eased into the dining area and kept backing up as Fred followed. Maybe it was just nerves, but even with Durley's gun steadily pointed at us, I wanted answers.

"Why did you set Aster and Maise up to take the blame for Cornell's death?"

"That wasn't intentional," he said offhandedly as he

dropped the bag of flour on the dining table. "I'd aimed to shoot the worm, but I couldn't resist making him suffer when I saw the snickerdoodles at the hot dog stand."

"So you went home and whipped up a batch of cookies using peanut flour?"

He narrowed his eyes. "How did you tumble to that?"

"My best friend is a baker."

"Hats off to your friend. My sister has gone gluten-free. It was child's play to borrow her bag of flour."

"How did you know about Cornell's peanut allergy?" I held my purse slightly behind my leg.

"I'm an investigator, Ms. Nix. I admit I lost track of him for a while. I had family issues to settle. Once I found him again, I learned everything about him, including that he had a peanut allergy and a heart problem."

I stopped between a faux-suede chair and a sofa, and Fred stood beside me. A small round coffee table sat in front of the sofa. Rope was coiled on the sofa back near where Durley stood. A lot of rope.

"Your purse looks heavy and lumpy, Ms. Nix. Put it there on the coffee table. Now."

I reluctantly lowered my purse, hoping the concrete piece inside didn't clunk. If I kept him talking long enough, maybe reinforcements would arrive. The seniors had sent texts. They had Durley's home address. And if they didn't storm the house themselves, they would've called the local police. Time to use my gift for gab.

"You were in the square when Hamlin beat up Cornell," I said. "I saw you on the sidewalk."

Durley chuckled, but it wasn't a pleasant sound. "For a few minutes, I thought he'd do the killing for me."

"How did you keep track of Cornell after he left the square Sunday morning? It wasn't dumb luck that you were at the convenience store on Sunday night when he was," I said.

"You have been busy," he said, his brows climbing to his

forehead. "Did you know it was me this morning when you called for the appointment?"

I shifted so Fred would be behind me. "We put everything together about an hour ago."

"We?" he asked sharply. "How many people know about me?"

I shrugged. "About a dozen, including two Lilyvale detectives and a county deputy. Trite as it sounds, you really won't get away with this."

"Oh, I will, because I think you're bluffing." He tilted his head. "Out of curiosity, how did you decide I was guilty?"

"Fred's sweetheart saw you with Cornell last Sunday night in the parking lot."

"Ida ain't my sweetheart, missy."

I flapped a hand at him but kept my gaze on Durley. "And then the Lilyvale librarian remembered that Dennis Moreno had a stepbrother who was a PI. That's when we knew for sure. We hatched this fiasco on the fly."

He chuckled. "All in all, you didn't do a bad job of it."

"You caught us, Durley," I said. "How is that good, and why didn't you keep the appointment?"

"I had a hunch, so I asked my partner to take the meeting. This isn't what I'd planned for today, but it'll do. I know how to disappear."

From the corner of my eye, I saw Fred hide something in one hand. I didn't know what it was or what he meant to do, but I needed to keep Durley distracted.

"So how *did* you get to Cornell? Didn't he know who you were?"

"Not a clue." He smiled widely. "I followed him after the fight Sunday morning. Told him I was investigating Hamlin and chatted him up. Put a tracker on his car."

"And later you met up with him and gave him the bag of cookies? Did you put them on the plate or did he?"

"What's funny is, he did it. He had one lone cookie left

from the ones he'd bought but put mine on top. It was all I could do to keep a straight face when he ate one after the other."

"You waited for his allergy to kick in."

"I didn't go to all that trouble just to walk away before the job was done. I offered to take him to the hospital and put him in the passenger seat."

"And then parked the car, and let him die."

His eyes grew cold. "I watched him die."

I suppressed a shiver. "And then you shot Dex Hamlin for attempting to blackmail you?"

"My, my, Ms. Nix," he mocked. "Your talents are wasted working in that little store."

"Two of my family members had to spend the night in jail because of you. They're still under a cloud of suspicion."

"No need to fret. I've written a confession letter. It'll go out in the mail Monday."

I gaped. "Wait. You're sending a confession to the police?"

"Like I said, I'm not a monster. The confession will clear your friends, but the police won't find me. You and I will be in Mexico in a matter of hours, then I'll let you go before I disappear for good."

Fred snorted. "You can't take her to no foreign parts. She ain't got a passport."

"A fake passport is easy enough for me to get. I have connections, and one of them is the pilot waiting to fly me out of here." His expressed hardened, and he gestured at the rope with his gun. "Stop stalling, Ms. Nix. Tie him to the chair behind you. It'll be comfortable enough until help arrives."

"Him's name is Fred," Fred grumbled, then thumped me on the back. Was he urging me to move, or signaling he had a plan? I hoped it was something other than throwing a screwdriver.

I reached for the rope slowly, not making any sudden

moves, and hyperaware of the weapon pointed at me. He might not shoot to kill, but I'd bet Fred's nuts and bolts Durley would shoot to wound and not think twice about it.

Once I had the coil in hand, I fumbled around looking for a rope end. Fred awkwardly pushed his walker toward the chair so his tool belt sat by the arm. I knew it was for show. Fred was never awkward with his walker. He wanted those tools close by.

I knelt as he lowered himself to the cushion. "Not too tight, missy. I have the bad circulation in them legs."

"Okay, Fred."

Before I'd finished tying off one end, Fred yelled, "Now, missy!"

Something whizzed over my head. Adrenaline flooded my body. Durley cursed, and the gun fired. I flinched as another projectile flew from Fred's hand, and then I acted.

Faster than I thought possible, I pivoted, grabbed my bag, and launched myself at Durley. I swung the bag at his startled face, and it connected with a solid and satisfying thud. Durley dropped to the floor, and I frantically searched for his gun. I saw it under the dining table, well out of his reach. Which didn't matter now, because he was down for the count.

With the immediate danger over, I looked at Fred to be sure he was okay. He was on his feet, leaning on his walker and wearing a pale, horrified expression. In the next moment, the front door burst open, and people swarmed the room yelling, "Police!"

My shoulder hurt and dizziness swamped me. I leaned to brace my hands on my knees, and my heavy bag whacked my shin. Should've let go of the bag. That would leave a mark.

"Nixy, dear God, are you okay?"

I didn't straighten but looked up into my Aunt Sherry's face, saw the rest of the Silver gang staring, mouths agape, and then saw darling Eric hunkered at my feet.

"Honey, you're hit."

I nodded, then put a hand on his shoulder to steady myself when another wave of wooziness rolled over me. "I know. I hit him good, and so did Fred."

His hands covered mine. "I mean your shoulder is bleeding."

I glanced half cross-eyed at my right upper arm, where blood stained my emporium polo shirt. Dang, I'd never get that out. Then I thought of something else and looked into Eric's bedroom brown eyes.

"Does this mean our Eureka Springs trip is off?"

TWO DAYS LATER, ON A BRIGHT, BEAUTIFUL MONday, the El Dorado hospital released me with a sling and some lovely pain meds. Eric picked me up and took me to the farmhouse to recuperate for a few more days. Me being in the hospital almost an hour away had been a strain on the Six, so when Sherry insisted I come home, I couldn't refuse.

The Six plied me with pillows and pure kindness. Aster sprayed me with so much lavender water, I'd smell it on my skin for months. Neighbors and friends heaped enough food on us to last until Thanksgiving. Judy came to lecture me for a full five minutes before she hugged me and presented us with a plate of chocolate croissants and eclairs. Even Debbie Nicole visited. She brought a pamphlet titled "Investigating for Lame Brains." She'd created it herself, and the number one tip was, "Don't get shot."

The Six chuckled over that for hours.

Well, except poor Fred. He blamed himself for the incident. The first screwdriver he'd thrown had been aimed at Durley's gun hand but hit him in the upper arm instead, and the gun discharged. The second throw hit its mark, knocking the gun from his hand, but the damage to my shoulder was done.

When I told Fred in no uncertain terms that I preferred being shot over being kidnapped and dragged to Mexico, he lightened up. When I asked him to teach me the fine art of screwdriver throwing, he positively beamed.

The blow I'd delivered with my bag had knocked Durley cold but hadn't killed him. I asked Eric the questions I hadn't had the chance to ask Durley, and Eric answered every one. Durley did have a sister and had taken her to the folk art festival on Saturday, but she lived in Shreveport, not Lilyvale or El Dorado. She'd known nothing of her brother's plot, and neither had his PI partner, Sally Maynard. She thought he'd had a family emergency and would simply be late for the meeting with us.

My biggest question was why Durley had carried out his revenge on Cornell at all after so much time had lapsed. Durley had lawyered up as soon as he'd come to, but the file of notes I'd stashed in my purse were fair game for the authorities to seize.

Durley had written about Dennis's confession that Cornell had elbowed, punched, and shoved the librarian in his back several times before he'd nearly run Dennis down. His back injury had been aggravated to the point of requiring surgery, and the procedures hadn't been effective. Dennis wasn't paralyzed, but he was disabled. That, in turn, had caused severe depression, and he needed constant care. Durley contended that if Cornell had left Dennis alone, his brother would be well, and likely still living and working in Lilyvale.

He had a point. No matter how much Cornell had changed, he'd made life hell for the Ozark Arms residents.

Still, I preferred remembering him with the little boy and with my critters.

Who, by the way, left my side only to eat and do their business. Yes, they paid attention to the Six, especially Fred, and they had raptures when Eric came over. Otherwise they remained my constant companions. Amber curled up in the bend of my legs, and T.C. draped herself on the sofa arm, one paw always touching my head.

Charlene Vogelman brought the official notice that all charges against Maise and Aster had been dropped. She even apologized in a roundabout way for her suspicions, and the Six graciously forgave her.

I did, too, though a little more grudgingly.

The best medicine of all? Planning the Eureka Springs trip with Eric. I could hardly wait!

Epilogue

THE TRIP WAS EVERYTHING I'D HOPED FOR, AND SO much more. I don't know if we hit leaf-peeping peak season, but the autumn colors were truly breathtaking. Especially from the cabin on the ridge overlooking Beaver Lake that Eric had rented from his friend. Eric and I sat there on the deck overlooking the spectacular trees of every color and talked for hours.

We also explored the downtown, uptown, and underground of Eureka Springs. Eric booked both walking and riding tours of the city, and then we explored its historic charms on our own. We visited Basin Spring Park, and all the old hotels, including Basin Park Hotel, the Palace Hotel and Bathhouse, and the Crescent Hotel and Spa. We saw St. Elizabeth Catholic Church, one of the many buildings that seemed to grow out of the mountains, and we were in the glass Thorncrown Chapel during a thunderstorm. Sitting there surrounded by lightning was a bigger thrill than riding any roller coaster.

Grotto Spring, the Carry Nation House, the many bed-

and-breakfasts, some stately, some funky. I couldn't have picked a favorite because doing anything and everything was special with Eric. The things we saw and did in the daytime . . . and at night.

Our four days came to an end too soon, but I loved the new closeness I'd found with my darling detective.

The weekend before Thanksgiving, we went to dinner at the farmhouse. Eric wore his usual jeans and boots but wore a long-sleeved shirt and a lightweight jacket. Not that it was all that cold, but I'd donned jeans and a light sweater against the nip in the air.

Sherry hustled us directly into the dining room, but when I asked if we were late, she pooh-poohed me. Eric and I sat at the end of the table, which was laden with food. Conversation centered on what Maise had on the menu for Thanksgiving. When I said I was afraid to ask what she was serving for Christmas, every one of the Six beamed at me, then wiped the goofy grins from their faces and changed the subject.

But that didn't mean the covert glances at Eric and me stopped. I wasn't wearing my sling tonight. Maybe they were concerned about my wound. Eric shifted in his seat and fiddled with his napkin as if he was nervous, but I chalked it up to him being on call.

At the end of the meal, I got up to ferry plates and the leftovers to the kitchen, but Sherry shooed Eric and me to the huge front porch. Amber and T.C. came with us.

"Sit, relax," she said before hotfooting it back inside.

We sat in the swing, Eric gently pushing it with his foot because my legs were too short to touch the porch floor. The critters had raced down the steps to chase around the yard.

Since we'd been back from Eureka Springs, I'd been to Eric's refurbished bungalow several times, mostly to watch football or movies. His parents had died years ago, so we'd naturally agreed to spend at least part of the Christmas holidays with the Six. He wanted to decorate and I promised

I'd help, but I was iffy about putting up a tree in my apartment. I didn't really think T.C. would climb it, but bat at the lights and ornaments? All bets were off.

As for New Year's Eve, we'd discussed dinner and dancing but hadn't made a final decision. It was enough to know we'd be together.

Eric's phone buzzed with a text message. He checked it, then said we needed to go inside. I figured he'd caught a case, so I went in with him.

Instead of grabbing his jacket, he ushered me down the long hall to the back door. It seemed awfully bright in the yard, and I realized why when he took my hand and led me onto the deck.

A galaxy of patio lights hung from the house to the barn and back. More lights were arranged in a circle in between. Music softly played somewhere, and Amber and T.C. sat just outside the circle, their ears perked.

"Eric, what in the world did you do?"

"Wait and see."

He escorted me down the deck steps and over to the circle of light. Then he aimed a thumbs-up toward Bernice Gilroy's house, and the music gradually swelled until I recognized it as "Kiss the Girl" from *The Little Mermaid* movie.

"The first time I kissed you, Bernice was playing our song."

"I remember," I said. "How did you get her in on this?"

"She summoned me while you were in the hospital. I set this up with her after we got home from Eureka Springs."

"Set what up?"

He reached into his jeans pocket even as he went to one knee and held up a diamond ring.

"Nixy, I love you. Life is never a given, but what we have of it, I want to spend with you. Will you marry me?"

I don't know when tears began sliding down my cheeks. I didn't think of myself as a particularly sentimental or even romantic woman, but Eric's softly spoken, sincere declaration melted my heart. The sizzle between us would never fizzle.

I smiled at him, nodded, and hoped my nose wasn't running. "Yes, Eric. Yes."

He took my left hand, slid the ring onto my finger, and stood.

As the music swelled, I heard Bernice cackle, heard the Six applaud, and heard the critters bark and meow as they rubbed against our legs.

Then Eric's mouth met mine, and all I felt was the forever warmth of his kiss.

Crafting Tips

MAKING SOAP THEN AND NOW

By Deborah Baker
Magnolia Cove Luxury Soaps
facebook.com/magnoliacovesoaps

The first cold day of winter was always deemed by my South Arkansas grandmother as hog-butchering day. Even though it was a gruesome process, the yield of pork chops, hams, and bacon were worth the mess. Nothing was wasted—even the fats were rendered in the cast-iron washpot. A portion of the rendered lard was mixed with lye to make lye soap. It was strong and smelly and would clean anything, especially dirty laundry.

By definition, soap is made from an acid/alkaline reaction, combining the oil acids with alkaline sodium hydroxide (lye) in a process called saponification. It creates glycerin, which is typically absent from grocery brand soaps. Today's lye soap is luxurious, moisturizing, and beneficial to skin.

My soaps are made using a complex formula of shea butter, palm oil, olive oil, coconut oil, and castor oil. These oils are balanced to ensure long-lasting lather, creaminess, and moisturizing properties. I use the cold process method for my soap making. The oils are heated to 100 degrees F and mixed with dissolved lye cooled to the same temperature. Lye is caustic and dangerous, so safety precautions such as gloves, goggles, and long sleeves are essential. Remember, it's the same stuff you use to dissolve nasty clogs in the sink lines!

The mixture is stirred with an immersion blender until it reaches "trace" and is like pudding. At this point, additives such as essential or fragrance oils, color, or tea leaves are added to the soap mixture. The fragrance oil volume is calculated based on the amount of carrier oils that are used. The fragrance develops completely as the soap dries. Fragrances can be combined to create similar characteristics as perfumes with top, middle, and bottom notes. This is the fun and unique part of soap making!

Once the additives are in the soap, the thick mixture is poured into a mold and allowed to harden overnight. By the next day, I cut it into bars and let it dry for thirty days. It is now ready to use for a relaxing bath.

For those of you who would like to make soap, I recommend researching the process thoroughly before attempting it. The use of lye is very dangerous, and care must be used when handling it. Brief yourself on safety precautions. Purchase the right equipment. Find a recipe that is tried-and-true. Books and online sources are rich with information on soap making. Once you've mastered the process, it is fun and rewarding to experiment with different oils, colors, and fragrances.

Real soap. Really luxurious!

Happy Soap Making!
Deb

EASY ESSENTIAL OIL WATER SPRAYS

By Nancy Haddock

I don't remember when I learned to make sprays with essential oils, and I wish I could remember who taught me about them, but I was using various essential oils decades before aromatherapy became a discipline.

Aromas and our responses to them are unique and personal. Lavender is primarily touted to be a calming scent, which is why it's added to so many products. But not everyone will be calmed by lavender, and some individuals are allergic to it. So, if you make your own essential oil sprays, chose the scents you like, whether they calm you, energize you, lift your mood, or help you focus. Oh, and be cautious about how much you use, especially if you'll be out and about. Triggering someone's allergy does not win a friend!

You will need a small spray bottle, a bottle of essential oil, and any kind of plain water. (I've never tried the fizzy kind, so l can't speak to how it would work.) I generally use tap water and plastic bottles from a drugstore or dollar store.

Fill your bottle as much as you like, but probably not more than three-quarters full so the mixture will blend well when you shake it. To the water, add drops of essential oil until you're happy with the strength of the scent. I add 15 to 25 drops, depending on the size of the bottle. Cap the spray bottle, shake, and spritz. If you want to increase the scent's intensity, add oil. If you want to cut it, add water.

Although oil and water aren't supposed to mix, this method of making sprays has always worked fine for me. I do shake the bottle before each use. Do NOT use essential oils or oil sprays in your mouth or on an open wound, or allow contact with any mucous membranes without having specific, expert information on such use. For instance, I dilute clove oil in a carrier oil (virgin olive oil) and apply the mixture to my gums with a cotton swab. If not properly diluted, clove and other oils will burn like crazy, and possibly cause tissue damage!

In addition, the purity and quality of oils will vary, so educate yourself about the companies bottling essential oils. I buy therapeutic grade always, and buy the less expensive oils for some applications.

What are my favorite oil scents? Rosemary, mint, and lavender are my top three at the moment, but I also find uses for coconut and pear scents. Tea tree oil has antibacterial, antimicrobial, antiseptic, and antiviral properties. It also helps when I have a sinus headache, and so does tei-fu oil. Citrus scents are great for boosting mood. (I wonder if that's why so many cleaning products are lemon scented!) My friend Deb Baker created a soap for me to give as swag, and the scent is lavender and lily of the valley. It is divine!

Have fun experimenting with the scents you enjoy! And remember to spritz responsibly!

Recipes

SNICKERDOODLES

Fun to Say—to Sniff—to Eat

From Mrs. Floyd Rich

Presented here as it appeared in the cookbook compiled by the First Presbyterian Church Guild Committee, 1956

Edited for clarity

1 cup shortening
1½ cups plus 2 tablespoons sugar
2 eggs
2¾ cups flour
2 teaspoons cream of tartar
1 teaspoon baking soda
¼ teaspoon salt
2 tablespoons cinnamon

Cream the shortening and 1½ cups sugar together, add the eggs, and beat well. Sift the flour, cream of tartar, baking soda, and salt together and add them. Mix well.

Roll the dough into small balls (about the size of walnuts). Roll the balls in a mixture of the cinnamon and 2 tablespoons sugar. Place 2 inches apart on an ungreased cookie sheet. Bake for 8 to 10 minutes at 400 degrees F or until lightly browned but still soft.

These cookies will puff up at first, then flatten out with crinkled tops. Makes about 5 dozen 2-inch cookies.

"Give schoolchildren these snickerdoodles hot from the oven with a glass of milk."—Mrs. Floyd Rich

DANIEL'S BANANA ICEBOX CAKE

Contributed by Daniel Stefanic

Hello, bakers! Making this banana icebox cake is a process. You'll be preparing 4 "elements" in the recipe and then assembling those parts into a whole. The process takes more than 9 hours, including 6 hours or more in the fridge (actual prep and cooking time is about 2 hours). A time-saving tip is to make the banana bread and crust the day before and let it cool overnight before making the mousse and assembling the cake. Have patience! The result will be worth it! The recipe serves 12 to 14 people.

BANANA BREAD

1½ cups all-purpose flour
¼ cup cornstarch
1 cup granulated sugar
½ cup (1 stick) unsalted butter, room temperature
2 large eggs
3½ ripe bananas
1 tablespoon milk
1 teaspoon ground cinnamon
½ teaspoon ground nutmeg

1 heaping teaspoon cream of tartar
1 teaspoon baking powder
1 teaspoon baking soda
1 teaspoon salt

Preheat the oven to 325 degrees F. Butter a 9 × 5 × 3 inch loaf pan.

Sift together the flour and cornstarch.

Cream the sugar and butter in a large mixing bowl until light and fluffy. Add the eggs one at a time, beating well after each addition.

In a small bowl, mash the bananas with a fork. Mix in the milk, cinnamon, and nutmeg. In another bowl, mix together the flour-cornstarch mixture, cream of tartar, baking powder, baking soda, and salt.

Add the banana mixture to the butter-sugar mixture and stir until combined. Add the flour-cornstarch mixture, mixing just until the flour disappears.

Pour the batter into the prepared pan and bake for 1 hour to 1 hour 10 minutes, until a toothpick inserted in the center comes out clean. Set aside to cool on a rack for 15 minutes. Remove the bread from the pan, invert onto the rack, and cool completely before slicing.

CHOCOLATE COOKIE CRUST

1 cup graham cracker cookie crumbs
1 cup Oreo cookie crumbs (white centers removed)
2 tablespoons granulated sugar
⅔ stick unsalted butter, melted

Preheat the oven to 375 degrees F.

In a bowl, mix the cookie crumbs, sugar, and butter with your hands. Press the mixture evenly into the bottom of a 9-inch springform pan. (It will seem like an excessive amount of crumbs, but it will compress down quite a bit with pressure.) Press the crumbs down quite firmly to make a smooth surface. Bake for 5 minutes for a soft crust or 10 minutes for a crisp crust.

Remove the crust from the oven and let cool completely before filling.

CHOCOLATE MOUSSE

9 ounces quality bittersweet chocolate chips
2 ounces espresso or strong coffee
3 tablespoons butter
1½ cups heavy whipping cream
½ teaspoon plain granulated gelatin
2½ tablespoons confectioners' sugar
½ teaspoon vanilla extract
1½ containers (5.2 to 6 ounces each) banana-flavored Greek yogurt

Chill a metal mixing bowl and beaters in the freezer.

In the top of a double boiler, combine the chocolate chips, coffee, and butter. Melt over barely simmering water, stirring constantly. Remove from the heat while a couple of chunks are still visible. Cool, stirring occasionally, until no longer warm to the touch.

Pour ¼ cup of the cream into a metal measuring cup and sprinkle it in the gelatin. Allow the gelatin to bloom for 10 minutes. Then carefully heat by swirling the measuring cup over a low gas flame or candle. Do not boil or the gelatin will be damaged. Stir the mixture into the cooled chocolate and set aside.

Whip the remaining 1¼ cups cream with the sugar and vanilla using the chilled bowl and beaters. When the cream starts to thicken, add the yogurt and continue whipping until soft peaks start to form. Slowly fold the whipped cream into the chocolate mixture, mixing and folding as little as possible. There may be white streaks still visible in the mousse in the end; this is fine.

WHITE CHOCOLATE MOUSSE

1½ cups plus 2 tablespoons heavy whipping cream
1 heaping teaspoon plain granulated gelatin
3 tablespoons butter
8 ounces white chocolate, coarsely chopped
1 tablespoon confectioners' sugar
½ teaspoon vanilla extract
1½ containers (5.2 to 6 ounces each) banana-flavored Greek yogurt

Keep in mind that white chocolate is much more temperamental than regular chocolate. When making white chocolate mousse, you want to use the lowest temperature possible when melting your white chocolate—barely simmering water in your double boiler—in order to produce a smooth end product. If your melted white chocolate appears grainy, like it has sand in it, this is due to crystallization of the sugar in the chocolate, and your resulting mousse will not be smooth.

Chill a metal mixing bowl and beaters in the freezer.

Pour ¼ cup of the cream into a metal measuring cup and sprinkle in the gelatin. Allow the gelatin to bloom for 10 minutes. Carefully heat by swirling the measuring cup over a low gas flame or candle. Do not boil or the gelatin will be damaged.

Melt the butter and very slowly stir it into the gelatin mixture. Allow to cool to room temperature.

In the top of a double boiler, melt the white chocolate and 2 tablespoons of the cream. Cook and stir until the white chocolate is melted and the mixture is smooth.

Whip the remaining 1¼ cups cream with the sugar and vanilla using the chilled bowl and beaters. When the cream

starts to thicken, add the yogurt and continue whipping until soft peaks start to form. Then add the butter-gelatin mixture and continue whipping until stiff peaks form. Fold about ¼ cup of the whipped cream into the white chocolate mixture.

Carefully fold in the remaining whipped cream.

ASSEMBLY

After the chocolate cookie crust and banana bread have cooled, trim the crust off the bread and cut the bread into 1-inch cubes. Slice 3 bananas into about ¼-inch-thick slices. Put a layer of banana slices directly on the chocolate cookie crust so they come to the outer edge, touching the walls of the springform pan.

Spread a layer of chocolate mousse, about ¾ inch thick, on top of the sliced bananas. Add another layer of sliced bananas on top of the mousse, assembling the bananas the same as the first layer to the outer edge of the pan.

Put a layer of banana bread cubes on top of the banana slices, bringing the layer of bread cubes to the edge of pan.

Add a very thin layer of chocolate mousse on top of the bread cubes, just to fill the gaps in the bread and barely covering the bread cubes. Be careful not to go all the way to edge of the cake, to ensure that the bread layer is clearly visible and separated.

Finish with a layer of white chocolate mousse. Cover the cake completely so the mousse comes slightly above the top of the pan. Scrape the white chocolate mousse smooth with the back of a bread knife to be even with the top of the pan.

If desired, decorate the top of the cake to your liking, for instance, with melted chocolate drizzle. Chill the cake in the refrigerator for at least 6 hours, preferably overnight. Keep refrigerated until serving time, and serve cold.

Enjoy!